The Saladin Murders

An Omar Yussef Novel

Matt Rees

W F HOWES LTD

This large print edition published in 2008 by
W F Howes Ltd
Unit 4, Rearsby Business Park, Gaddesby Lane,
Rearsby, Leicester LE7 4YH

1   3   5   7   9   10   8   6   4   2

First published in the United Kingdom in 2008
by Atlantic Books

A CIP catalogue record for this book is available
from the British Library

ISBN 978 1 40741 947 3

Typeset by Palimpsest Book Production Limited,
Grangemouth, Stirlingshire
Printed and bound in Great Britain
by MPG Books Ltd, Bodmin, Cornwall

To Jamil Hamad

The crimes in this book are based on real events in Gaza. Though identities and circumstances have been changed, the killers really killed this way, and those who died are dead just the same.

CHAPTER 1

As Omar Yussef came along the passage, the flies left the flooded toilets to examine him. The filth in the latrines soon lured most of them back, but a small, droning escort orbited him as he sweated toward Gaza.

The passage was wide and empty, haunted by the thousands who shoved through there twice a day. Its whitewashed walls were soiled gray to the height of a man's shoulder, marked by the touch of laborers jostling at dawn to their construction jobs in Israel. The mid-morning sun slopped under the raised tin roof, sickly and urinous. The air was pale and stinking and every surface was repugnant.

Omar Yussef struggled along the uneven concrete, scuffing his mauve loafers and bracing his overnight case against his knee with each step. He touched the back of his hand to his nose, fighting the toilet stench with a hint of his French cologne.

Magnus Wallender came alongside him. At forty, the Swede was sixteen years younger than Omar Yussef and three inches taller, not quite five feet ten. His wavy hair was a blondish gray and his light beard was trimmed very short. He wore khaki

1

slacks, a well-pressed blue shirt and tasteful glasses, horn-rimmed and rectangular. 'Oh dear,' he said, raising a pale eyebrow at the putrid puddle in front of the toilets.

'The scent of Gaza,' Omar Yussef said.

Wallender smiled and turned to Omar Yussef. 'Would you like me to help you with your bag?'

The Swede was trying to be kind, but Omar Yussef hated to think it was obvious that the weight of the bag was a discomfort to him in the heat. Had it been anyone else, he would have snapped, but Wallender was his boss. *Kiss the hand that can't be bitten*, he thought. 'Thank you, Magnus. I can manage,' he said.

A Palestinian officer sat behind a battered desk in the shade of the grubby passage wall, beyond a squeaking turnstile and a tall roll of barbed wire. When he saw Omar Yussef approaching with a foreigner, he straightened, preparing to process important guests. He reached for the green plastic wallet that held Omar Yussef's ID card and for Wallender's dark red passport. The officer examined the photo page of the passport. 'Mister Magnus?' he said.

Wallender nodded and smiled.

'Welcome,' the officer murmured, in English. 'For what do you come to Gaza?'

'I'm with the United Nations Relief and Works Agency, in the Jerusalem office,' Wallender said. 'We're making an inspection of the UN schools in the Gaza refugee camps.' He gestured toward

Omar Yussef. 'My colleague is the principal at one of our schools in Bethlehem.'

The officer nodded, though Omar Yussef was sure the man's English wasn't equal to Wallender's explanation. Omar Yussef noticed that he transcribed the Swede's name incorrectly in the large, dog-eared tablet on the table.

'How long since you were in Gaza, *ustaz*?' the officer asked Omar Yussef.

'Twenty years, my son. The permit isn't easy to get.'

'You'll notice some changes in Gaza.'

'Gaza will notice some changes in *me*.' Omar Yussef gave a short laugh that sounded as though he were preparing to expectorate. 'When I was last in Gaza, I had nice curly hair and I could carry an overnight case without breaking into a sweat.'

The officer grinned. He glanced from the ID card to Omar Yussef and his smile wavered, betraying polite confusion. *Is he surprised that I'm not as old as I look?* Omar Yussef thought. Just below average height, Omar Yussef appeared even shorter because his shoulders stooped like those of an old man. His hair was white, liver spots stained his balding scalp, and his tidy mustache was gray.

'At least, you still have your mind, uncle.' The officer handed back the ID card. 'Unlike Gaza.'

Wallender stepped into the light beyond the passageway and gazed at the sun, stretching. 'We're being met here by the UN security officer for Gaza,' he said. 'A fellow named James Cree. I'm told he's Scottish.'

Omar Yussef came up beside him. 'A security officer?'

'Apparently Gaza is a bit dangerous, you see.' Wallender laughed.

Taxi drivers lazed in the shade cast by a one-room police post. A few of them approached, calling vaguely predatory welcomes and pointing to their shaky, yellow vehicles. From the shadow beyond the police station stepped a bald, thin man, peering at his mobile phone. He was nearly six and a half feet tall, and his face and scalp were red from the sun.

'I'd say that's our Mister Cree, don't you think?' Wallender said. 'He looks even more foreign than I do. Which is a rare feat.'

James Cree put his mobile phone in the breast pocket of his short-sleeved shirt. His sunburned face was soft and seemed wavily rounded, like a poached egg on a plate. His eyes were a delicate, faded blue, and he wore a ginger mustache no wider than a pinkie finger from top to bottom. His limbs were long and narrow and suggested the sinewy strength of an endurance athlete.

Wallender shook Cree's hand. 'This is our colleague Omar Yussef, principal of the Girls' School in Dehaisha refugee camp,' he said. 'I'm lucky enough to have obtained permission from the Israelis for him to pass through the checkpoint to work with me on this inspection.'

4

The Scot bent to shake Omar Yussef's hand. Omar Yussef felt small, slow and paunchy before the tall, lean man. 'Mister Wallender takes you to all the best places,' Cree said dourly, barely moving his lips.

Wallender reached up to slap Cree's shoulder and went laughing to the white Chevrolet Suburban with black UN markings that rolled out of the parking lot for them.

They settled into the vehicle's air-conditioned cool. From the front seat, Cree looked at Wallender over his shoulder as the driver pulled into the road. 'We've got an emerging situation here, Magnus. The office called me as I was waiting for you, and they've been messaging me more details on my cellphone. One of our teachers was arrested early this morning.'

'Who?' Wallender said.

'A fellow named Eyad Masharawi. He teaches part-time at our school in Shati refugee camp. The rest of the time he's a university lecturer.'

'At the Islamic University?' Omar Yussef said.

'No, the other one, whatever the hell it's called.'

'Al-Azhar.'

'Aye. Well, the poor bugger's been arrested. So I'll drop you at your hotel, if you don't mind, and I'll get along sharpish to Masharawi's house to see what can be done.'

Magnus Wallender looked at Omar Yussef. 'We don't want to delay you, James. Why don't we come with you? You can take us to the hotel later.'

'I'd just as soon drop you first.'

'No, really, we'd prefer to go with you.'

Cree wasn't looking at them now. 'What about your inspection?' he said, softly.

'I'd say this would be part of our inspection, if one of our teachers is in custody,' Wallender said. 'Don't you agree, Abu Ramiz?'

Omar Yussef noticed Cree's blue eyes flicker across him when Wallender called him Abu Ramiz, 'the father of Ramiz,' a respectful and yet familiar form of address. The Scot didn't give Omar Yussef a chance to respond. 'All right, if it's like that, then.' He turned to the driver. 'Nasser, we'll go to Masharawi's place first.'

As the Suburban weaved around the potholes and picked up speed, Omar Yussef wondered where this poor Masharawi might be held and what might have led to his arrest. As a teacher of history to refugee children, he felt an affinity with others who chose such work for little money and less respect.

Outside, the heat flamed off the road and the dunes burned white. *Even Bethlehem is more welcoming than this*, he thought. His hometown in the bare hills south of Jerusalem had its deadly problems, but it maintained its historic core and the dignity of its old stones. His friend Khamis Zeydan, Bethlehem's police chief, traveled to Gaza regularly, and he maintained the place was so broken that it ought to be pulled out into the Mediterranean and sunk, along with the gunmen and corrupt ministers who ran it.

Yet this small strip of land – rather than Bethlehem – seemed to represent the desperate reality of the Palestinians: Gaza bellowed and struggled like an injured donkey, while its rulers played the role of the angry farmer, furiously beating the stricken beast, though they knew it couldn't get up.

Nasser hit the brakes as he raced up behind a slow-moving military convoy, and swore. Omar Yussef glanced at the UN men. They showed no sign of comprehending the crude Arabic curse. He leaned forward and spoke to the driver.

'Shame on you,' he said. 'Watch your mouth.'

The driver kicked down a gear and sent the Suburban roaring into the opposite lane to pass the military vehicles.

There were five trucks. The three at the back were small and camouflaged, each filled with so many soldiers that they had to stand. They held onto the shoulders of the men next to them and swayed with the rolling of the trucks across the torn surface of the road. They wore green and khaki camouflage, red berets, and red armbands that bore the words *Military Intelligence* in white.

The second truck from the front was a flatbed of medium length. At its center, a coffin was draped in the green, white, red and black of the Palestinian flag. A row of soldiers stood on each side of the casket, their legs braced against the movement of the truck, facing forward and trying to stand at attention. Omar Yussef thought they strove for a tough look, but their callow faces were bony and nervous.

The UN driver slowed as he passed the coffin. 'There is no god but Allah, and Muhammad is his prophet,' he muttered, in benediction for the dead man. Omar Yussef leaned forward in his seat to get a better view of the coffin. Under the flag, there would be a simple box of unfinished planks with no lid. The dead man would be wrapped in a shroud, his legs tied at the ankles. When they buried him, they would save the coffin to use again.

'You're on the wrong side of the bloody road, Nasser.' Cree spoke to the driver through his teeth.

Nasser stamped on the accelerator and shot past the coffin, pulling back into the right lane.

Omar Yussef wondered who was in that coffin. This was his first sight of death in Gaza, neatly packaged in a box. He was not a mile from the checkpoint and already death was riding the same road.

CHAPTER 2

The Masharawi home in the Tuffah neighborhood of Gaza City was stuccoed white over concrete and the doorways were framed with faded purple paint. Its two floors lay behind a shoulder-height garden wall graffitied with the Palestinian flag and a yellow Dome of the Rock. Spiky barbed-wire curlicues encircled the cartoon mosque.

Omar Yussef stepped out of the sandy lane where the Suburban was parked. The path to the house led through a tangle of lemon trees that stood twice as high as the wall. The trees gave off a warm citrus scent, as though they'd been boiled for herb tea by the strong sun. The low cooing of doves came soothingly through the heat. In a corner of the garden, there was a shady olive grove and a bulbous clay *taboun*, where Masharawi's wife might have been baking on any normal day. A strange silence reached out from the open doors and windows of the house into the thick midday stillness.

A thin, gangly boy in his teens, whose left ear stuck out at ninety degrees to his head, appeared at the door. His eyes stuttered between the foreigners and the floor. Omar Yussef spoke to him first.

'Greetings,' he said.

'Double greetings, *ustaz*,' the boy whispered.

'Is this the home of *ustaz* Masharawi?'

The boy dropped his eyes to the cheap plastic thongs on his feet and nodded.

Cree stepped up to Omar Yussef's shoulder. The boy leaned backward to look at the towering man. There was a small quiver in his jaw and his eyes were blank and fearful.

'Is Missus Masharawi at home?' Cree said.

'My mother?' the boy asked, in slow English.

'That's the girl,' Cree said.

The boy didn't understand. He looked at Omar Yussef, who spoke to him gently in Arabic. 'These men are with the UN. They're here to find out what has happened to your father. Can we talk to your mother?'

'Welcome,' the boy said, again in English.

They followed him inside. The dark hallway was a relief from the hot sun flashing off the white exterior walls. While his eyes adjusted, Omar Yussef blindly trailed the sound of the boy's plastic thongs slapping against the tiles. The boy led them to the back of the ground floor and gestured to the several thick, floral couches crammed around the edge of the dim, cool room.

'Welcome,' he said again, as Wallender and Cree entered. Then he turned to Omar Yussef and spoke

10

in Arabic: 'Like the home of your family and your own home.'

Omar Yussef acknowledged the greeting. 'Your family is with you.'

'Do you want tea or coffee, *ustaz*?'

Omar Yussef translated for Wallender and Cree.

Wallender smiled, asked for coffee and sat quietly. Cree spoke to the boy in a loud voice that was deaf to the unhappy silence of the house. 'A coffee it is. Thanks, laddie.'

'I'll have mine *sa'ada*,' said Omar Yussef, who always took his coffee like this, without sugar. 'And ask your mother to come talk to us, please.'

The boy left the room. The three men sat unmoving on the sofas. There were low sounds from a corner of the house, as though skirts moved quickly in the hush. A cozy hint of burning gas and brewing coffee floated into the room.

In the corner between Omar Yussef and James Cree stood a cheap bookshelf of chipboard covered with a fake wood finish. A row of photographs lined its top. The shelves were bowed by the weight of volumes on education and history in Arabic, French and English, except for one shelf, which was empty. Omar Yussef stood and examined it. He saw no dust, though the lip of each of the other shelves hadn't been cleaned for months. Something that had covered the entire shelf had been removed.

Omar Yussef assumed the center photo on top of the bookcase was of Eyad Masharawi. The man in the shot held his head slightly to the left. Omar Yussef

11

smiled and wondered if Masharawi had a wildly protruding ear like his son and was vain enough to hide it from the photographer. The man was bald, but the hair at the sides of his head was as richly black as the bitter coffee being prepared in the kitchen. His eyes were hooded, aristocratic, and dark. The mouth was tense and resigned, as if accustomed to exasperating news.

The boy returned with a tray covered, like the bookshelves, with fake wood. He pulled out two small cherry-varnished side tables and put them beside the guests' knees. Then he laid down the coffees, the first cup before Wallender.

'Allah bless your hands,' said Wallender, quietly using the traditional Arabic formula of gratitude. Omar Yussef smiled at him.

'Allah bless you,' the boy mumbled. He slouched into an armchair in the corner.

Wallender leaned forward and whispered to Omar Yussef. 'Should we refer to Mister Masharawi as *ustaz*?'

'He's an educated man, a teacher, so it would be respectful to refer to him as *ustaz* Masharawi,' Omar Yussef said.

He tasted the cardamom-scented coffee and put his cup on the side table. Two women entered the room with measured, silent steps.

The first woman nodded to each of them and whispered her greetings. She wore a long black housecoat with large gold buttons that hung loosely almost to the floor. Her headscarf rounded her face to a gold clasp under her chin. The scarf was cream with a brown floral print around the bottom edge, which fell across her shoulders. Her skin was a light brown, like her melancholy, preoccupied eyes. Her black eyebrows were raised, as though she had taken a breath and was about to sigh. Her features were small, despite the thickening of age around the jaw. Omar Yussef thought she was in her mid-thirties. She carried a thin manila folder in front of her upper belly like a clutch bag, tapping it edgily with the finger which bore her simple gold wedding ring. She sat on the edge of the unoccupied couch, holding her neck erect and her back straight, with her palms flat on the folder she now placed in her lap. Her ring finger made tiny nervous circles on its surface.

The woman behind her was a few years older and dressed similarly, though her headscarf was plain, her gown was gray and her body beneath it was bulkier. Her mouth was wide and shapeless and pouting. When she moved, her fleshy cheeks quivered with each step. She smiled at the guests and sat on the same sofa as the first woman. Her plumpness reminded Omar Yussef of his neighbor Leila back in Bethlehem and, with a shiver of shame, he recalled the sexual attraction he had often felt for her. He experienced a similar physical curiosity about the thick-set woman on the couch. He caught himself holding his breath as he watched her stroke her friend's shoulder blade reassuringly.

That comforting gesture gave Omar Yussef his clue.

He spoke to the woman in black. 'You're the wife of Eyad?'

She nodded and lifted her head a little higher.

'I'm Abu Ramiz, Omar Yussef Sirhan, from Bethlehem. These are my colleagues from the UN.' Omar Yussef introduced Wallender and Cree, then addressed them quietly in English. 'I'll ask her what happened during the arrest?'

'There's no need for you to translate, Abu Ramiz,' the woman said. 'I'm a teacher of English.'

Cree and Wallender smiled with appreciation. 'Where do you teach?' Wallender asked.

'Sometimes at the same UN school where Eyad teaches. I give lessons to the local children here, too.' She turned to the woman beside her. 'This is my friend, Umm Rateb. She works at the university as secretary to the president.'

The chubby woman smiled, showing big teeth along the wide mouth, and looked a long time at Omar Yussef with an expression of amused curiosity.

'Eyad was arrested because of something that happened at the university, not because of his work at the UN school,' Masharawi's wife said.

'Why do you say that, Missus Masharawi?' Cree asked.

The woman paused. That form of address must have sounded as odd to her as it did to Omar Yussef. 'I am Salwa Masharawi. You are welcome to call me Umm Naji – the mother of Naji. This is Naji, my eldest boy.' She gestured to the lanky kid, folded on the armchair in the corner.

14

Cree nodded, with a hint of impatience.

'Fourteen armed men came to our house very early this morning, when everyone was asleep,' Salwa said.

'Israeli soldiers?' Wallender asked.

'Palestinian security agents.'

'What did they want?' Wallender took out a small notebook and a pen.

'The agents asked my husband for his papers.'

'His identity papers?'

'No, his papers from the university. There have been exams at the university recently and he kept the test papers here.' Salwa pointed at the book-case in the corner. 'They took all the papers from that empty shelf.'

'Why did they want these papers?'

'There has been trouble at the university, Mister Wallender.' Salwa closed her eyes and touched her forehead. 'Well, at least, Eyad has done things which, as I believe one says in English, are asking for trouble.'

'What kind of trouble?'

'Three days each week, Eyad teaches at your UN school. He likes to be there, because he is from an old Gaza City family, and he often says that we should work with the refugees to show that they are always welcomed here. It seems silly, perhaps, because they are just as much Gazans as anyone else, after sixty years in their camps, but they are still the poorest people in town and Eyad thinks it's his duty to work on their behalf. The other two days each week, he works at the university. He teaches in the Education Department.' Salwa hesitated and glanced at her friend, who gave her a nod. 'Unlike his UN job, the work at the university is no longer a source of pleasure for Eyad. It is a battle.'

'Against whom?' Omar Yussef asked.

'Perhaps you think that the corruption of Palestinian life should not infect the university, Abu Ramiz? That academia should be above such dirtiness?' Salwa shook her head. 'Sadly, this is not so.'

Cree drank the last of the coffee in his tiny cup, wiped the thick dregs that clung to the tips of his mustache, and put the cup down on the side table with a rattle.

'Naji, make tea, now,' Salwa said. She puckered her lips and blew out a breath, as though in relief that her son would be spared her story.

'He's a good boy,' Omar Yussef said, after Naji left the room.

'He looks just like his father, even down to the ear. You saw, it sticks out?' Salwa said. 'But he's quiet and calm. Not like Eyad.'

'What went wrong for Eyad at the university?' Omar Yussef asked.

'Eyad discovered that the university is selling degrees to officers in the Preventive Security.'

'Preventive Security?' Wallender frowned. 'What's that?'

'The plainclothes police force,' Cree said.

Salwa nodded.

'Why would a policeman need a degree?' Omar Yussef said.

16

Umm Rateb put her hand on Salwa's wrist and took over. 'To be promoted quickly, these policemen need to show that they have studied law or had some other higher education. It puts them on what you'd call the fast track to the highest posts. Of course, that means a better salary and more power.'

'So the university gives them the degree in exchange for payment?' Omar Yussef said.

'Yes, they have to show up to a couple of classes, but they don't really study,' Umm Rateb said.

Salwa clicked her tongue and her tone edged into anger for the first time. 'They couldn't study if they tried. They aren't qualified to be at the university. These men didn't even graduate high school. They were on the streets making trouble when they should have been in class. But now the troublemakers are the law in Gaza and they want to receive something valuable without working for it.'

'What did Eyad do when he discovered this?' Omar Yussef said.

Salwa shook her head. 'My husband is not a calm man. If he sees something he dislikes, he has to act against it. I always say to him, "Please, Eyad, slow down. Let us live in peace." But that isn't what he wanted. Three weeks ago, he set an exam for his class at the university.'

'The exam that was confiscated this morning?' Omar Yussef said.

Salwa handed him the folder. 'They didn't get this copy of the exams. Eyad left it on his bedside table.'

Omar Yussef translated from the first page: '*Write*

an essay about corruption in the government.' He looked at Cree, whose face was measured and unreadable. Wallender bowed over his notebook.

Umm Rateb spoke up. 'The head of the university, Professor Adnan Maki, was very angry. He called Abu Naji to his office and they did a great deal of shouting. When Abu Naji left, he forgot even to say goodbye to me at my desk outside Professor Maki's office, though I am a good friend of his family. For the rest of the afternoon Professor Maki was extremely irritable.'

'Did the university punish Eyad?' Omar Yussef asked.

'My husband didn't wait to be punished,' Salwa said, with a sad laugh. 'He went straight to his classroom that afternoon and set another exam for his students. Have a look.'

Omar Yussef turned to the second page in the file and read: '*Write an essay about corruption at the university.*'

'All the students wrote about the university selling degrees to the plainclothesmen,' Salwa said. 'Professor Maki immediately suspended Eyad.'

Wallender looked up from his notebook. 'If the students already knew about the selling of the degrees, why would Eyad be punished?'

'It was not something to talk about in public, not something to set exams about,' Umm Rateb said.

'It's more than that,' Salwa said. 'It became personal.'

'Between Eyad and Professor Maki?' Omar Yussef said.

'Worse.' Salwa waved her hand. 'Colonel al-Fara.'

'Bloody hell,' said Cree.

'Who's that?' Wallender asked.

'The head of the plainclothes police. One of the most powerful men in Gaza and certainly one of the nastiest bastards you'll ever come across.' Cree slapped his thigh. 'He's tortured more prisoners than you've had pickled herring and Aquavit, Magnus.'

'James,' Omar Yussef said, flicking his eyes toward Salwa.

Cree looked at the woman's solemn face. 'Sorry, dear,' he said, with a little cough.

Salwa nodded, but her mouth was tense. She shivered slightly before she continued. 'Professor Maki told my husband that he had embarrassed him in front of Colonel al-Fara. As you point out, Mister Cree, that's not a favorable situation in which to find oneself in Gaza these days. With men like Maki and al-Fara, all kinds of politics are involved which, as I told my husband, he couldn't possibly know about.'

'Shouldn't the head of the university protect academic freedom?' Wallender asked.

Salwa and Umm Rateb shared a glance that suggested the Swede might as well have dropped in from Mars. 'Professor Maki didn't become head of the university because he's a notable academic. Rather, it was because he's involved in politics,' said Salwa. She turned once more to Umm Rateb, who nodded with grim approbation. 'He's a member of the Fatah Party's Revolutionary Council and very senior in the PLO. So is Colonel al-Fara. No doubt many secret deals could be strained by a conflict between them. I warned my husband they would need a scapegoat to allow them to patch up their differences.'

'After he was suspended, what did your husband do?' Wallender asked.

'He should have waited until next year and the suspension would have been lifted, when everyone had forgotten about what he did. But he went to one of the human-rights organizations, which has campaigned against corruption. They decided to make this an issue of academic freedom. They wrote to Professor Maki about my husband's case.'

Omar Yussef felt a darkness enveloping him. He thought of this woman's impulsive husband, determined and arrogant. Those aloof eyes in the photo were too proud for Gaza, debased as it had become. To live here, you would have to accept the shadows, swelter in airless rooms, choke on your resentment.

'They also wrote to Colonel al-Fara,' Salwa said.

Omar Yussef knew where that letter must have led. The boy returned with a tray of small glasses filled with mint leaves and dark tea. Omar Yussef saw a flicker of fear on Salwa's face and her lips tightened, as though the boy before her were in as much danger as her husband. Naji set a cup before Omar Yussef and glanced at the open file on the older man's knees. Omar Yussef reached for the tea. His hand shook and he withdrew it. His pulse raced.

'Did Colonel al-Fara make any reply to the letter from the human-rights group?' Cree said.

'The arrest was his reply,' Salwa said.

'You said they asked for his papers,' Omar Yussef said. 'We can see from the empty shelf that he gave them the papers they wanted. Why did they arrest him, as well?'

'The policemen insulted him. I heard one of them say that the papers looked very suspicious and that they would need to interrogate him about them. Eyad lost his temper and shouted at them. I'm sure they wanted to provoke him, so they could arrest him.'

'Where were you?' Omar Yussef asked.

'I was upstairs. As I came down, I saw them taking Eyad through the door of this room and out of the front of the house. He was in hand-cuffs and one of them made him bend forward as he walked, pushing his neck down. I called out to him, but an agent stood at the bottom of the stairs and refused to let me pass.'

Omar Yussef heard the desperation of that moment even now in Salwa's voice. 'They were Preventive Security agents?'

'Yes. They wore leather jackets, even though it wasn't cold. They took Eyad through the garden and went away very quickly.'

'Did anyone tell you why he was arrested?'

'First thing this morning I went to their local office. They told me Eyad was held at their head-quarters in the south of the city. They said he was being investigated, that perhaps he worked for the CIA.'

'The CIA?' Cree shouted.

'That's right.'

'Jesus Christ, they're aiming for the bloody top.' Cree clapped his hands. 'No messing around with piddling accusations of collaboration with the Israelis here. No, he's a big CIA hotshot. Christ.'

Salwa drew herself straight. Her voice was soft and precise. 'I agree, Mister Cree. If my husband is a spy, then take him to Palestine Square and shoot him, I told them. But he should be put on trial first. There should be justice.'

'They didn't mention a trial to you?' Omar Yussef said.

Salwa shook her head.

Cree scoffed and waved his hand. 'Trial? No chance.'

Magnus Wallender looked up from his notes. He rested his elbow on his knee and rubbed his short beard. 'Your husband will have the backing of the United Nations, Umm Naji. We will see to it that he's freed or, at least, allowed to have a fair trial. We will work with all our contacts here in the government, and we will inform our diplomatic representatives.'

'Thank you,' said Salwa.

Omar Yussef sensed the meeting was at a close. His hand felt steady enough to lift the glass of tea from his side table. He put it to his lips and took a sip.

Umm Rateb sat forward. 'Perhaps, Mister Wallender, you will visit Professor Maki at the university to discuss the case?'

'Yes, Umm Rateb, I think we shall.'

'Leave it a few hours,' the plump woman said. 'He was in Rafah this morning, and he'll go home for lunch and a siesta before he goes to the office. You will find him there after four or four-thirty. Go to the main entrance of the university and ask directions from there.'

'Thank you.'

Umm Rateb stood, resting her weight on one leg and pushing out that hip. Omar Yussef liked the way she held herself. 'Salwa, I have to go and prepare lunch for my family. I'll talk to you later.'

Salwa stood and kissed Umm Rateb's round cheek.

Umm Rateb smiled at Omar Yussef, showing the teeth in her wide mouth. 'I'll meet you later today, Abu Ramiz.'

Omar Yussef was taken aback. Had she sensed his attraction to her? Could she be propositioning him in front of these people? His hand shook and dropped splashes of tea onto the manila file and the crotch of his trousers.

Wallender covered Omar Yussef's embarrassment. 'At the university, Abu Ramiz. Umm Rateb is Professor Maki's secretary, you remember.'

'You will have to pass my desk to reach his office,' Umm Rateb said.

Omar Yussef put down his tea and cleared his throat, composing himself. 'If Allah wills it,' he said.

CHAPTER 3

Omar Yussef heard gunfire as the UN Suburban pulled down the drive of the Sands Hotel. Wallender looked toward him nervously. The guns sounded close, short resonant bursts.

'You boys get nice and comfy here and I'll pick you up later this afternoon on my way to the university,' Cree said. He winked at Omar Yussef, and the UN car spun in the drive and left.

The hotel lobby hid behind smoked-glass doors smeared with splashes from a dirty rain. Despite the brightness of the day, Omar Yussef could feel a dust storm's approach in the building air-pressure and the tiniest of headaches threading like a burning needle from his right eye to the center of his ear. The hotel workers didn't bother fighting the elements: there would always be another dust storm and it would end by settling in a layer of filth, no matter how much they cleaned.

The reception desk was cut in dark, stained wood. Beyond another set of smoked-glass doors on the far side of the lobby, Omar Yussef saw the white tablecloths of the breakfast room. To the right of the reception desk, an open staircase of polished stone led to the rooms. The landings on the stairs overlooked the front desk and each was decorated by a pair of crossed scimitars mounted on the wall above a small, crimson carpet in a thick Bedouin stitch.

The woman behind the reception desk turned from her computer. She was small, slim and young. She wore a blue headscarf and her eyes were big and dark and long-lashed. She took Wallender's passport and Omar Yussef's ID card.

'You're lucky to find a room, gentlemen,' she said, as she photocopied their documents. She handed them forms to fill out with their names and addresses. 'The Revolutionary Council is meeting here in two days. Many of the most important Fatah men and their staffs have come to town already. They like to stay at our hotel.'

'What do they like so much about it?' Wallender clearly had seen more attractive lobbies. 'Not that it isn't a fine hotel.'

Omar Yussef turned to the Swede. 'Fatah's the biggest faction in the PLO, which owns all kinds of things, from airlines to chemical plants. And hotels. I'd guess that this hotel's owned by the PLO and that the party hacks like to stay here because, as the owners, they can behave as badly as they like.' He laughed.

'Is that so?' Wallender said.

'Of course, only the PLO has enough money to

25

afford the most polite, educated and beautiful staff.' Omar Yussef smiled at the receptionist.

The woman laughed. '*Ustaz*, you should tell that to my poor father. He has a simpler way of judging his daughter. A woman with good, wide hips brings a dowry of seven camels, because she will bear many children. I am small and I have narrow hips. So even though I have my degree in Business Administration, my father complains he will receive only one camel for me.'

Magnus Wallender joined the joke. 'Abu Ramiz, you can surely afford a single camel.'

'Let's go,' Omar Yussef said. 'We'll come back with a camel.'

The receptionist laughed again.

'How much could a camel cost, after all?' Wallender said, pretending to count the cash in his wallet.

A voice called from the door of the breakfast room. 'Sir, put away your money. Your friend is a Palestinian. He will *steal* the camel.'

Omar Yussef turned from the reception desk. Brigadier Khamis Zeydan came out of the breakfast room, laughing. He wore a checked sports coat and a cream shirt open at the neck. His thinning, white hair was cropped short and combed forward. His scalp, usually protected from the sun by a military beret, was starkly paler than his face. He stubbed his cigarette into a glass ashtray on the reception desk, breathed the smoke over his nicotine-stained mustache and kissed Omar Yussef three times on the cheeks.

'Magnus, this is Bethlehem's police chief,' Omar Yussef said. 'Abu Adel, this is Magnus Wallender, from the UN.'

Khamis Zeydan shook hands with Magnus Wallender. He lit another cigarette.

'Have you known Abu Ramiz a long time?' Wallender said. He pointed to his cheeks, to show that he asked because of the kisses.

'We go way back and, then, even a little further back than that,' Khamis Zeydan said, with his hand on Omar Yussef's shoulder. 'I've known him since we were at university in Damascus together. I remember him when he had nice, curly black hair and a little black mustache. He looked like Charlie Chaplin.'

Omar Yussef noticed Wallender squinting with curiosity at the black leather glove tight on Khamis Zeydan's left hand as it rested on his own shoulder. He wished he'd had an opportunity to tell the Swede about the prosthetic hand beneath that glove. He thought of the hatred Khamis Zeydan felt for the plastic limb when he was drunk and miserable. He didn't want the Swede's glance to draw his friend's attention to it and infect his mood with memories of the grenade that had maimed him during the Lebanese Civil War.

'I didn't recognize you without your uniform,' Omar Yussef said.

'Am I so scary that you can't imagine me in human

27

clothing?' Khamis Zeydan said. 'Actually, it's simply less hassle to pass through the Israeli checkpoint into Gaza without a uniform. But I'm wearing blue socks so that you can tell I'm a policeman.'

'Are you in Gaza for the Revolutionary Council meeting?' Omar Yussef asked.

'Yes. Come and drink a coffee with me.' Khamis Zeydan pulled Omar Yussef's elbow. 'You, too, Magnus. I invite you.'

'That's very kind,' Wallender said. 'But I ought to call the office in Jerusalem. To update them.'

Khamis Zeydan protested, but Omar Yussef squeezed his shoulder. 'All right,' the police chief said, 'I've lived in Europe. I'm not going to be one of those provincial Arabs who takes offense when his hospitality is rejected.' He winked at the smiling receptionist. 'Anyway, Magnus, come down and drink coffee after you've made your phone call.' He lowered his voice. 'Or perhaps you'd like to come to my room later. I have a bottle up there that's very much against the laws of Islam.'

Omar Yussef frowned, but not out of respect for the proscriptions of the Prophet. Though he had foresworn alcohol a decade ago, he kept some Scotch in his home, just for Khamis Zeydan's visits. Lately, he had noticed that the police chief emptied those bottles faster than usual. He cleared his throat and glanced at the receptionist.

Another volley of gunfire crackled down the street.

'What's that shooting?' Wallender asked.

'Don't worry. They're burying a soldier who was

killed in Rafah last night,' Khamis Zeydan said. 'The funeral is along the beach at the president's compound. You just missed the main part of the parade. It left the house of General Moussa Husseini a few minutes before you arrived.'

'Who's that?' said Wallender.

'The head of Military Intelligence. He lives directly across the street from the hotel. Now his soldiers are firing into the air. Gunfire is the sound of Palestinians in mourning.' Khamis Zeydan gave a little punch to Wallender's arm. 'Of course, if you go to a wedding, you'll discover that gunfire is also the sound of Palestinians celebrating. Gunfire is the music of the Palestinians.'

Omar Yussef recalled the coffin they had seen transported by the military convoy on their way into town. That must have been the soldier whose funeral was the source of this gunfire.

'What's the difference between these Military Intelligence people and the other lot – Preventive Security?' Wallender rubbed his beard.

Khamis Zeydan took a long drag on his cigarette. 'Imagine you wanted to set up a police state, Magnus. You'd need a uniformed force to do the day-to-day brutalizing and intimidation – that's Military Intelligence. Then you'd have your secret police, plainclothesmen who'd be involved in sinister, shady operations – that's Preventive Security.'

'Gaza is a police state?' Wallender frowned.

'It was meant to be a police state, but it ended up more of a banana republic.' Khamis Zeydan laughed and gave a phlegmy cough. He lowered his voice and moved close to Wallender. 'Military Intelligence is a private army for General Husseini. His rival, Colonel al-Fara, the head of Preventive Security, has bigger ambitions than Husseini. He's very close to the CIA.'

'Hell,' Wallender said. He glanced at Omar Yussef.

He's thinking of Salwa's husband in al-Fara's jail, Omar Yussef thought.

'Don't worry about the different names of these organizations, Magnus,' Khamis Zeydan continued. 'The only thing a foreigner like you needs to remember is that they're all bastards and nothing they do is in the interests of ordinary Palestinians.'

'I'll bear that in mind.'

They left Wallender at the reception desk filling out more registration forms and went into the breakfast room.

Khamis Zeydan headed for a table by the long window that faced the beach. He wiggled his open hand to call a waiter.

Omar Yussef stood at the window and watched the waves come in to the narrow beach. It was a long time since he had seen the Mediterranean from the coast of Palestine. The sea rippled a deep turquoise, as though it were a tide of gemstones. Its motion was so beautiful and free that his eyes filled with tears.

He looked along the sand. There was trash on

the beach, burned out oil drums and plastic bottles protruding from shiny black sprays of kelp. Two boys were throwing stones at another kid as he untangled his fishing net.

Khamis Zeydan ordered coffee, sweet for him and bitter for Omar Yussef, and dropped his pack of Rothman's on the white tablecloth. 'What're you doing here, Abu Ramiz?' He put another cigarette in his mouth.

Omar Yussef looked again at the sea. The boy with the net threw it angrily at one of the stonethrowers and wrestled him to the sand.

'The Swedish fellow is my boss,' he replied. 'We're supposed to be inspecting the UN schools here.'

Khamis Zeydan cocked an eyebrow. 'Supposed to be?'

'One of our teachers has been arrested. Magnus wants to help get him released.'

'You know the proverb: *It's the business of the muezzin to make the call to prayers.* In Gaza, it's safest to stick to your own tasks and not to go freelance.'

'Oh, so it's time for proverbs, Abu Adel? How about this one: *Every knot has someone to undo it.* Maybe fate brought us to Gaza to help this poor man.'

'You're not going to undo the knot. You're going to get tied up.'

The waiter brought the coffee. Khamis Zeydan lit his cigarette. 'I want to tell you something, as one who cares about his dear old companion from university days, Abu Ramiz. Don't get involved in the case of this schoolteacher.'

'You don't even know why he was arrested.'

'I'll bet you don't, either. Not really. In Gaza, nothing is what it seems. The truth will be far below the surface. You can't predict how deep it will go, but you can be sure that it will reach out to touch other victims and other crimes. You can't solve all the crimes in Gaza.'

'Perhaps I can solve this single crime.'

'There *is* no single, isolated crime in Gaza. Each one is linked to many others, you'll see. When you touch one of them, it sets off reverberations that will be felt by powerful people, ruthless people.' Khamis Zeydan squeezed his prosthesis with his good hand, thoughtfully. 'By Allah, it's dangerous here, Abu Ramiz. Do you think, for example, that I wander around unprotected?' The police chief gestured toward the corner of the room. A young man sat at a table smoking and nursing a glass of mint tea. He nodded to Omar Yussef. He was about twenty-five, lean and powerful. His hair was short and tightly waved. He had high cheekbones in his spare, bronzed, clean-shaven face. He sat with the absolute self-contained stillness Omar Yussef had observed in men who had spent time confined in Israeli jail cells. 'You know who he is?'

'Isn't that Sami Jaffari?' Omar Yussef asked. 'From Dehaisha?'

'The Israelis deported him to the Gaza Strip,

because he was a gunman in Bethlehem. Even the Israelis consider Gaza adequate punishment for a bad guy.'

'His father is my neighbor. Is Sami really a bad guy?'

'Sami was my best officer. He was only involved with the gunmen because I sent him undercover to keep tabs on them. Now he works for me in Gaza.'

'As a bodyguard?'

'During my visits, yes. But when I'm not in Gaza, he's my eyes and ears here. Being a deportee earns him a lot of credibility with the local gangs and he gets a good deal of information that way. He also has friends in the security forces.' Khamis Zeydan leaned toward Omar Yussef. 'Listen, I've told you in the past to keep your nose out of dirty business – you're not suited to it. You didn't pay attention to me then, and I have to admit you were right to ignore me in that case.'

Omar Yussef grimaced and waved his hand.

'No, it's true,' Khamis Zeydan said. 'I can only assume you won't listen to me this time, either. If you're determined once more to dig into things best left untouched, you should do so with Sami's help. Gaza is a minefield and Sami knows where to step.'

Omar Yussef didn't think Wallender would take to the idea of working with a man deported by the Israelis as a terrorist, no matter how innocent Khamis Zeydan said he was. 'Thank you. But I think I'll be okay. I'm not alone here. I'm with the UN.'

Khamis Zeydan inhaled smoke through his nostrils and stared at Omar Yussef, shaking his head. His pale blue eyes were sad and incredulous.

'Let's not argue, Abu Adel.' Omar Yussef tried a light, raspy laugh. 'Tell me, what's the big Revolutionary Council meeting about?'

Khamis Zeydan clicked his tongue bitterly. He crushed his cigarette and warmed his fingertips on the coffee cup. 'I hate this air-conditioning. It's so fucking cold in here.'

'It's your diabetes. It's messed up your circulation. You should cut back on the cigarettes and watch the sugar.'

'Now *you* know what's good for *me*?'

Omar Yussef's jaw stiffened. He raised his voice. 'Why is the Council meeting? To decide who should be killed next?'

'It's more appropriate to wonder who's *not* going to be killed.' Khamis Zeydan swept his arm to indicate the whole of Gaza beyond the hotel walls. 'This place is at war. Not with the Israelis – the only people fighting *them* any more are the Islamists. We're at war with ourselves. The meeting is a hopeless attempt to stop us all from killing each other.'

'Why *are* you killing each other?'

'Colonel al-Fara wants to be the next president and has the CIA behind him. General Husseini wants to overtake him in the favor of the Americans.

So far, Husseini and al-Fara are each trying to force the other into a corner, to cut off their sources of power in the party. As soon as that's done, the victor will strike. The loser and his supporters will be wiped out.'

'That's what the Council meeting's really about, right? To decide which of these two wins.'

'Perhaps.' Khamis Zeydan rubbed his eyes. 'No one knows which of them to get behind. It isn't a bet you'd want to lose, after all.'

'Who're you supporting?'

The police chief squinted at Omar Yussef. He lit another cigarette and looked toward the sea.

'Why won't you tell me? Don't you trust me?' Omar Yussef said.

'The less you know about all this, the safer you are. It's going to get very ugly, believe me.'

'Are you in danger?'

'Everybody's in danger,' Khamis Zeydan said. 'This is Gaza.'

Omar Yussef touched his friend's hand and smiled. 'I'm going to get settled into my room.'

Khamis Zeydan leaned across the table and held Omar Yussef's fingers between his hands. Omar Yussef felt the cold leather of the gloved prosthesis against his knuckles. 'Remember what I said about Sami's help. May Allah protect you.'

'May Allah lengthen your life.'

Omar Yussef waved at Sami Jaffari as he left. The young man smiled and cut a slow salute.

Omar Yussef climbed the staircase to the second

floor of the hotel. His knees ached. Perhaps Khamis Zeydan was right and Gaza was too dangerous for him. Ruthless people like al-Fara struggled for the grand prizes of the presidency and absolute power here. A vital, cunning young man like Sami Jaffari could infiltrate their networks and negotiate the dark relationships within. How could a history teacher in his mid-fifties, slowed by the effects on his body of youthful dissipation, hope to encounter such a dirty world and retain his decency, even his life?

He entered his room. The porter had placed his overnight bag on the bed. Omar Yussef drew back one of the curtains. Like the hotel entrance, the window was streaked by the marks of the rain that had broken the last dust storm.

The empty room made Omar Yussef feel lonely. He picked up the phone. It took him a few attempts to get an outside line. Then he dialed his wife.

'Maryam, it's me,' he said.

'Omar, my darling, how are you?'

'Fine, may Allah be thanked.'

'How is Gaza?'

'I think there's a dust storm coming.'

'Stay inside and drink a lot of mint tea. And don't forget to put on a jacket, or the sand will get to your chest.'

'I will. How're the children?'

'Nadia is here. She's reading stories to Dahoud and Miral.'

Omar Yussef smiled. His eldest grandchild was twelve and so much like his own mother had been that he couldn't help but favor her over his other grandchildren. He imagined her sitting now with Dahoud and Miral. He had taken in the two children last year, at Nadia's suggestion, after the deaths of their parents, who were friends of his. He could hear her voice in the background, modulated and expressive, not droning and bored like the children in his classroom at the UN Girls' School in Dehaisha when they read aloud. 'Let me speak to her, Maryam.'

While the line was quiet, Omar Yussef thought of Salwa and Eyad Masharawi, separated by a sudden arrest. He wondered what it would be like for Maryam if she didn't know when he would return to their old, stone house on the edge of Bethlehem. Or for him, if he were unsure when next he would eat her food and listen to her good-humored scolding. He felt lonely and cold. He looked about for the control to the air-conditioning to turn it off, but he didn't see it.

Nadia came on the line. 'Grandpa, it's me.' She sounded far away from him.

Omar Yussef swallowed his loneliness. 'No, it's me,' he said.

Nadia laughed. 'You can try that joke with my little brother, but *I* know how to use a phone, Grandpa.'

'Evidently.'

'In fact, I know how to use a computer, too.'

'Daddy's computer?'

'That's just for playing. I'm taking a new class

at school in computers. I've decided to build you a website.'

'A what? Ah, one of *those* things. What for?'

'Daddy has one already for his business, so I can't make one for him.'

Omar Yussef didn't understand computers, but he wanted to be encouraging. 'Go ahead. I'm sure it'll be the best website in Bethlehem.'

'The best website on the web.'

'Where?'

'Grandpa, even Grandma knows about the web.'

Did she really? Omar Yussef often felt discontented with his wife's perception of the world. He thought her simple and conventional, though he couldn't help but treasure the bond that had formed between them over the years. Could Maryam really know of things that were beyond him? It was true that sometimes she seemed to know his thoughts, even when he wanted to hide them from her. He recalled Salwa Masharawi's friend, the university secretary Umm Rateb, and wondered if Maryam would detect in his voice some trace of the sexual attraction he had felt for another woman.

Maryam came to the phone. 'Omar, did you eat lunch? Make sure you don't let Magnus work you too hard without eating.'

Omar Yussef relaxed and sensed his love for his wife as surely as if her voice were a hand caressing his skin. 'I'll look after myself, Maryam.'

CHAPTER 4

The sky was clear blue, but Omar Yussef knew it was filling with dirt. He felt the first grains of the dust storm on his tongue and it left him short of breath. He stopped to blow his nose, then shuffled on through the hot yard of al-Azhar University behind Magnus Wallender and James Cree. The campus was a snaking collection of three-story rectangles, like a giant game of dominoes washed to the color of milky coffee. Palestinian flags twitched on the roof of the administrative building in the brief stirrings of the wind.

Ahead, Cree held the door open for Wallender, who waited for Omar Yussef to catch up. The door was entirely covered in posters. Most were decorated with the fervent, apprehensive faces of suicide bombers preparing to depart on their missions.

At the end of the hall, they entered an anteroom with two desks, each seating one secretary. Salwa Masharawi's friend Umm Rateb rose and welcomed them. She smiled, with her head lilting to the left. 'Peace be upon you, *ustaz.*'

'And upon you, peace,' Omar Yussef responded.

'Professor Maki has just arrived from his home after lunch,' she said in English.

Omar Yussef noticed Wallender glance up at the clock on the wall. It was 4:30 p.m.

'I will tell him you're here,' Umm Rateb continued. 'Please take a seat.'

Wallender and Cree sat. Omar Yussef leaned against a filing cabinet. He read the label on the top drawer. *Degree Records: Alif to Ha.* He thought of Nadia and her computer: *Palestinians always want things on paper. Computers will never really catch on here.* The other secretary tapped at her keyboard and the printer next to her desk hummed.

Umm Rateb returned from the inner office. 'Please come in,' she said.

Omar Yussef followed the foreigners into the office. The shades were down, but the overhead light was bright, and the air-conditioning was stealthily effective. Professor Adnan Maki stood behind a desk designed to look stylish and expensive. Varnished to the color of strong tea, it swept in a curve that took it ninety degrees from the flashy black telephone at one end to a computer at the other, its shiny surface uninterrupted by papers or any other sign that work was performed upon it. Behind the desk, a Palestinian flag was draped from an upright pole. On either side of the flag, Maki had hung photographs of himself, smiling with the current president on the left and, on the right, embracing the old president.

40

Maki had a long, protruding upper lip and a receding chin that made him look equine, but not thoroughbred. Deep lines ran from his nostrils to the corners of his mouth. He was about the same age as Omar Yussef, but he carried no paunch and moved quickly. His small, greedy eyes were so black and wet, they looked like tadpoles spawning.

'Welcome, welcome,' Maki said, eagerly, in English.

He bent forward, almost flat across the desk, to shake hands as they introduced themselves. He smelled strongly of expensive cologne. When he asked Umm Rateb to bring drinks, he leaned still closer to his guests and reached out an arm with the palm quizzically opened. 'Tea or coffee?' He looked at his watch. 'Or is it late enough for something a little stronger?' He giggled and put his hand to his mouth, exuberant to the point of clownishness.

Umm Rateb wagged a finger. 'Hamas will come and burn down your office for your bad morals, Abu Nabil.'

Maki laughed loudly. 'Umm Rateb, Mister Cree is English—'

'Scottish,' Cree said.

'Even better. The land of whisky. Surely, Umm Rateb, you will allow me to welcome my guests as their culture sees fit. Where are you from, Mister—'

'Wallender. I'm from Sweden.'

'Sweden? You are all drunk all the time in Sweden.'

Wallender flinched.

'Umm Rateb, you see? I know what our friends

would like. And I'm sure that our brother here—'
he gestured to Omar Yussef '—is no Islamist.'

'I no longer drink alcohol,' Omar Yussef said.

'A hellraiser in your younger days, were you,
Abu Ramiz?'

'The hell was all on the inside,' Omar Yussef
replied.

'I will have tea, please,' Wallender said.

'Very well, tea for everyone, Umm Rateb, and
for me a coffee.'

Wallender watched the secretary go. 'Is it accept-
able to drink alcohol in Gaza?'

'Not in public. The Islamists actually burn places
down if alcohol is served – the old Windmill Hotel,
your UN Club. But I'm only teasing Umm Rateb.
She's religious, you know, with the headscarf. She
understands that I don't open the special bottom
drawer of this desk until she goes home for the
day.' Maki tapped the wood playfully. 'Mister
Cree, last year I went to Scotland. An old professor
at the University of St Andrews invited me to
lecture about the Jews and the occupation and the
suffering of the people in Gaza. A very sympathetic old gentleman. He served me a fine whisky
in his office. Now, when my secretaries go home
at the end of the day, I imagine that I'm not in
Gaza. Instead, I'm transported to the office of that
jolly professor in Scotland.'

'I'd rather be in Gaza myself,' Cree said firmly.

That surprised Omar Yussef. He snapped his
head around to look at Cree.

42

'Then you will agree to swap passports with me, Mister Cree,' Maki said.

Cree smiled, but it could just as easily have been a contortion of pain. 'Only if I get your VIP card.'

'I don't have one. The Israelis refuse to give me one. Me, a member of the Revolutionary Council and head of the national university. No VIP card.' Maki lifted both his arms wide to indicate the astonishing and incomprehensible nature of this outrage. 'Of course, I should be among the VIPs. All the top officials are issued this card by Israel under the terms of our peace agreement. The VIPs pass easily with their vehicles through the Israeli checkpoints. They don't have to wait in long lines with the ordinary workers.'

'That doesn't seem fair to the workers,' Wallender said.

Umm Rateb brought the tea, placing the glasses along the curving edge of the desk.

'Fair, Mister Wallender?' Maki's arms reached wider still and his voice touched falsetto. 'Is it fair that someone like me, with such senior positions and such pressure on his time, should have to wait in the cattle pens with ordinary workers?'

'Cattle pens?'

'Surely on your arrival you passed the metal barriers and the cages? It's crowded and there's pushing and shoving. The smell is repulsive.' Maki laughed and slapped the desk top. 'Last week, I traveled through the checkpoint. One of the Israeli soldiers, he saw my clothes.' Maki lifted the lapel

43

of his sports coat and rubbed it between his fingers to illustrate its fine cut. 'The workers wear dirty old T-shirts and trousers covered in paint and filth from their construction jobs in Israel. So the soldier asked me who I was. When I told him, he lifted his rifle and pushed a path through all the workers for me to pass.' Maki mimed the action of the soldier thrusting aside the laborers with his rifle-butt to make way for him. He laughed and clapped his hands.

Wallender and Cree watched the professor with unsettled smiles. Omar Yussef looked down at his hands.

'Were we processed in the VIP office this morning, Abu Ramiz?' Wallender asked.

'Yes, we were.'

'Ah,' said Maki, jabbing a finger at Omar Yussef, 'but you are no VIP.'

Omar Yussef looked at the tiny, wet eyes. This was no time to speak his mind. He lifted the lapel of his jacket and rubbed it between his thumb and forefinger as Maki had done.

Maki laughed and reached his hand high. Omar Yussef held out his palm and Maki slapped it in appreciation, then repeated the lapel-rubbing gesture and clapped in delight. 'Welcome, welcome,' he said.

Omar Yussef nodded to Wallender. They could move on to business now.

'Thank you for receiving us, Professor,' Wallender said. 'Abu Ramiz and I have come to Gaza to inspect the UN schools in the refugee camps.'

'Fine work.'

'But our inspection begins with a troublesome note,' Wallender continued.

'Difficulties with the Israelis at the checkpoint?' Maki flicked his hand at Omar Yussef, whom he clearly assumed would have been the source of any such problem.

'No, one of our teachers has been arrested. He works part-time for you at the university and—'

'This arrest was not to do with his work at the university.'

'You know who I mean?' Wallender sat up straight.

'Yes, yes. This terrible Masharawi fellow.' Maki's hand flicked once more, this time dismissing the incarcerated husband of Salwa Masharawi.

'Eyad Masharawi,' Wallender said. 'He was arrested this morning.'

'It's nothing to do with the university, as I say.'

'But when he was arrested, the police took away all the exam papers he set for his university students.'

'How do you know this?' Smiling and exuberant, Maki swiveled his head back and forth between Cree and Wallender. 'Did the police tell you?'

'We went to see Masharawi's wife,' Wallender replied.

'How can you believe a word she says? She's a troublemaker like her husband.' The professor's nostrils flared, as though confronted with a smell so vile it could penetrate even the wall of cologne around him.

'She showed us where the papers had been. Now they aren't there.'

'And what papers? Just university papers? Who knows? I believe the security forces are investigating more than the shocking examination questions alone.'

Wallender looked at Cree. Cree nodded.

'Masharawi accused the university of selling fake degrees to policemen,' Wallender said.

'I'm not short of students who wish to pay for an education. Why should I sell fake degrees?'

'I said it was the university that was accused of selling the degrees, not you,' Wallender said.

'I *am* the university, sir. I've built it from nothing since 1991, when the Old Man told me to set up an institution here to rival the Islamic University.' He gestured toward the photo on the wall of himself in a clinch with the deceased president. 'We have two hundred teachers. One of them makes complaints – this is Masharawi. One hundred and ninety-nine don't complain. And we have tens of thousands of students. Are they all to understand that their degrees are devalued by the accusations of one man? It's a scandalous attack.'

Omar Yussef sipped the last of his tea and put the glass back on Maki's desk. 'Are there students at the university who belong to the security forces?' he asked.

'Yes, and from all the struggling groups.'

'Struggling groups?' Wallender said.

46

'The professor means the militias that fight the Israelis,' Omar Yussef said.

'You might know them as terrorists.' Maki laughed and shrugged.

'Are there students who are officers in the Preventive Security?' Omar Yussef asked.

'If you bring me a name, I can get the file on that student from the office there where Umm Rateb sits. In the file, you will find his high school certificate, to show that he's qualified to study for a degree here. Then, when they graduate, you will see the record of all the classes they passed to earn their rightful qualification, as well as the payments they made for tuition.'

'Did the Preventive Security contact you about Professor Masharawi?' Omar Yussef asked.

'Please, he's not a professor. He's a part-time lecturer.'

He's no VIP, either, Omar Yussef thought. 'Did they contact you?'

'I went to *them*. Masharawi made dangerous allegations against the university and against me, and even the government itself. He refused to retract. So I went to the Preventive Security about this.'

'You asked them to arrest Masharawi?' Wallender sat forward on his seat, his back stiff.

'No, they didn't arrest him for this offense, as I told you. But still, I believe he should be brought to account for this, too.'

'Then why *was* he arrested?' Wallender asked.

'I asked Colonel al-Fara about Masharawi this

47

morning and he told me there are far more serious allegations against him than the responsibility for distributing scandalous exam papers.' Maki lowered his voice to a whisper. 'There's evidence of a connection between Masharawi and the CIA. I'm as astonished as you. Yes, perhaps even the CIA.'

Cree blew air through his pursed lips and clicked his tongue. Omar Yussef gripped the arms of his chair. Wallender cleared his throat.

'You understand, Professor Maki, that we must pursue this case, because Masharawi is also an employee of the UN,' Wallender said. 'He's our responsibility.'

'Surely it's an internal Palestinian matter. You needn't concern yourselves.'

'The international community will view this very seriously.' Wallender's voice betrayed some impatience. 'For a university administrator to request police intervention in a matter of academic freedom is a shocking development.'

'Academic freedom? It was a slander.'

'You believe the allegations were a slander aimed at you personally?' Wallender said.

'Me and the university. It's the same thing.' Maki made himself smaller, calmer. He put a hand to his forehead and lowered his voice. 'It's upsetting for me, too, gentlemen. As a gesture of my good faith, let me suggest that I make contact with the people conducting the investigation and report to you tomorrow. Perhaps if the brother Abu Ramiz would consent to come to my house tomorrow night for dinner, I will give him good news about this case. At least, I will be able to impart details of which you are currently ignorant, about the depths of Masharawi's crimes.'

Omar Yussef knew why Maki wanted to split him away from the foreigners. There would be appeals to him in the name of the Palestinian struggle. There might even be a payoff to persuade him to throw the UN men off the scent. Still, Omar Yussef considered that, just as Maki thought he could better persuade his fellow Palestinian alone, he also might be able to manipulate the university president through the subtleties of their native language. 'I would be very happy to come, Abu Nabil.'

'Welcome, welcome,' Maki said, turning up his volume again.

CHAPTER 5

The cold air sounded a single, long, deathly exhalation. Omar Yussef lay awake, freezing in his hotel bed because he couldn't fathom how to turn off the air-conditioning. He wished its drone were the low, rattling snore of his wife. Whenever he dropped off to sleep, a key would turn loudly in a lock down the corridor or a voice would call goodnight to a friend. The noises seemed so close that at one point he thought someone had entered his room, and he sat up half-awake with a racing heart and sweaty pajamas, despite the chill. He went to the bathroom for a glass of water just before dawn, wrapped himself in the thin towels for warmth, and drank the water at the window. Peering past the edge of the curtain, he watched the detachment of soldiers outside the home of the head of Military Intelligence across the street. Through the dimness of the dust storm that had whipped up in the night, he counted the tips of their cigarettes, glowing orange each time they inhaled, until he felt sleepy.

When Omar Yussef came downstairs in the

morning, Magnus Wallender was at the reception desk, laughing with the pretty young clerk.

'Abu Ramiz, morning of joy,' he said.

'Morning of light, Magnus.'

'Meisoun here tells me they don't have the English-language newspapers in Gaza, as they do in Jerusalem.'

'Do you want me to translate the headlines for you from the Arabic newspapers? I'll tell you if there's an article about our friend Masharawi or if Sweden has invaded Norway. Any other news, believe me, you can live a few days without knowing it.'

Wallender laughed. 'You're right. Hungry?'

Omar Yussef took one of the Arabic newspapers from the reception counter. The main story was about the Military Intelligence officer's funeral. He noticed a small item at the bottom of the page. He tapped it with his forefinger and waved the newspaper at Wallender. 'Gaza is full of the most cheerful news, Magnus. Look: *Body exhumed from grave, dumped near Deir el-Balah,*' he read. 'That's the headline. Here's the story: *A farmer discovered the remains of a man near the town of Deir el-Balah yesterday. The farmer reported to police that he discovered the bones in a corner of his cabbage field near the Saladin Road.*'

'Where's Deir el-Balah?'

'South of Gaza City, halfway to the Egyptian border.' Omar Yussef read on: '*At first the farmer thought he had found animal bones, but then he discovered the skull, which was clearly human. Police transported the remains to Gaza City's Shifa Hospital, where doctors were puzzled by the age of the bones. Doctor Maher Najjar, Shifa's pathologist, said it was hard to identify the precise age of the remains, but added that it could be as much as a century since the body was buried. There have been no reports of a grave being disturbed, but police are investigating in the hope that the bones can be returned to their original resting place.* Do you have an appetite for breakfast now?' Omar Yussef chuckled and folded the newspaper.

They entered the breakfast room, sat by the window overlooking the sea and ordered toast and a basket of croissants.

Wallender peered out of the window into the impenetrable dust storm. 'Hell.'

'We call it a *khamsin,* which means fifty,' Omar Yussef said. 'That's supposed to be the number of days each year in which clouds of dust like this descend upon us from the desert. But who's counting?'

'How long will this one go on?'

'A few days, a week. Until it rains a little or until the wind dies down. Did you sleep well?'

'I kept waking. It felt as though someone was smothering me.'

'That's the air pressure from the dust storm. It gives me a headache right here.' Omar Yussef drew a line from his right eyebrow to his ear.

'I have a bottle of aspirin. Do you want some?'

'No, I'll simply add this one to my collection of

headaches here, here, and here.' Omar Yussef tapped his head all around and smiled.

James Cree arrived at the same time as their breakfast. 'What've you got for me, son?' he called to the waiter.

'Coffee, sir?'

'That's right,' Cree said, lifting a croissant from the basket on the table. 'Coffee it is, laddie.'

'American coffee or Arabic coffee, sir?'

Cree grinned aggressively at Omar Yussef. 'What a polarized world we live in, eh, Mister Yussef? American or Arabic, that's all the choice there is. East or West. Capitalism or fundamentalism.' He leaned toward the waiter. 'I'll have a *European* coffee, son. Make of that what you will. Run along.'

The waiter smiled and turned toward the kitchen.

Cree stuffed the croissant into his mouth. 'Makes me bloody starving, this weather.'

'Here, have mine, too,' Omar Yussef said.

'You sure? All right.' Cree took the second pastry and bit, before he had swallowed the first. He wiped a buttery flake from his mustache and lowered his voice. 'I'm thinking the Masharawi arrest could be a real problem for the UN.'

'It's a bigger problem for Masharawi, though,' Omar Yussef said.

The waiter returned with a cup of drip coffee. 'European coffee, sir.'

Cree sniffed. 'Is that what I think it is, son?'

'Your double health, sir.' The waiter smiled and walked to his station by the swing doors.

Cree stared at the back of the waiter's white shirt. He sipped the coffee. 'Bloody hell, there *is* a drop of the hard stuff in here.'

Wallender leaned over the cup and inhaled. 'Not European coffee. I'd call it Scottish coffee.'

Cree clapped his hands and gave a thumbs-up to the waiter. 'I can see I'm going to become a caffeine addict,' he said. He drank, with a sigh.

Omar Yussef smelled the alcohol across the table. The raw scent of something he had forbidden himself made him resentful of Cree. 'We have to see Masharawi as soon as possible. The longer he's kept in jail, the harder it will be for us to persuade the security people that this is all just a misunderstanding,' he said.

'We?' Cree tilted his head. 'You're here to inspect the schools, Mister Yussef. I didn't intend to involve Magnus in this issue in the first place, and this morning I want to discuss with him whether he shouldn't simply withdraw from it now. Leave it to those of us who are trained professionals in our dealings with the security forces. Certainly, I think it'd be inappropriate for you to continue taking part in our enquiries.'

'I believe I can help. There may be subtleties that you would miss, because you are foreigners.'

'I speak a bit of Arabic, you know, and I've been here long enough to understand how to talk to these buggers.'

'Perhaps you know the security people,' Omar Yussef said. 'But Masharawi? I think you would treat him as a troublemaker, if you were allowed to speak to him.'

'Seems like he's made some trouble, doesn't it?'

'He merely spoke his mind.'

'Like I say, he *does* seem to be a troublemaker.'

Omar Yussef raised his voice. 'Then we need more troublemakers in Palestine.'

Cree put down his cup. 'You have to remember, Mister Yussef, that Magnus's responsibility is both to the school-children of Gaza's refugee camps and also to the United Nations. He and I have to consider the Masharawi situation not only from a humanitarian perspective. There's also the question of UN policy in the peace negotiations between the Palestinians and the Israelis.'

'How does Masharawi's case affect that?'

'It means that we need to balance our reaction to the Masharawi case against our diplomatic interests.'

'Surely the Palestinians need to keep the UN on their side, diplomatically,' Omar Yussef said. 'Which means that if the UN demands Masharawi's release, they will have to comply.'

'We only have a certain amount of capital to expend with demands like that.'

'What use is capital, if it isn't worth a man's life?' Omar Yussef brought his fist down on the table.

'No one's suggesting Masharawi's about to be killed,' Cree said.

'They're accusing him of collaboration. What do you think happens to collaborators?' Omar Yussef flicked his wrist with his palm downward to mime the sudden taking of a life.

'We all know that's just a cover story. They've arrested him because of the questions he asked his students about corruption. It's a warning to other teachers that they shouldn't delve too deep.'

'That, too, is something the UN should stand against. The UN should push for freedom of speech.' Omar Yussef turned to Wallender. 'Is this how the UN would react if I was arrested in Dehaisha? Would you tell my wife Maryam that there were big, diplomatic issues involved and that I was a small fish who didn't merit the attention of the mighty UN?'

Wallender frowned. 'James, it seems to me that if we go quickly to the Preventive Security, it can all be cleared up without the diplomats knowing anything about it.'

'That's just the problem – the Preventive Security,' Cree said. 'If Masharawi had been arrested by anyone else, we'd have more room to maneuver. There're a dozen security services here and we can basically ignore eleven of them. But Colonel al-Fara is the most important contact our diplomats have in the security forces.'

Omar Yussef growled and hammered his hand on the table once more, rattling the cups.

Cree laid his hands flat beside his plate and drew a long breath. 'It's like this: we want peace talks to go ahead between Israel and the Palestinians, but Israel won't talk if there's terrorism. If al-Fara keeps the terrorists quiet in his own nasty fashion, everyone's happy. But if al-Fara decides not to help us, there'll be terror attacks in Israel and everything goes to hell. *Ergo*, we need him happy.'

'So this bastard al-Fara can do whatever he likes to the people of Gaza, as long as he doesn't let them kill any Israelis?' Omar Yussef felt his hands shaking. He hid them below the tabletop in his lap.

'Mister Yussef, it's not that simple. If al-Fara chooses not to act against the terrorist groups, the Israelis will storm into Gaza to fight the terrorists themselves. Al-Fara's prepared to let that happen, because it'd illustrate that, without him, Gaza is helpless. Our alternatives: Israeli tanks on the streets, or carte blanche for al-Fara.' Cree sat back with a shrug.

'Why didn't you say this yesterday?' Omar Yussef said. 'Someone in New York who has no idea what a Palestinian refugee camp looks like or smells like told you how to handle this, didn't they? You spoke to someone high up in New York and they told you to bury the Masharawi case.'

'Mister Yussef—'

'I'm not 'Mister Yussef.' My family name is Sirhan. Omar and Yussef are my first two names.' He lifted a finger and pointed it at Cree, though he knew it would shake as he did so. 'You don't even understand Arab names. Yet you think you understand the duplicitous minds of men like al-Fara.'

Cree stared doubtfully at the pointing finger. 'Do you want me to call you Mister Sirhan instead?'

'No, I should be referred to as Abu Ramiz, the father of Ramiz. But by you, I prefer not to be addressed at all.'

Wallender took hold of Omar Yussef's hand. 'Abu Ramiz, calm down, please. Let's not forget that we all want Masharawi released. We need to secure his freedom without angering our diplomats in New York and without getting on the wrong side of Colonel al-Fara. It's going to take the ingenuity of all three of us to figure out a way to do that. We must work together. So please.'

Omar Yussef stared at his plate. He tapped his finger on a crust of toast. 'I apologize, James.'

Cree watched him. He pushed his chair back. 'The car's outside. Let's go to the jail. Maybe they'll let us talk to Masharawi.'

Omar Yussef looked up.

Cree smiled at him. 'The European coffee has made me reckless,' he said.

CHAPTER 6

The Suburban came into the wide streets of Tel el-Hawa, the neighborhood where the PLO's top hacks had built their gaudy mansions. Uniformed men hunched in the shade of mock Greek pillars, coughing out the swirling dirt. Nasser drove fast down a long, straight street. They reached an elongated, two-story white building, just before the road disappeared into rolling cabbage fields and dunes. It was surrounded by a white-washed wall about eight feet high. By the gate, a handful of men in leather jackets stood with their legs apart and Kalashnikovs across their chests. This was the headquarters of the Preventive Security.

Nasser pulled the UN vehicle up to the gate. One of the guards came to the window, unsmiling. 'Leave the car out here and bring your passports to the entrance,' he said.

Outside the car, Omar Yussef coughed against the dirt and hunched into the hot wind. In the gatehouse, a guard examined the passports of the two foreigners. He wore a loose black leather jacket with a gray synthetic fur collar and a black T-shirt. His face was thick and his hands and

59

stomach were bulky. It was the bullish kind of fatness that hides great strength, like the broad solidity of a Turkish wrestler. He cleared the dust from his throat and wiped his long, black mustache with the back of his hand. He took Omar Yussef's green ID card and stared at him with blank, sadistic eyes. 'What do you want?'

'We're from the UN,' Omar Yussef said. 'These gentlemen would like to talk to Colonel al-Fara about an important case.'

'You don't look so important to me, fellow.'

Omar Yussef touched the tip of his mustache and took an impatient breath. 'It's the case of the university teacher, Eyad Masharawi. We need to see Colonel al-Fara about it.'

'He isn't here.'

'Will he be back soon?'

The guard shrugged and dropped the ID card and the passports from enough of a height that they made a little slap on the desk.

'Is there somewhere else we could meet him?' Omar Yussef said. 'Or a time when we could set an appointment?'

'You're making a mistake, if you think I can help you with that. His secretary is much prettier than me.'

'The mistake is yours. If you don't correct it, the colonel will screw you, instead of his pretty secretary.'

The guard's big fists tightened. Omar Yussef estimated that together they were almost the size of his own head. The guard picked up a phone and dialed. He mumbled into the receiver, waited, and hung up, quietly. 'Go to the courtyard, up the stairs and all the way to the left.'

'The colonel arrived suddenly?'

The guard took the passports and Omar Yussef's ID and put them in a drawer of the desk. 'Collect these on your way out.'

'Thank you.'

The guard grunted.

'Smile. You'd look a lot prettier,' Omar Yussef said.

He followed Cree and Wallender into a broad courtyard. Near the staircase, a few low black Audi sedans were parked, their license plates marked with single digits. *Al-Fara's motorcade*, Omar Yussef thought. The cars were new and shiny, even under the dirty cloud that had come down on Gaza.

Cree was pleased. 'You seem to have a way of opening doors, Abu Ramiz,' he said.

'After they get slammed in my face,' Omar Yussef replied.

They followed the guard's directions to the end of a corridor, where a sign next to a dark wood double-door was emblazoned with the eagle crest of the government. It read: *Colonel Mahmoud al-Fara, Commander, Palestinian Preventive Security Service (Gaza)*.

Cree tapped the sign with his forefinger and smiled.

'Let's get him,' he whispered. Omar Yussef figured he was still feeling the European coffee.

Three men in leather jackets perched against an empty desk beyond the door. The smallest led them past a series of offices, scuffing his plastic soles against the floor noisily with each step. He nodded them into an empty waiting room and set his feet wide, watching them from the door. After a few minutes, a slim secretary showed them through the connecting door into al-Fara's office. The windows were lightly curtained to prevent anyone seeing inside and strong air-conditioning kept out the heat of the day. The walls were a blank cream, except for a single black-framed document at the far end of the room. *No photo with the president,* Omar Yussef noted. *This man doesn't pretend to owe allegiance to anyone.* Beside the door, ring-binders were scattered across a bookshelf. A television was tuned to an Arabic news station, with the sound muted. A long conference table extended down the middle of the room. At its head sat Colonel al-Fara in a tall black leather chair.

His hair was black and fine, parted at the side and drooping over one eye. His mustache performed the same service for his mouth. His forehead looked damp and feverish, and he slouched his skinny, medium-height body low in the chair. He dragged on a Marlboro in his left hand, expectorated into a tissue in his right, and dropped it into a waste-basket. There was the ex-prisoner's economy of motion about him, just as Omar Yussef had noted in Khamis Zeydan's bodyguard at the hotel.

Cree greeted al-Fara and reminded him that they had met during the recent visit of a UN delegation from New York. Al-Fara showed no sign that he remembered. Cree introduced Wallender and Omar Yussef. When Wallender gripped al-Fara's limp hand, the Swede followed the shake by placing his palm over his heart. It was an Arab gesture of sincerity and Omar Yussef smiled.

Al-Fara dispatched his secretary to prepare tea. He held a tissue before his mouth as he prepared another gob of sputum. The eyes that examined Omar Yussef over the top of the tissue were inflamed by the dust in the air, but they were shifty and dangerous, nonetheless. Omar Yussef squinted at the framed document on the wall. It was a law degree from al-Azhar University. *Maybe that explains why it's worth arresting a man who accuses the university of selling degrees to security agents*, he thought. When he looked back at al-Fara, he saw that the colonel had watched his eyes move to the degree certificate. Al-Fara kept his gaze on Omar Yussef and spat into the tissue.

'Colonel, we would like to discuss the situation of our schoolteacher, Eyad Masharawi,' Wallender said.

Al-Fara rumbled a damp cough in his throat and spat again.

Wallender continued. 'We believe there has been a simple misunderstanding. We would like to secure the release of *ustaz* Masharawi. We understand he's held here.'

63

'There is an investigation,' al-Fara said. He took a long drag on his cigarette. 'It must be completed before he can be released.'

'May I ask the substance of the investigation?'

Al-Fara clicked his tongue and lifted his chin. Negative.

'It seems that *ustaz* Masharawi was arrested because he made accusations of corruption,' Wallender said, 'about the university selling degrees to officers in the Preventive Security.'

'We are aware of this accusation,' al-Fara said.

'But surely that can be cleared up easily. A university professor is entitled to freedom of speech. He must be allowed to question the institutions of the state, so that they are kept from corruption. Academics can be expert watchdogs on behalf of the public.'

'You are from – what country?'

'Sweden.'

Al-Fara sucked on the cigarette, then blew his nose, loudly. 'Everything is peaceful in Sweden, so you can afford to have all these different rights. If your country was threatened by a wicked occupation, you would see that these freedoms about which you talk would be less useful. Later, when we have our state, we will have all these freedoms, of course. The Palestinian people deserve them.'

'It's the position of the UN that those freedoms are a prerequisite for the foundation of a true Palestinian state. And you can help that process by allowing *ustaz* Masharawi to go free.'

'It's more important to allow the security forces to investigate collaborators, because of the threat to our people from Israel.'

'Who said anything about collaborators?' Omar Yussef broke in. 'We were talking about corruption at the university.'

Al-Fara spat into a tissue and stared into it with a grimace.

'At least you can explain the charges against Masharawi, so that we can begin a defense,' Wallender said. 'It's possible that all this is just a mistake.'

The secretary brought small cups of tea on floral saucers. Omar Yussef waited for al-Fara to drop a third sachet of sugar into his cup. The nail on the colonel's right little finger was three-quarters of an inch long – a common affectation among those who wished to show that they didn't work with their hands. The long nail was dark yellow, like the urine of a dehydrated man. 'How do you answer the corruption allegation?' Omar Yussef asked.

'Corruption? This collaborator defends himself by making accusations against the very people who protect the Palestinians from men like him,' al-Fara said, watching his tea as he stirred it. 'There's no corruption. Mistakes have been made, that's true. If no one made mistakes, Allah wouldn't have to send prophets to show us the true way.'

'So someone sold these degrees by mistake? It wasn't really corruption; it was just some kind of slip?' Omar Yussef said.

'I don't know if degrees were sold. Anyway, whatever this building may be, it's not the university. You have the wrong address.'

'It would reflect on your own force, though,' Wallender said, 'if your agents were buying degrees so they could be promoted and get a bigger salary out of the government.'

'We aren't short of money. We could pay higher salaries if we wanted. We have two thousand officers. That's not a big number. It's not such a costly thing to increase their pay.' Al-Fara slurped his tea and wiped his mustache with a tissue. 'There are foreign influences in Gaza. Spies. This is what we're investigating.'

Al-Fara stared past his guests, along the table to the television at the end of the room. The news station repeated footage of the mass military funeral of the previous day. With the vaguest of sneers, al-Fara watched the crowd jostle the coffin, draped in the Palestinian flag. He extended his pinkie and picked his teeth with the long, yellow fingernail.

'You're investigating Masharawi for spying on behalf of the CIA?' Omar Yussef said.

'Perhaps.' Al-Fara didn't look away from the television.

Omar Yussef switched to Arabic. 'You also work with the CIA.'

Al-Fara didn't move, but a long breath like the sound of a distant jet engine sighed out of his throat.

'What would he be spying on, precisely?' Omar

Yussef asked. 'The nuclear reactor in Gaza? The tactics of the Palestinian soccer team?'

Al-Fara turned his dark eyes slowly toward Omar Yussef. 'You think there are no spies in Gaza?'

'I think it's easy to call someone a spy and make it stick these days.'

'That's because there are so many of them.'

'I admire your logic,' Omar Yussef said. He paused. 'Mister Wallender and Mister Cree would like to visit Masharawi on behalf of the UN, which employs him on days when he's not at the university.'

Al-Fara turned fully away from the television to Omar Yussef. His eyes tightened. *When they arrested Masharawi, this guy didn't know the teacher was a UN worker as well*, Omar Yussef thought. *Professor Maki didn't tell him. Now he's angry, because the foreigners are going to blame him. A domestic matter might suddenly turn into an international incident. He doesn't want that kind of scrutiny.*

'It's not possible for you to see him,' al-Fara said.

'The United Nations must insist that its representatives be allowed to see Masharawi,' Omar Yussef said, raising his voice, 'to examine his condition and to discuss his case.' He saw Wallender twitch his head toward him, wanting to know what these Arabic words meant, sensing the tension that glowed around al-Fara like a flame, but not wanting to interrupt.

Al-Fara watched the stub of his cigarette burn.

'As a humanitarian gesture, I will allow his wife to visit him. But I cannot allow anyone else to see him until the investigation is complete.'

'When can she see him?' Omar Yussef asked.

Al-Fara dropped the cigarette into a glass ashtray and held his hands wide. 'Today, of course.'

'Thank you. Will it be possible for us to discuss the case with you in more detail, once she has reported to us on his condition?'

'I won't be here.'

'Perhaps this evening, then?'

'It's not possible. I won't be in Gaza.'

'Where will you be?'

Al-Fara smiled and looked hard at Omar Yussef. 'I'll be in Tel Aviv. I have a meeting with the American ambassador.'

'The meeting will keep you away from Gaza all afternoon and evening?'

'All night. It's not just a meeting to say hello. I'm visiting the American ambassador, not my auntie. I'll be discussing serious issues and the talks are sure to go on into the night.' He switched back to English and looked at Cree. 'I'm sure the United Nations is aware of these security talks.'

Omar Yussef glanced at Cree. *Does he know about them?* he wondered.

'But, of course, those contacts are at the top level, far above your heads.' Al-Fara looked from Omar Yussef to Wallender.

In the courtyard, Omar Yussef stopped to blow the dirt from his nose. Above the line of Audis there were small, barred windows in the wall. Cells. He felt a flash of abandonment, cold across his chest, and he knew it for the way Masharawi must have been feeling, confined up there. He thought of calling the prisoner's name, but Wallender and Cree already were on their way to the gate, happy they had arranged a meeting for Salwa Masharawi with her husband.

Omar Yussef looked back at the windows. Behind the bars, there appeared to be no glass in the frames. The dirt that hung in the air would fill those rooms as well.

CHAPTER 7

Vivid orange spots vibrated behind Omar Yussef's eyelids, decaying to red and purple. His head ached. His breathing was shallow and the air was hot, thick and sweaty.

'This is a bastard place to make us wait,' Cree said.

Omar Yussef opened his eyes and the bright sun needled deep into his brain. Cree sat across the bare room on a plastic garden chair, his tall body folded awkwardly. He pinched the shoulders of his shirt and lifted them away from his sweating skin. Wallender's eyes were shut. He rested the backs of his hands on his knees and breathed slowly and deeply through his small nose.

The windows had been painted shut and there were no shades. Cree had propped open the door with a chair to circulate some air, but the corridor smelled powerfully of feces from a blocked toilet. This was clearly a room where people were put to make time drag excruciatingly, to render every breath a crushing effort, rewarded only with foul air virtually devoid of oxygen.

It was nearly two o'clock. They had brought

Salwa Masharawi to the Preventive Security headquarters at noon. The burly guard with whom Omar Yussef had first clashed at the gate led them to this room on the ground floor, while another took Salwa across the courtyard toward the cells. The guard locked the door at the end of the corridor to keep them from wandering the halls. All the open doors on the hallway led to rooms as bare and stifling as this one.

Omar Yussef's chest was tight. The dead air in the room was familiar to him, though it was a memory he had tried to bury. It rushed through his mind now in a cascade of heavy turning locks, filthy food and air that was hot and still. He felt an urge to confess to the two foreigners, but he wondered what they would think of him. *You know, a long time ago I was in jail, too,* he would say. *It was an injustice, a matter of political revenge.* They wouldn't believe him. They would assume he had been guilty, because, after all, they came from countries where there was law and justice. *Perhaps shame keeps me silent,* he thought. *Not shame that I was jailed, but shame that I was bullied out of politics by the threat of more time in prison. Shame that I chose to live a quiet, easy life for so long, while there was death and suffering all around me.* He stared at the sun and tensed his jaw to be sure he wouldn't speak.

A key turned in the lock at the end of the corridor and the door opened. They heard heavy feet shuffle into the hall, then stop.

'If you please,' the guard called. His voice echoed along the corridor.

Wallender opened his eyes and rolled his neck. 'A nice rest,' he said, with a gentle sigh of contentment.

Cree stared at the Swede with his mouth wide open.

Omar Yussef followed the foreigners along the dark corridor. He felt stiff, but he tried to move as fast as he could to keep up. The guard watched him all the way and he couldn't help but fear being left behind, closed into this place without the protection of the UN, imprisoned with the stink of filth and the maddening heat and the hopeless vulnerability.

Salwa Masharawi waited for them at the gate of the compound in her loose black gown and flowery headscarf. As they approached, she straightened the scarf and wiped her nose with a pink tissue.

'How are you, dear lady?' Omar Yussef asked.

Salwa smiled and toyed with one of the gold buttons on her gown. Her eyes were shot with red. She had been crying. 'May Allah be thanked, *ustaz*.'

'We'll take you to your home and you can tell us the news from Eyad.'

At her house in Tuffah, Salwa gave a long glance at the barbed-wire graffiti surrounding the cartoon of the Dome of the Rock as she entered the yard. Naji waited by the door, fiddling self-consciously with the ear that stuck out from his head. Salwa whispered to him and led her guests into the sitting room where she had met them on their first visit. Omar Yussef glanced at the photo of her husband, smoldering and aloof, his head turned to hide his malformed ear. He wondered if Masharawi cared about such vanities after a night in jail.

Salwa sat with her hands clasped in her lap. She looked at the picture of her husband, as though she needed to feel his presence before recounting their meeting to Omar Yussef and the foreigners. 'My husband asked me to send his greetings to you from the jail and to thank you for your efforts,' she said.

'How is he?' Omar Yussef asked.

'I regret to tell you he has been tortured, *ustaz*.'

Omar Yussef had considered the heat and dust and the stench inside the cellblock, but he hadn't thought the man would be tortured. Wallender groaned and rubbed his beard.

'Since you visited Colonel al-Fara this morning, they have fed Eyad, but before that he was without food and water for over twenty-four hours,' Salwa said. 'They kept him in the *shabbah*. You know this position?'

'I've read about it,' Cree said. 'A low crouch, bent forward with your hands tied behind your back and your heels off the ground. After a few minutes, your legs and back feel like they're on fire.'

Salwa covered her mouth and nose with her hand. She sobbed and lowered her head, then she sat upright and breathed deeply. 'They beat the soles of his feet and put on his head a dirty sack that smells of vomit. They tied his hands behind his back and suspended him by them from the ceiling. He passed out a number of times.'

'How could they?' Omar Yussef touched his fingers to his brow. He thought of the discomfort he had felt in the room where he had waited for Salwa. He was ashamed of the self-pity he had experienced there, a short distance from where Masharawi had been exposed to true suffering.

Salwa's eldest son entered with a tray of tea. Omar Yussef was thankful that the boy lowered his head and shoulders with the awkwardness of adolescence. He wouldn't have wanted him to see the pity and horror in the eyes of the guests as they watched him. Naji set out the cups and left the room.

'Eyad spoke to me at first in a very organized way. But when he told me about the torture, he broke down.' The memory of that moment halted Salwa and she reached for a tissue from the coffee table. 'I was able to see him only through a wire mesh. He entered the room hunched forward, shuffling, as though every motion was an agony. He smiled and asked me about the children. I told him about your help, Abu Ramiz. He was very grateful. He sends his regards.'

'What have the interrogators asked him?' Omar Yussef said.

'They asked no questions. They only commanded him to sign a confession.'

'Confessing what?'

'That he's a CIA spy, whose mission was to spread rumors against the government. They said the university will stop his salary and there will be no money for me and the children.'

'He will receive his UN salary,' Wallender said.

Salwa nodded her thanks. 'He asked his interrogator when he would go to his trial. The interrogator laughed and said, "When the Palestinian state is established, you will have a trial." You understand—' she turned to Wallender and Cree '—that this is what people here say when they mean that something will never happen. It's supposed to be a joke. Then my husband cried and said to me that he felt he had died five hundred times already. I'm so worried, Abu Ramiz. If Eyad is in this condition after one day, perhaps they really do mean to kill him.'

'Certainly not,' Omar Yussef said. 'You said that they fed him after they realized the UN was following the case. The tortures will surely stop now, too. Yesterday, he was just a Palestinian, and we all know how the security forces treat their compatriots. Today, he's in the international eye. In case they have to bring him before UN investigators, they won't want him to look like he has been tortured. They need to be able to deny that, to say that he's just telling lies about them and that he was treated well.'

Wallender stood. 'Umm Naji, we'll be in contact with our office in New York. We'll go to send a report

75

on the torture right away, to bring pressure on the government to end this situation immediately.'

'Magnus, if you don't mind, I'd like to stay with Umm Naji for a while,' Omar Yussef said.

'Good idea, Abu Ramiz. We'll go back to the hotel and report to the office.'

'Fine. I'll probably be back late in the afternoon. I have to leave time to get ready for dinner with Professor Maki tonight. Will you be having dinner at the hotel?'

'Don't you worry about your old Magnus,' Cree said. 'I'm going to take him out for the best fish dinner in Gaza.'

Wallender and Cree left. Salwa and Omar Yussef sat in silence, while the UN Suburban labored out of the sandy alley in reverse.

'I invite you to join us for lunch, Abu Ramiz.'

'Allah bless you.'

She lowered her head and her headscarf shook. Omar Yussef pulled a tissue from the box on the coffee table and handed it to her. She dabbed below each eye, but the tears weren't finished. 'Abu Ramiz, I'm scared.'

'It's a terrible, frightening story, my daughter. But you don't have to face it alone.'

'I'm scared for my son Naji. You know what happens to the sons of collaborators – they're so desperate to make amends for their family's damaged reputation that they volunteer for suicide missions against the Israelis. He's such a quiet boy. He could plan something dreadful, and I wouldn't know about it until I heard it on the news.'

'He doesn't seem like that kind,' Omar Yussef said. 'Besides, he's only the son of an *accused* collaborator, so far. And we'll make sure it goes no further.'

Salwa sniffed. 'Thank you, *ustaz*. I'd better prepare lunch.' She left the room.

Omar Yussef heard the sound of plates being removed from a cupboard in the kitchen. After the big, empty breakfast room at the Sands Hotel, it was a calming, domestic sound.

The boy came to the door. He linked his fingers and stared at the backs of his hands.

'Yes, Naji?'

'*Ustaz*, would you like to see my birds?'

'I'd be delighted.'

The boy led Omar Yussef upstairs to a big, light room at the back corner of the house. He heard the doves whose muffled throatiness he had noticed in the olive grove when he first arrived at the house. The room was spartan. A cheap, fluffy blanket covered the bed, colorful and synthetic. A small desk stood against the wall, neat piles of exercise books and textbooks flush with its edges.

Naji opened a glass door to a balcony. A cage of chickenwire and plywood about four-feet-square stood in the corner farthest from the bedroom. A pair of doves perched on a thick, twisting olive branch propped inside the cage. Two canaries flitted in orbit around them. Naji bent to the seed tray. He fed in some new seed from a small sack. He looked up and a smile broke through the rigidity of his desolate face. Omar Yussef felt his lips tremble with pity.

'Do you hear what they're saying, *ustaz*? Listen, they're saying *uzcouru Allah*. You hear it?'

Remember Allah. Those words of the dove were a traditional childish conceit. Omar Yussef listened to the repetitive call of the white birds and watched the tender expression on Naji's face.

The boy straightened. He hooked his fingers through the chickenwire. One of the canaries perched on his thumb. 'Will my father be okay, *ustaz*?'

Omar Yussef sniffed and cleared his throat. 'Of course.'

'Did he do something wrong?'

'The exact opposite. Your father stood up for what is right. In a place full of wrongs, that's a dangerous thing to do.'

Salwa called up the stairs for Naji. Gently, he let the canary fly from his thumb. He watched it land by the seed tray. 'I think there's food downstairs,' he said.

The table was in a small dining room at the front of the house. As Omar Yussef entered, Salwa set down a final plate of eggplant salad. '*Babaganoush* is Eyad's favorite,' she said. 'Please, Abu Ramiz, sit here.'

Omar Yussef sat at the head of the table. Salwa introduced him to the other four boys. The older ones watched him inquisitively. The two youngest looked about six and seven, and they ripped their bread into strips without seeming to notice the visitor.

The table was spread with *hummus* and other salads – spicy, red *Turkiyyeh* and creamy, white *labaneh*. The boys seemed to favor the pickled radish: each had a plate of these, sliced, with a few olives at the side. Omar Yussef broke open a *kubbeh*. From within its cracked-wheat crust, the ground lamb gave off a sweet scent of cinnamon and pine nuts. He smiled at Salwa. 'Umm Naji, I very rarely eat any food except what my dear wife Maryam prepares – she's so good in the kitchen. For this reason, I don't like to travel. But your skill as a cook has made my absence from Bethlehem less of a hardship today.'

Salwa smiled. 'Welcome. Your double health,' she said. 'Your family is from Bethlehem, Abu Ramiz?'

'No, we're refugees from a village on the edge of Jerusalem. My dear father arrived at Dehaisha Camp in 1948, when I was a baby. But I belong to Bethlehem. I'm not aching to go back to the village.'

'Is the village still there?'

'The village fields are covered by an Israeli shopping mall now, like one of those shiny places you see on the Gulf television channels. I've seen nothing like it in any of our towns, although I'm told they're building something similar in Ramallah.'

'Did you ever visit the place?'

'I went back to the village once, in the days when it was easy to get a permit. To tell you the truth, not much remained, except the mosque, which is in disuse. I was just a baby when we left, so my memories are only the stories my dear father told me about the old life. By now, those stories seem real enough to be my own memories, though.' Omar Yussef looked at the kids and thought of their father. 'Children, everything that seems bad passes. Life is very long. When you're young, it's easy to feel that some bad event is bigger than it is. But, look, I lived through even the great Catastrophe of our people and I'm a happy man. I studied hard at school and I work hard at my job and I have a good family.'

'Did you take exams at school?' one of the younger boys asked. He watched Omar Yussef and took a mouthful of *hummus*.

'Yes, I took lots of exams. I went to university in Damascus.'

'Why didn't they arrest *you*?'

'They don't arrest you for taking an exam, Sufian,' Salwa said.

The boy looked unconvinced. He watched Omar Yussef with a frown, as though failing to be arrested for taking an exam made the older man part of the conspiracy that robbed him of his father. 'Why didn't they arrest you, instead of Daddy?'

Omar Yussef chewed the *kubbeh*, but he didn't feel like swallowing it any more.

'Are you a policeman?' the boy asked.

'Sufian, shut up.' Naji shook his little brother's shoulder.

'I'm a schoolteacher, like your Daddy,' Omar Yussef said.

'Daddy says teachers have to be like policemen,' said Sufian. 'They have to find out what's true, and then they make sure all the children know about it.'

'I'm looking forward to meeting your Daddy. I think I'll like him.' *When the police aren't interested in the truth, adults keep quiet,* Omar Yussef thought. *When it's dangerous, only children ask questions. And maybe their teachers, because they care about the minds of the children and the future in which they'll grow up. That's why Masharawi wouldn't be silent, despite the danger. Maybe that's why I'm here, too.*

CHAPTER 8

Revolutionary Council delegates were crowding the front desk of the Sands Hotel when Omar Yussef returned from lunch at the Masharawi house. His two visits to Colonel al-Fara's headquarters that morning had drained him. His shirt was damp and his sweaty hair straggled down his neck to his collar. His eyes stung from the dust storm. He wanted a coffee, but the breakfast room was full of politicians and their aides, chatting noisily.

Khamis Zeydan was at a table near the door. Six other men in suits sat around the table, as did Sami Jaffari, wearing the black T-shirt that accentuated the lithe muscularity of his shoulders and chest. Everyone smoked cigarettes or pulled on the pipe of a *nargileh*. The suits were rapt by the story Khamis Zeydan told. Omar Yussef couldn't hear what his friend said, but he could tell the punchline was coming by the way Khamis Zeydan leaned back in his chair and lifted his arms wider and higher with each phrase. When the arms were above his head, the table exploded with laughter.

Sami noticed Omar Yussef through the doorway.

He winked and raised his eyes, as though he were suffering patiently.

Omar Yussef went up to his room. He sat quietly on his bed. Someone locked a door nearby and walked down the corridor, arguing into his cellular phone. Then it was silent. Omar Yussef listened to his breath. He thought of Eyad Masharawi, beaten and tormented, and of the children who missed him at home. Masharawi's chances of escaping further torture might depend on how Omar Yussef handled Professor Maki at dinner that evening. He felt such sudden, desperate loneliness that his jaw dropped and the skin of his cheeks felt heavy. He picked up the phone and struggled to remember how to get an outside line. Then he dialed his home.

Nadia answered.

'Greetings, my darling,' Omar Yussef said. 'How are you?'

'May Allah be thanked, Grandpa. What's happening in Gaza?'

'There's a dust storm here,' he said. 'How's the weather in Bethlehem?'

'Very hot. No dust storm.'

'You're lucky. What have you been doing?'

'I was reading one of your books this afternoon, Grandpa. The big one about ancient Egypt, with the pictures of the pyramids and the Egyptian gods.'

'I'm quite sure I wouldn't be allowed to bring such a book to Gaza. Hamas would object to its paganism.'

'Exactly. Shame on you, Grandpa.'

Omar Yussef tried to remember how old his sons had been when they developed a sense of sarcasm. He couldn't help feeling that Nadia, at age twelve, was advanced even in this.

'So I read in the book that Seth, who had the head of a jackal, was the god of the desert and that he made the dust storms,' Nadia said.

'Then the jackal-headed god is hard at work in Gaza. Unlucky for the men of Gaza.'

'I also read about men. About where men came from, according to the Egyptians.'

'Where did they come from?'

'The god of creation was called Atum. He made everything. First, he snorted the god of air out of his nose. Then he spat the goddess of water out of his mouth. And then some others that I can't remember, but they all came out of his body. When he looked at the result of all his work, Atum cried and each of his tears became a man to populate the world. So, you see, we all began with a god crying.'

Omar Yussef remembered the myth. He also recalled that it started with Atum arousing himself and engendering other gods with his orgasm. He hoped that hadn't been in the book Nadia had read.

'What do you think of the myth?' he asked.

'I think it makes sense. It explains why so much of life is sad and why we face so much wicked-ness, no matter how good we are.'

'Perhaps Atum was crying tears of joy.'

'I hadn't thought of that, Grandpa. But I don't think he was, anyway.'

'I'm glad that you're reading about history and how ancient people understood the world. There's much more to life than the views expressed by people in our own town and in our own time. I have other books like that one. I'll show them to you when I get home.'

'Grandpa, I made you a homepage.' Nadia was suddenly excited.

'You drew something for me?'

'What? No. For your website. I started it yesterday, after we spoke. I registered your domain name, and I wrote the text for the homepage and I posted a photo of you and I did some graphics, too.'

'What's a homepage?'

'When people type in the address of your website, the homepage is the first one that will come up. Of course, I have to make other pages, so they can navigate through the site.'

She has grown up more than I realized, Omar Yussef thought. *She understands the sadness at the core of the world in the story of the Egyptian god's tears. But she also has this technological excitement, which suggests she believes in the future.* He wondered how this change in his favorite grandchild had crept up on him. Perhaps he missed other changes in the world around him, too, simply because they didn't directly affect him. He remembered that he had been surprised when Salwa Masharawi told him her husband had been tortured. Now his surprise seemed alien to him, as though he would take it for granted that any man arrested for criticizing the government would have the soles of his feet beaten. Since that time in jail so long ago, he had spent decades building a wall of innocence around himself, but he had lost some portion of it in Gaza. Perhaps it hadn't been innocence, after all, but blindness. He understood why the god Atum had cried when he looked on the world he had made.

'Grandpa, is there a computer in your hotel?'

'Yes, there's a computer at the reception desk.'

'Do they have internet access?'

'I can ask them. There's a very nice lady at reception.'

'Write down your homepage address. It's *www.pa4d.ps.*'

Omar Yussef wrote the web address on a piece of hotel notepaper. 'What does that mean?'

Nadia laughed. 'You'll see. You have to go and call it up on the web. Do you want to talk to Grandma?'

'Yes, please, my darling.' Omar Yussef folded the slip of paper with the web address on it and tucked it into the breast pocket of his shirt.

He pulled back the drapes on his window. The hotel drive rose twenty yards from the lobby doors to the main beach road. The haziness of the dirt-filled air was thickening into twilight. A donkey trotted along the road, pulling a cart piled with boxes of tomatoes. A string of yellow taxis followed, sounding their horns and jockeying to be the first to overtake. A detail of red-bereted soldiers leaned against the guardpost outside the chief of Military Intelligence's home across the road. The building was a plain apartment block six stories high. Only one floor was illuminated, a sickly fluorescence glowing through the dust.

Maryam came on the line. 'Omar, dear, what did you have for lunch?'

He felt the loneliness again, sharply. 'Maryam, my life, I love you.'

'Omar?'

'I'll come home soon, I promise.'

'Omar, is something wrong?'

Omar Yussef's eyes stung. He thought it might be a good idea to cry out all the dust from the storm. He felt ready for it. His room was cold and he imagined himself imprisoned in it, far from home. *You know what it's like to be shut away, terrified and alone*, he thought. He was nauseous and he feared ruining everything that night by nervously throwing up his meal at Professor Maki's dining table. He breathed deeply and fought to visualize his wife's face. 'I had a good lunch at the home of a friend.'

'Good. Don't let Magnus take you to a restaurant. They cut corners with their recipes.'

'I'm eating at the home of a – a friend tonight, too.'

'Did Nadia tell you about your homepage?'

'Yes, did you see it?'

'No, she won't show it to anyone until you've approved it.'

'She's very clever.'

'Are you surprised?'

'No, I'm proud. I should get ready for dinner now, Maryam.'

'Go ahead. Everyone is fine here, may Allah be thanked.'

He hesitated. 'You're my whole life.'

Maryam laughed. 'Omar, are you going to start singing me old songs? Allah bless you, darling.'

Omar Yussef hung up. Three jeeps halted at the home of General Moussa Husseini across the street. He assumed they were changing the guard shift, but the men at the gate remained at their posts and the jeeps didn't leave. Instead, they formed a cordon around the entrance. The soldiers in the jeeps jumped from the rear of their vehicles and jogged through the door of the apartment building. On every floor, the lights came on. Then they all went out at once.

Omar Yussef turned off his lamp and watched Husseini's house. Nothing happened. He waited. Perhaps it had been only a routine bolstering of the guard. This might have been how they always prepared for the onset of night. *Except that tonight there's a dust storm*, he thought. *The darkness will be doubled.*

CHAPTER 9

A taxi dropped Omar Yussef on Emile Zola Street at seven-thirty. He rested his hand against the smooth bark of a tall sycamore and coughed. Dirt gusted through the air. With the falling darkness, the thick dust storm turned Omar Yussef's vision into a monochrome blur. The branches of the tree danced above him, jousting with the tricolor behind the wall of the French Cultural Center. The metal loopholes in the flag scratched rhythmically against its pole.

The wind came from behind him, caught his white hair and blew his little combover into his eyes. He moved carefully. Even here, in Gaza City's most expensive district, the sidewalk was uneven. He caught his toe on a protruding brick, forced out of its place in the diamond pattern underfoot by the roots of another old sycamore, and stumbled. With relief, he came to a gate and found a buzzer. Next to it, scribbled on the white-washed wall, was the name *Maki*.

Beyond the tall garden wall, the wind abated. Omar Yussef fixed his hair with a plastic comb from his shirt's breast pocket. He rubbed his shoes on the back of his trousers to clean away the dirt. The garden was lush and tropical. Omar Yussef wondered if Maki might be to blame for Gaza's water shortage, the grass was so thick and the spiky feet of the date palms were swamped by so many low fern bushes. The path to the house was short, but it wound around a fountain of molded concrete and turquoise tile. A large plastic doe peered from behind a bush next to the bubbling water. Omar Yussef pressed his palm to her snout and stroked her head as he passed.

The plain mahogany door opened as Omar Yussef came up the steps to the porch. A tiny maid in a brown nylon housecoat held it for him and greeted him in deferential, whispered English. She was narrow and straight and bony, almost like a little girl. Omar Yussef assumed from her look and accent that Maki had shipped her in from India or Sri Lanka. Omar Yussef thanked her and looked around. He had never seen such luxury in the home of a Palestinian. The floors were a milky brown marble polished to shine like the surface of a summer lake. At the center of the room, there was a brilliant chandelier so large that the last Shah might have thought it ostentatious, and a dining table and chairs not less sparkling than the floor. For a small girl, the maid put in a lot of elbow work.

'Professor Adnan will be with you soon, sir,' she said. 'May I bring you a drink?'

'Thank you. Soda water, please.'

The table was laid with two dinner settings of shimmeringly expensive silverware and crystal. Mentally, Omar Yussef set a place at the table for Eyad Masharawi and reminded himself that he must think carefully over every stage of his conversation tonight. Masharawi's freedom depended upon it.

The maid brought him his soda water and disappeared. The glass shook in his hand.

The low strains of a Fairuz love song drifted through the room. Amid such opulence, Omar Yussef half expected the Lebanese diva to step from behind a curtain with a string quartet.

Instead, Professor Adnan Maki made his appearance. He came from a corridor whose entrance was disguised by a black cloisonné Chinese screen decorated with blue and red birds. He wore a loose cobalt-blue silk shirt that made him look like a movie pirate and dark linen pants. He reached his arms wide. 'My dear *ustaz* Abu Ramiz,' he said.

Omar Yussef advanced carefully across the marble, in case it was as slippery as it looked.

Maki gave him three kisses on his cheeks. The smell of cologne was once again powerful. 'Consider this your family and your home,' he said.

'Your family is with you.'

'Welcome, welcome, welcome, Abu Ramiz. Merciful Allah bless you.'

'Allah bless you.'

Maki held onto Omar Yussef's hand and led him to the table. He pulled out a chair for him and slid it in under his guest. He glanced at the soda

91

water. 'Abu Ramiz, you are not in Hamastan any longer. The interior of this home is not even in Gaza, as far as I am concerned. It's wherever I want it to be, and it can be a place for any enjoyments I care to arrange.'

I'll bet, Omar Yussef thought. Maki certainly was right that his salon didn't look like it was in Gaza. 'As I mentioned earlier, I don't drink alcohol, Abu Nabil.'

'Surely just one glass,' Maki said. 'Your namesake, the ancient Persian poet, rhymed *divine* and *wine*. Was he not correct? Let's toast to him.'

'Much as I enjoy the poetry of Omar Khayyam, my health doesn't allow me to join you in your toast, Abu Nabil,' he said, gesturing vaguely toward the internal organs of his abdomen.

Maki raised a cautious eyebrow.

'But I don't object to your partaking,' Omar Yussef obliged.

Maki snapped his fingers and the maid appeared, holding a silver tray with two fingers of whisky in a crystal tumbler. Maki took it without a glance and put it away. Even as he swallowed, he spun his finger to signal that he wanted another, and sat. He looked suddenly serious and leaned forward.

'Abu Ramiz, it's such a pleasure to have cultured company.' He let out the groan of a man who has long suffered ignorant fools. 'You can't imagine how I'm stifled by Gaza and its provincialism. My wife can't stand to be here longer than a few weeks. As you can see from the place settings, she's not eating with us. No, she is eating in a far better establishment tonight. She's in Paris.'

The maid poured another whisky and Maki dived into the glass as if he were coming down from the high board at the beach club in the dunes north of Gaza City. He came up, shivering as he swallowed, and peered across the table with the staring wide eyes of a man swimming underwater. 'We have an apartment in Paris. *A pied à terre*, as they say. A little place built in the seventeenth century. It's in the Marais. You know this part of Paris? It used to be the Jewish quarter, but now it's rather exclusive.' Maki laughed. 'I like that very much, to be an occupier of the Jewish quarter. Yes, this is my small revenge for the occupation of our land in Palestine.'

He emptied the second glass and, while his throat recovered, he wagged a finger to signal that he had a story to tell. 'Some old Jews still live in our building in the Marais. I like to watch their little heart attacks when I tell them they share their staircase with a senior member of the PLO. They refuse to acknowledge me, so I just whisper *Allahu akbar* as I pass them on the stairs. My wife is there now, as a refugee from the dust and the heat of Gaza. The only negative thing about her absence, from her point of view, is that she will not meet you, dear brother Abu Ramiz.'

Omar Yussef felt he was supposed to smile. He twitched his cheeks and blinked. 'Your children are in Paris, too?'

'Yes, a boy and a girl, may Allah be thanked. Both are doing graduate studies at the Sorbonne.'

'Did they do their undergraduate degrees here at al-Azhar?'

Maki laughed and reached forward to tap Omar Yussef's hand, as though he were a delightfully naughty boy. 'It's a shame you don't drink, Abu Ramiz. You're so witty, even when you're sober. You'd be hilarious if you would join me in a whisky. Of course they didn't study here.'

The maid brought a bottle of red wine and poured for Maki. Omar Yussef covered the top of his wine glass with his palm, so that she wouldn't give him any. The crystal sounded a light, full note as his hand brushed its rim.

'So you're a schools inspector for the UN, Abu Ramiz?'

'I'm on a schools inspection at the moment. Usually I'm the principal of the UNRWA Girls' School in Dehaisha camp.'

'Ah, the finest people are those of Dehaisha. Progressives, leftists. Not all Islamists, as they are in Gaza.'

'Although I'm the principal, my main activity is still teaching. For three decades I've been a history teacher.'

Maki threw his arms wide. 'That's my field also. Abu Ramiz, we are two historians. This is a wonderful night. Welcome, welcome, Abu Ramiz. We shall talk history all night and forget about the present troubles of Gaza.'

Omar Yussef smiled, politely. Moroccan soap operas or Egyptian soccer would have been more neutral distractions. But if Maki was relaxed, perhaps he would be more inclined to help Omar Yussef with the Masharawi case.

The maid brought a tray of *mezzeh*, distributing the small plates of salads and spreads in a spray across the table. Maki handed Omar Yussef a wide, flat bread with which to eat the salads and pushed each plate solicitously toward him. 'Your health,' he said.

Omar Yussef scooped a deep red paste of ground nuts, cumin and chilis onto a corner of his bread and ate it. 'This really is the best *mouhammara* I've tasted in a long time,' he said.

'These Sri Lankans know Arabic cooking better even than Arabs. However, I fear that your colleagues, the Swede and the Scot, don't have the same feel for Arab culture. They can't truly understand our situation here in Gaza,' Maki said. 'And why not? Because they don't understand the history. If one only knows recent politics, then everyone looks bad – the nationalists, the Islamists, the refugees, the resistance. One can't see why Palestinians behave as they do unless first one traces the dim reaches of our history.'

'Do you think the men in the resistance know our history?'

'They may not have studied for a doctorate, but I believe they fight in the name of the Prophet Muhammad, who was a real historical figure, or

Saladin, who personally fought for Gaza against the Crusaders.'

'What lesson should my foreign friends draw from that?'

'That our people were fighting invaders long before the Jews came. It has been a constant battle throughout our history.' Maki picked up an oily vine leaf, bit through to the rice wrapped inside and chased it with a hearty swig of claret. 'Two thousand years before we began to reckon time from the foundation of Islam, the Pharaoh Thutmose was our first invader. The Canaanites took Gaza from the Egyptians, only for the Philistines to capture it from them. In the oldest part of our city, you can still see a ruined stone building popularly known as the very temple which Samson pulled down on the heads of the Philistines. It's nonsense, naturally – what's left of the building is no more than five hundred years old, but it has a place in our historic memory.'

'The Jewish Bible says Gaza was allotted to the tribe of Judah,' Omar Yussef said.

'Of course, but don't mention that – a thunder-bolt may come down from the skies to strike us.' Maki looked up in mock terror. 'Or one of the homemade *Qassam* rockets that our resistance fires into Israel.'

'You recounted these ancient invasions. But what importance do they have for the present conflict?'

'Great importance, indeed. They're the roots of today's conflict. Your foreign friends look at Gaza

96

and see what? A shithole, of course. Who can blame them? The Scot is probably from Edinburgh, the Athens of the north, as they call it. Very cultural. Maybe the other one's from the highly organized city of Stockholm, where no one crosses the road and farts at the same time. To them, Gaza is the epitome of absolute, worthless chaos. But Gaza was a crossroads of international trade when they were still painting themselves blue to raid the next village and steal its pigs.'

Maki took such a long drink of his claret that he was momentarily out of breath. 'Look, if you read the surveys, you'd see that Swedish women have the smallest breasts, on average, in the whole world.' Maki rubbed his silk shirt in illustration. 'Why? Because they don't understand how to *share* life and its bounty. They're individualists. Now Gazan women: under their robes they carry enormous breasts, big and heavy and full, like the hump of a camel.' He pursed his lips, screwed up his eyes and held his palms upward as though they supported a great and sensuous weight. 'This is because we're surrounded by the desert, so we understand the value of life, of food and nourishment and community. Nature around us is harsh. We can't look to it for easy sustenance, as they can in Sweden, with their lakes and forests. We must find nutrition in each other, in the fulsome bodies of our wives and in the feeling of belonging to a clan and in the shared struggle against the Jews. That's the story of Gaza.'

Omar Yussef nodded and stretched his lips into some kind of a smile. He was glad Maki was enjoying his cultured evening discussion.

The Sri Lankan maid brought a platter of grilled, fatty lamb chops and kebab on metal skewers and charred chicken flecked with red grains of sumac. Maki slid the kebab from the skewers with a folded piece of bread and filled Omar Yussef's plate. He picked up a roasted onion and pulled it apart with his fingers.

'The invaders continued to come. Saladin fought the Crusaders here, and then came the Turks.' Maki made circles in the air with the onion pieces, daintily, like a conductor with his baton. 'The British fought three battles here before they took Gaza in 1917. Can you imagine? Do you suppose the British people know this, riding the London Underground and shaking their heads with a tut-tut as they read stories about Gaza's violence in *The Daily Telegraph*?' Maki waved a segment of onion dismissively. 'As they see it, the violence here is all about our immediate conflict with the Jews – we could have peace, if only we were reasonable, like the British. They don't understand our three thousand years of oppression.'

'The problem isn't that the *Telegraph* readers don't know our history, Abu Nabil,' Omar Yussef said. 'Our own people don't know it, either. They learn history only in nasty cartoon form or from the mouths of politicians. How many people who claim to fight in the name of Saladin know anything

98

about him, except that he was a hero who fought the Christians? They probably think he was a Palestinian, rather than a Kurd.'

Maki stared over the top of his wineglass. He made his voice serious and quiet. 'As a historian, I should like to sit in on your classes, Abu Ramiz,' Maki said. 'But I'm also a politician. I'd like to talk to you now about politics.'

'I welcome the opportunity to be your student.'

'The situation with Masharawi is very delicate,' Maki said. He rolled his wine around in his glass and watched the light of the chandelier filter through it. 'I must appeal to you as a brother Palestinian that this case should go no further.'

'That's not up to me.'

'I think it is.'

'Did I arrest him? *I* didn't report him to Colonel al-Fara. Oh, and I forgot to bring the keys of his jail cell with me tonight.'

Maki stared at his wine.

Omar Yussef reminded himself to stay calm. He needed Maki on his side if he was to secure Masharawi's release. He made his voice sweet. 'Forgive me. Do you have any new information about the investigation into Masharawi, Abu Nabil?'

'It's a very serious case, Abu Ramiz. There's evidence of his involvement in espionage.'

'How could a teacher possibly help a spy agency?'

'By disrupting the work of our university and

poisoning the minds of our best students against the government and the security forces.'

'What evidence is there of this?'

'He has signed a confession.'

'He signed?'

Maki lifted his chin and held his palms forward in a gesture of finality. 'Confessing everything.'

'Under torture.'

'We don't torture prisoners.'

'We? I'm not referring to the university, Abu Nabil.'

'Neither am I. I mean that *we Palestinians* do not torture prisoners.'

Omar Yussef waited as the Sri Lankan slid a platter of fruit onto the table. The professor took a paring knife to an orange and cut it into sections.

'Then he will be put on trial?' Omar Yussef said.

'If the security forces brought him to trial, it would only allow him to spread his false propaganda once more.'

'Then what do you intend to do with him?'

'That depends on whether the UN makes a big deal out of it. If the UN remains quiet, then it's possible that we might be able to allow Masharawi to go free.'

'Release a spy?'

'After a suitable period in jail undergoing some punishment for his crimes.'

'More torture.'

'Punishment.' Maki raised his eyebrows and waved a segment of orange at Omar Yussef. 'But it would be necessary to persuade the UN to remain quiet. If it becomes a diplomatic issue, it will be difficult for Colonel al-Fara to back down. Masharawi might have to be executed, as a traitor.'

'Wallender already has been told that Masharawi was tortured. He won't just let that go.'

'The Swede is at your mercy, Abu Ramiz. He doesn't speak Arabic, right? He doesn't understand the culture or the players. He knows only what you let him know.' Maki smiled like a contented man sinking into a hot bath. 'I don't expect your cooperation just because of my beautiful eyes, Abu Ramiz. I can offer you incentives.'

Omar Yussef glanced around the room. He thought of the furnishings in his own home. He and Maryam were comfortable, but there was something seductive about a room of such lavish excess. The Sri Lankan brought a coffee and put it before him. She smelled of spices and kitchen sweat.

Maki grinned and nodded toward the Sri Lankan as she left. 'Incentives of whatever taste you may have.'

'She's too skinny for me,' Omar Yussef said. *Keep a grip*, he thought. *Don't let him know that you won't help him*. 'I shall do what I can, Abu Nabil. But you have to give me something I can offer the Swede. Some way for him to feel he saved Masharawi. Perhaps if Masharawi were simply suspended from teaching for a semester.'

'He would have to be suspended from opening

his mouth. The fool can't help but broadcast ugly accusations every time he talks.'

'If Colonel al-Fara allowed me and Wallender to visit Masharawi, we might be able to persuade him to reach a deal. To keep his mouth shut.'

'I would prefer to make *you* happy in some way.'

'We shall discuss that, of course, but you must give me a little help, so that I can persuade Wallender.'

'We understand each other?'

Omar Yussef nodded. He looked at his watch and rose to say goodbye.

'Shall I call a car for you?' Maki asked.

'No, thanks. I must walk off some of this excellent food you've presented to me tonight. It's not far to my hotel.'

When Maki saw Omar Yussef to the door, he held his hand and kissed him. The dust blew in and Omar Yussef stifled a cough. Maki looked at him closely and all the softness of the evening was gone from his face. His eyes were hard in the half-light. *He doesn't believe me*, Omar Yussef thought.

He went down the steps. At the fountain, the plastic doe nuzzled his hand again. He came to the gate. Maki was in the doorway, silhouetted against the gleam of the big chandelier. The professor buzzed the gate and it swung open in the wind, faster than Omar Yussef expected. It caught him painfully on the wrist as he reached for it. Out on the street, the dust storm had picked up.

CHAPTER 10

The darkness stalked Omar Yussef, watchful and predatory. With each indistinct movement he perceived in the blackness, he halted and squinted into the dusty wind until he was sure he was alone. And he was. The streets were as empty as at the loneliest hour of night, though it was not quite eleven.

At the corner of Maki's street, he looked along the beach road in the direction of his hotel. The dust cloud shivered in the ocher glow of the streetlights, as though all those who passed this way during the day surrounded Omar Yussef now, raising the dirt into the air with their silent tread. The wind sounded in Omar Yussef's ears with the same heavy rush as the waves of the Mediterranean, a hundred yards beyond the road. It was humid and his shirt stuck to his back. He wondered if he had been sweating throughout dinner, or only since he began to walk. The tension he had felt with Maki had exhausted him. It seemed to have turned his knees to ice, and he swayed like a child standing for the first time. He had to keep moving.

Omar Yussef started along to his hotel. He walked

on the roadway, rather than the sidewalk, because there was at least some light down the middle of the street. Gaza City was already an hour in bed, and lights were out on all but the most important thoroughfares so as to deprive Israeli raiders of geographical reference points – whether they lurked above in a helicopter or sped through town in the car of an undercover squad. A few windows glimmered with fluorescent light, but most were blank and shuttered against the hot wind.

He reached the first streetlamp and found himself out of breath. He sat on the high curb of the narrow median and coughed into his handkerchief. He knew this dust storm might not break for another day or two; he cursed it and wished desperately for its end. He wanted to breathe and to see clearly. He wanted the atmospheric pressure to lift and the pain in his temples to stop. He wanted to hear silence and calm, not the hot rumbling pant of the *khamsin*. He spat gritty phlegm onto the road.

Under the hum of the storm, Omar Yussef heard the sound of engines. Two jeeps came around the corner from Emile Zola Street. Their motors growled so loudly that it seemed as though they might be the source of the moaning wind. Omar Yussef wondered if the center of the storm was about to suck him up and toss him into the skies above Gaza. That would be a turbulent ride, but if it dropped him somewhere outside Gaza, he wouldn't object.

The jeeps rolled to a halt in front of Omar Yussef. They were dark green and unmarked and their headlights were off. He made out the shapes of four gunmen inside each one, their assault rifles upright between their legs.

The front window of the first jeep slid down to reveal a man wearing a stocking cap over his face, with holes cut for his eyes and mouth. Around his brow, he had tied a black strip of cloth with white writing across it: *The Saladin Brigades*. Below the stocking cap, there was a camouflage jacket. The arm of the camouflage jacket led to a big hand that trained an automatic pistol on Omar Yussef. The schoolteacher stood, stiffly, and took the handkerchief away from his face. He wanted them to see him.

'Peace be upon you,' he said.

'And upon you, peace,' the man with the pistol said. 'Where are you from, uncle?'

'Bethlehem.'

'You're a long way from home.'

'I'm visiting Gaza. I was walking back to my hotel. I didn't think the weather would slow me down so much, but I had to sit down. I can't catch my breath.'

'Which hotel?'

'The Sands. Will you put down the gun, please? It doesn't help me to breathe any easier.'

The gunman withdrew the pistol. 'Sorry, uncle. There are Israeli undercover units on the streets.'

'If I'm one of them, then the rest of my squad

left me behind because I was slowing them down. Don't worry, I imagine I'm a lot less deadly than they are.'

The gunman looked at the man in the seat next to him, who also wore a stocking cap and Saladin Brigades headband, and whispered. He turned back to Omar Yussef. 'We would take you to the hotel, uncle, but we're on a mission.'

'That's okay. I'll walk. I'm getting used to the dust now. I'll be fine.'

'It's only a five minute walk to your hotel, uncle. But you shouldn't be in a hurry. Take longer than that.'

'What do you mean?'

'Our mission is close to the hotel. I don't want you to be caught in the middle of anything. So don't rush.'

'Your mission?'

'Allah grant you grace, uncle.' The jeeps howled into motion.

Omar Yussef watched them fade into the dust cloud. Their mission was near the Sands Hotel? It must have had something to do with General Husseini. Perhaps he had boosted his guard for the night because he knew these gunmen were coming for him. But why? And what were the Saladin Brigades?

He waited in the orange glow. There could be a shootout in front of his hotel. He knew he ought to remain at a distance, but he wanted to see what was going to happen. He noticed that he was firm on his feet, his exhaustion erased by adrenaline. He moved along the beach road toward the hotel.

With each step, he expected to hear gunfire. There were only eight men in the two jeeps; they would be outnumbered by the guard at General Husseini's house. But they might not be the only gunmen heading for the battle, if indeed it was to be a battle. He laughed to think that, if they hadn't been on an operation, they might have given him a ride to his hotel. *I don't have change for a tip*, he thought.

He came to the end of the row of hotels along the beach. Perhaps it would be safest to wait where he was. If there was to be a gun battle, he wouldn't want to be in the open when the two sides started to fire. He looked along the strip of hotels. Each was set back from the road, down its own short drive. Bright neon lights flickered over the driveways, smoldering in ugly pink and green through the dirty air. Where were the gunmen and their jeeps? Perhaps their mission was inside the Sands Hotel. They might be in there already. The Revolutionary Council was at the hotel. The delegates might be the gunmen's target, rather than General Husseini. He moved forward.

Omar Yussef was less than two hundred yards from the hotel when at last he made out the set-up through the dirt and wind. The two jeeps were outside the entrance to the drive of the Sands Hotel. One idled in front of the gate and the other sat in the middle of the road. As he approached, he saw the guards outside General Husseini's house, quiet and still. He moved more quickly. Perhaps he could get past them before anything started, whatever it might be. If he stopped where he was, they'd be suspicious. He didn't want a gun held on him twice in one night.

As Omar Yussef closed in on the jeeps, one of the gunmen looked in his direction and seemed to recognize him. Hoping this was the gunman who had spoken to him earlier, Omar Yussef pointed at the entrance to the hotel drive, to remind him where he was heading. The gunman looked undecided, then the sound of an engine cut through the wind and he turned to face it.

A UN Suburban came to the far end of the hotel strip. Its white bulk showed clearly through the darkness. It seemed somehow naïve of the car's occupants to drive with their headlights on, rather than creeping through these dangerous streets in the dark. The car headed toward the jeeps. Omar Yussef stared. If that was Cree and Wallender, they were driving right into the middle of a gun battle. At the very least, the gunmen would stop them and give them a fright.

The UN car slowed. It moved in second gear past the furthest jeep. Omar Yussef stepped away from the sidewalk and waved both his arms above his head. He felt sure Cree and Wallender were in the car, returning to the hotel. He had to warn them.

The first jeep roared, as loud as a low-flying jet.

It jerked across the entrance to the Sands Hotel and blocked the road. At that moment, the second jeep pulled across the back of the Suburban, hemming it in. The gunmen jumped from their vehicles and held their Kalashnikovs on the UN car. Omar Yussef glanced at the Military Intelligence chief's house. The guards were gone.

He hurried forward, coughing through the dust and waving his arms. The warm wind seemed to rush directly into him, slowing him, suffocating him. He had to get to Wallender and Cree.

The gunmen pulled the two foreigners from their car, their hands in the air. Omar Yussef couldn't make out the shouts above the wind. Wallender looked terrified. He was bent backward across the hood of the car with a Kalashnikov jutting into his ribs.

Cree refused to bend. He seemed taller even than he had when Omar Yussef first saw him. His hands were in the air, but he was talking calmly and without pause, engaging the two gunmen who faced him.

Omar Yussef reached the first jeep. He put a hand on the driver's open door to steady himself. He took a breath, ready to shout, but choked on a dusty cough. His face grew hot with frustration. He spewed out a mouthful of bile and rubbed his lips with his handkerchief.

'Stop it,' he yelled. 'What're you doing?'

The gunman who had seemed to recognize him turned, but kept his gun on Cree. He shouted at

Omar Yussef, so that he could be heard over the excitable yelling of the other gunmen. 'Go to your hotel, uncle.'

'These are my colleagues. They're innocent. They're here to help the Palestinian people.'

'Go to your hotel.'

Omar Yussef advanced on the gunman. He managed a smile in Cree's direction. 'It will be okay, James.'

'Don't get yourself hurt, Abu Ramiz,' Cree said. 'They won't do anything silly with us foreigners, but they might get pissed off at you.'

The gunman put his hand flat against Omar Yussef's chest. 'Uncle, this isn't your business.'

'I told you, these are my friends.'

'Get out of here, uncle.'

'Is this a kidnapping? Are you taking them somewhere? Then take me.' Omar Yussef tried to hear himself, to measure the calm in his voice. But the words sounded like someone else's. Someone desperate and shrill.

Cree was talking, stating his role at the UN, and the gunman was shouting and shoving Omar Yussef in the chest and Omar Yussef was pushing himself forward and a gun that had been trained on Cree was turned on Omar Yussef and he looked at the gun and stepped forward onto the barrel and felt it below his collar bone.

'They're from the UN,' he shouted.

'That's why we're taking them, uncle.'

'Then take me. I'm with the UN.'

'We need a foreigner.'

'I'm much more important to the UN than they are. I'm important to the UN's whole operation in Palestine. Take me.'

'No, uncle.' The gunman growled each word with a thrust of the rifle. His eyes were yellow behind the stocking cap.

'Abu Ramiz, it's okay. Go to the hotel—' Cree barely had opened his mouth to speak, before the gunman spun and smashed his rifle barrel flat into the Scotsman's teeth. Cree went to his knees. The gunman pulled his pistol.

He's going to shoot him. Omar Yussef frantically grabbed the gunman's arm, but the thickset man shook him off.

The gunman lifted his arm and brought the side of the pistol down flat on the back of Cree's head. The Scotsman pitched forward toward the dusty blacktop, out cold.

Omar Yussef tried to catch the falling man. He couldn't hold him, but he lowered him quietly. He stood. 'You're a fool,' he shouted at the gunman. He knew this wasn't the way to talk yourself out of a hostage situation, but he'd spent an evening dissimulating before Maki for the sake of Eyad Masharawi's freedom, even hinting that he might be as corrupt as the professor wished him to be. He'd had enough diplomacy. 'You've killed him. You've killed a UN official.'

The other gunmen saw the tall foreigner laid out on the ground and their shouting grew louder

111

with panic. Two of them grabbed Wallender and shoved him into the back of the second jeep. One of them cuffed the Swede across the cheek as he entered the jeep. It roared into the dark, taking four of the gunmen with it. Wallender's ghostly face glimmered through the window and was gone.

The gunman who had struck Cree stood over the body. He ordered the other gunmen to get going.

Omar Yussef grabbed the gunman's forearm. 'I said, you've killed him. Where are you taking the other one?'

'You'll find out soon enough. This one's not dead, and I wouldn't have had to hit him at all if you'd done as you were told, uncle.'

'Don't call me *uncle*, you bastard. You're not from my people. You're a destroyer of Palestine. Dogs like you disgust me and every decent Palestinian. No one ever tells you how much they hate you to your face, because everyone's frightened of you. But they hate you nonetheless. I'm not scared, though. I don't care what you—'

In the dark and the dust and with tears coming to his eyes, Omar Yussef failed to see the pistol, flat in the gunman's hand. He felt a white flash that shot from the left side of his head through his entire body and exploded out of his eye sockets. The eruption lit Gaza as bright as day and Omar Yussef saw the place clearly. He heard the words Khamis Zeydan had spoken to him in the breakfast room: *There is no single, isolated crime in Gaza. Each one is linked to many others, you'll see. When you touch one of them, it sets off reverberations that will be heard by powerful people, ruthless people.* What wickedness had he uncovered that these men should strike back like this? In the split second that the white light flashed around his head, Omar Yussef saw every crime ever committed in Gaza. He would start to solve those crimes when he woke up. He wondered if he would wake up.

The white flash was over and the dust storm had stopped. There was calm inside Omar Yussef. He must have been gone from Gaza.

CHAPTER 11

It was cold and dark when Omar Yussef came to. He shivered and hugged himself, and he heard a voice noting that he had moved. *Where is Magnus?* he thought. *Are they holding us in the same room?* He listened for signs that Wallender was there.

Omar Yussef shivered again. A hand lifted his head and fed him water. The movement of his neck was like a spike through his brain and he cried out. The water spilled onto his chin and chest, but he sucked down as much as he could. It tasted like an Alpine spring and he wondered if he was outside in the chilly night. He hoped it was true, because there were no Alps in Gaza, so perhaps he was somewhere else. When he choked, he rolled onto his side. His head gave a single massive pulse of pain with the motion and he bellowed again. A hand rested on his shoulder and patted him. *Friendly kidnappers*, he thought. *Bastards.* He pushed the hand away. 'Fuck off,' he said.

There was a laugh. 'I swear by Allah, he's almost back to his normal cheerful self,' a voice said, and there was another laugh. He recognized the voice,

114

but its owner was in Gaza, and Omar Yussef had convinced himself that the gunman had hit him so hard he had cleared the border fence, right out of the stinking Gaza Strip.

'Sami, help me get him upright.'

The familiar voice again, and he knew the name it spoke. His brain jarred as they propped him against the padded headboard. The friendly kidnappers had given him pillows and – now he felt it beneath him – a mattress. His squirming brain dropped the pain down into his neck and shoulders and on into his stomach, where it rolled like the boys he had seen roughhousing on the beach beside their fishing nets. The pain blotted out the lovely mountain views he had imagined when he tasted the water and forced him to remember that he was in Gaza. He was in bloody Gaza, he knew it, and he cursed again.

'Shame on you,' said Khamis Zeydan.

Omar Yussef breathed heavily. He put his hand to his face, on the left where the pain was worse. His eyes were covered in cloth. He put a finger beneath the cloth to lift it and a shiver of light bolted into his eyeball. Slowly, he rolled the bandage up to his forehead and exposed both his eyes to the light.

'We tried to fix your glasses,' Khamis Zeydan said. 'The lenses aren't broken, but the frame is a little bent.'

Omar Yussef took the glasses. He slid them on. They sat awkwardly on his nose, the right lens half an inch higher than the other one. His hotel room came into focus. Perched on the bed either side of him sat Khamis Zeydan and Sami Jaffari. They smiled, their faces pale, sensing the pain of the blow that had knocked him cold. Beyond the foot of the bed, James Cree sat in a gilt rococo chair with his elbow on the small vanity table. A bandage wrapped his head and his eyes were open wide, staring, drawn and sleepless.

'Sami found you outside,' Khamis Zeydan said. 'He was down in the lobby and he heard shouting, so he went to look. He found the two of you, unconscious. It looks like you were both pistol-whipped. James came to about an hour ago. You've been awake for a while, but you haven't made much sense.'

'Magnus?'

'Kidnapped by the Saladin Brigades. How do you feel?'

Omar Yussef groaned. 'Can you turn off the air-conditioning? I'm very cold.'

Sami went to the corner of the room by the door, out of Omar Yussef's sight. The infuriating purr halted and he felt warmer. He closed his eyes and listened to the silence, but he couldn't get back to the mountains, so he opened his eyes and straightened his back.

'Are you okay, James?' he said.

Cree lifted a glass of whisky. 'I'm well looked-after.' There was a bottle on the vanity next to him.

Khamis Zeydan laughed. 'Scotch was the first

thing James asked for when he came around in the lobby. Fortunately, there were no Islamists present. He was surrounded by delegates of the Revolutionary Council, who, as you know, are not strong adherents to the proscriptions of the Prophet, peace be upon him. A number of delegates were able immediately to oblige our Scots friend with their hipflasks. Though one of them, who claims to be a doctor, wanted to give you smelling salts.'

Omar Yussef looked confused.

'I said to him, *Does it look like my friend has simply fainted? Put away your stupid smelling salts.* Our party is full of people who obtained their medical degrees behind the Iron Curtain.' Khamis Zeydan smiled. 'For medicinal purposes, I also gave James a bottle from the supply in my suitcase.'

'Who are the Saladin Brigades? That's what was written on those headbands the gunmen wore. But how did you know they kidnapped Magnus?'

Khamis Zeydan pulled a sheet of paper from his jacket pocket. He unfolded it and gave it to Omar Yussef.

The top of the page bore a crest with a rampant eagle and two scimitars. When Omar Yussef tried to read, his brain pitched and rolled and, in his stomach, the rough and tumble started again. He handed it to Khamis Zeydan. 'I can't. Please read it to me.'

'*The Saladin Brigades demand the release of the brother and struggler Bassam Odwan of Rafah.*

Corrupt forces in the ranks of Military Intelligence wish to transfer the guilt for their cruel crimes to the brother Odwan and the Saladin Brigades. The Brigades demand Odwan's release in return for the freedom of the supposed UN official currently in the custody of the Brigades. The foreign UN official, who is under investigation for spying activities, will be handed over to the authorities in return for the release of Odwan. Odwan must be returned to his comrades in Rafah to continue his resistance against the Occupation.' Khamis Zeydan folded the paper and put it on the nightstand. 'There's more of the usual sort of heroic verbiage, but that's the essence.'

Omar Yussef gave an exasperated, furious exhalation. 'What is this all about? Who the hell is Bassam Odwan?'

'Bassam Odwan was arrested for killing the officer who had the big funeral yesterday. You heard the officer's comrades firing into the air during his funeral when you arrived at the hotel.'

Omar Yussef remembered the truck and the coffin draped in the Palestinian flag on the way into Gaza City. 'Why did Odwan kill the soldier?'

'Odwan is a member of the Saladin Brigades.' Khamis Zeydan glanced at Sami. 'Usually, the police don't touch the Saladin Brigades. It's the most powerful gang in the Gaza Strip. On this occasion, a Military Intelligence officer tried to arrest Odwan. Apparently Odwan didn't want to be arrested and he killed the soldier.'

118

'What does that have to do with Magnus? And he isn't a spy.'

'Don't get excited about that accusation,' Khamis Zeydan said, laying his hand on Omar Yussef's leg. 'They can't announce that they kidnapped a foreigner just to use him as a hostage. They have to make it look as though they did this to protect the Palestinian people.'

'We must find Magnus.'

'I don't think it's that simple.'

'What are you talking about?' Omar Yussef grabbed Khamis Zeydan's arm.

'This needs to be handled at a senior level. Even if we could find out where they're keeping Magnus, they wouldn't just give him up after we knock quietly on the door. And if we take along the security forces, there'll be one hell of a shootout. That'd be a lot more dangerous to Magnus than whatever they're doing with him now. After all, this isn't Iraq – they aren't about to chop off his head.'

'Then we need to persuade whoever's holding Odwan to let him go. After that, Magnus can be freed.'

'The commander of Military Intelligence, General Husseini, personally went to Rafah to coordinate Odwan's arrest. Do you think he'll just allow the killer to stroll away?' Khamis Zeydan grimaced. 'Look, the Saladin Brigades run tunnels under the Egyptian border into Rafah to smuggle weapons into the Gaza Strip. A Military Intelligence officer named Lieutenant Fathi Salah tried to arrest Odwan, to stop the smuggling. Then Husseini paraded the coffin all over the Gaza Strip and put on a hero's funeral for Salah, as a way of showing that his men make sacrifices to preserve law and order. He can't just let Odwan go a day later.'

Omar Yussef pushed himself up onto his elbows. The dizziness spotted his vision with bright colors. 'In the flyer, the Saladin Brigades claim Odwan is innocent. If Odwan killed Lieutenant Salah, we need to prove to the Saladin Brigades that their man is in the wrong. Or if someone else killed Lieutenant Salah, we can show General Husseini that Odwan's not guilty. But we need to investigate, to find out the truth.'

'They really did hit you hard on the head. You've lost all sense of reality.'

The spots cleared from Omar Yussef's eyes and he sat upright. 'They knocked my head clean out of Gaza,' he said. 'I'm thinking the way people think out there in the real world, not as they do in this madhouse.'

Khamis Zeydan shook his head and lit a Rothman's.

'Don't smoke in here,' Omar Yussef said. 'I feel nauseous.'

Khamis Zeydan hesitated, stared at the cigarette, horrified to forgo its nicotine, then stubbed it into the ashtray by the bed. He drummed his fingers against the nightstand and jiggled his knee up and down. Omar Yussef thought it might be less irritating just to let the man smoke.

Cree took a swig of whisky. 'I think you're correct, Abu Ramiz. Your summary of our options is right on the nose.'

Khamis Zeydan stared at Cree, incredulously. 'I'm not sure which one of you is more badly concussed.'

'They hit me at least twice, but I'd be willing to bet that I've got a thicker skull than Abu Ramiz.' Cree laughed and toasted Khamis Zeydan.

The Bethlehem police chief poured himself a drink from the bottle on the desk beside Cree. 'Look, when you two were out cold, I confess that I had the same thought as you, Abu Ramiz. But I discussed the reality of what you're suggesting with Sami. He understands Gaza best. That's why I know your idea's crazy.'

Omar Yussef put his hand on Sami's lean forearm. 'What's he talking about?'

Sami grinned. His teeth were discolored but healthy, and it was a sympathetic smile. 'I've heard from the guys in the Saladin Brigades that Lieutenant Fathi Salah had gone to meet Odwan late that night in Rafah when he was killed.'

'To meet him? Not to arrest him?'

'To meet. The Saladin Brigades people in Rafah wouldn't tell me much, because I'm tight with their outfit here in Gaza City and there's a big rivalry between the two wings,' Sami said. 'But I managed to get a little information out of them. They're adamant that Odwan didn't kill Salah.'

'Who would have framed him?'

121

Sami shrugged and looked at Khamis Zeydan.

The Brigadier nodded. 'There would be so many candidates, so many enemies for a man like Odwan. There are rival smugglers down in Rafah. Then the security forces, which want to make trouble so they can get bigger budgets. Gaza's in a state of anarchy. You can see that from your window by the guard General Husseini has outside his home.'

'He has extra soldiers there tonight. I saw them arrive.'

Khamis Zeydan glanced at Sami. 'These military men are all fighting for power,' Sami said. 'Particularly General Husseini and Colonel al-Fara.'

'Sami, there's a rivalry, you said, between the Saladin Brigades in Rafah and in Gaza City?' Omar Yussef frowned. 'I don't understand.'

'They're the same organization in name alone, Abu Ramiz,' Sami said. 'They're arguing over the profits from weapons smuggled under the Egyptian border. Parts for missiles are the big thing at the moment. In Rafah, the Brigades leaders say that they're the ones who bring in the weapons, so they should get the majority of the money. The Gaza City gang says it faces a greater risk of Israeli attack, so the big money should come to them.'

Omar Yussef took another drink of water. It no longer tasted cool like the mountains. It was lukewarm and there was a bitter aftertaste. He put his hand on Khamis Zeydan's forearm. 'It's strange. When the gunman hit me on the head,

I remembered what you told me in the breakfast room, about each crime in Gaza being connected to every other apparently separate offense. Could there be a connection between the case of Eyad Masharawi and Magnus's kidnapping?'

Khamis Zeydan scoffed and drank his whisky.

'I was walking home from Professor Maki's place,' Omar Yussef said. 'The gunmen who did the kidnapping came down Maki's street after me.'

'Are you saying the professor set up the kidnapping? Come on. Those same gunmen were here at the hotel while you were out,' Khamis Zeydan said.

'Here?'

'While you were still dining with Professor Maki, they came into the lobby. Sami was sitting there making eyes at the pretty receptionist, and he saw them come in a little after nine. Some of them spoke to the desk clerk and went upstairs. Then they left. Sami checked what they wanted. It turns out they asked the desk clerk what rooms the Swede and the other UN schools inspector were in.'

'We need to see this Odwan,' Omar Yussef said.

'You want to break him out of jail?' Khamis Zeydan said, pouring another glass of Scotch.

'We'll have to ask General Husseini to let us interview him.'

'If you ask politely, why not?'

Omar Yussef was angry with his friend's poor humor and the whisky scent in the room that made him wish for a forbidden drink. 'His home is just across the street. Why don't *you* stroll over and ask him? You're buddies with all these bastards. Husseini's on the Revolutionary Council, and so are you. Give him the secret handshake.'

Khamis Zeydan looked hard at his Scotch. 'The secret handshake usually has ten thousand dollars in it, at least.'

'I could try to set up a meeting with General Husseini,' Sami said. He turned to Khamis Zeydan. 'I don't want you to risk involvement in this affair, Abu Adel. It would be dangerous for you. Politically.'

Khamis Zeydan slugged down his whisky. He tapped the empty glass against his prosthetic hand and shrugged.

'I know a few people close to Husseini,' Sami said. He put a hand on Omar Yussef's leg. 'I warn you, General Husseini is a really bad type. Obviously he's a liar and a thief – that goes without saying. But Husseini is also a sadist. He personally tortures some of his prisoners, for his own entertainment. He likes to slice off the tips of a prisoner's fingers and wrench out the fingernails. At the prison, they call it a *Husseini Manicure*.'

Omar Yussef linked his fingers and rested them on his belly. He pressed them tightly together so no one would see his hands shaking. This was no longer a matter of a misunderstanding at the university, or even a case of a vindictive, corrupt boss punishing a whistleblower. It had extended into kidnapping and murder. His friend's life was in danger. He remembered his sense on the road into Gaza City, when the UN car passed the coffin of Fathi Salah, that death was pursuing him. He felt the dead man's breath cold on his neck.

'The *Husseini Manicure*,' Khamis Zeydan said, refilling his tumbler with whisky. 'He started that back in Beirut during the civil war. I knew the bastard well at that time. We both worked on the Old Man's personal staff. Husseini was dirty, cruel and corrupt even then.'

'He must have fit right in,' Omar Yussef said. He stared at Khamis Zeydan. The police chief met the stare, rolling the Scotch around in his glass.

Cree poured another long glass of whisky. 'Before the gunmen stopped our car, Magnus said to me, 'Oh, look, it's Abu Ramiz.' There you were, hurrying toward us with your arms waving.' He drank slowly. 'It was as though you knew what was about to happen.'

'The gunmen stopped me a few minutes before on the street,' Omar Yussef said. 'They said they were on a mission. When I saw your car heading toward them, I thought you might be in danger. I was trying to warn you.'

Cree swilled the whisky around in his cheek and was silent, but he kept his gaze on Omar Yussef.

'So you don't trust me, now?' Omar Yussef raised his voice. 'You think I tipped the gunmen off, pointed out your car, made sure they didn't grab the wrong UN people? Of course, and then they bashed me on the head to make it look like it wasn't a set-up.'

Cree swallowed. 'I suppose not.' His voice was low and dark.

Omar Yussef cursed and slammed a hand down on the nightstand. The motion bounced him slightly on the bed and his glass of water spilled on the crotch of his pants.

Cree seemed to take pity on him. He put a convivial hand on Khamis Zeydan's back, pointed at Omar Yussef and lightened his tone. 'My Arabic's not so great, but I made out some of what Abu Ramiz said to the gunmen during the hold up. 'I'm much more important to the UN than they are. I'm important to the whole UN operation in Palestine,' he said. Look, here he is, the UN's big fish, with his trousers underwater.' Cree and Zeydan laughed. Sami squeezed Omar Yussef's knee, reassuringly.

Khamis Zeydan clinked glasses with Cree to celebrate the joke. 'You used to have a nice quiet life, Abu Ramiz,' he said. 'These days you seem to attract trouble. Last year with the gunmen in Bethlehem, and now here with the Saladin Brigades and only Allah knows who else. What happened?'

'I'm the same as I ever was,' Omar Yussef said. 'There's just more trouble to go around.'

CHAPTER 12

Khamis Zeydan woke Omar Yussef every two hours, in case he had a concussion. Each time he awoke, Omar Yussef stared in confusion and wondered why James Cree was drinking and humming a tune at the foot of his bed. At eight, the Brigadier roused him as Sami entered the room.

'General Husseini will see us at nine-thirty,' Sami said. 'He wants you to have breakfast with him at his home.'

Omar Yussef breathed slowly. *I recall who General Husseini is, but why does he want to have breakfast with me?* It took him some seconds to remember. He rubbed his head. Clearly it had been a stronger blow than he had realized. He glanced at Khamis Zeydan. He saw from the tension in his friend's tired eyes that his confusion had been noticed.

'You need to have all your wits about you to handle a snake like Husseini,' Khamis Zeydan said. 'You're in no condition to go up against him.'

'I'll play the strong silent type and leave the talking to James,' Omar Yussef said. 'He seems fine.'

Cree was whistling 'Flowers of the Forest.' He raised his glass. The whisky was down near the bottom of the label on the bottle. 'I'm on top of my game, lads. Fresh as a daisy. You leave it to me.'

Khamis Zeydan whispered to Omar Yussef. 'That one phoned the UN people to alert them about Magnus while you were sleeping. He slurred his speech. He's in no better shape than you.'

'By Allah, I'm not afraid,' Omar Yussef said. He reached out, caught Khamis Zeydan's elbow and pulled him close. 'I just feel as though Gaza is too complicated for me to understand where I'm treading.'

'I warned you.'

Omar Yussef rubbed his eyes and growled. 'Military Intelligence, Preventive Security, the Saladin Brigades of Gaza City and their rivals in the Saladin Brigades of Rafah. It's as though I have to find room in my head for every square kilometer of Gaza and space for every soldier in all these different groups, to keep track of them.'

'Do you want me to draw you a diagram?'

'Magnus's life depends on these people and I don't know which of them to trust.' Omar Yussef could hear the desperation in his voice. *Am I breaking down?* he wondered. *I mustn't. Magnus needs me.*

'Let me make it simple for you.' Khamis Zeydan took both of Omar Yussef's hands and looked hard at him. 'Forget all of these groups. Trust none of them. Think only of the man who sits in front of you at any given time. Forget his name and his organization. Just remember that at that moment he's first in line to eat you alive.'

'It's a long queue.'

'Gaza is full of nasty gourmands.'

Sami brought newspapers from the lobby. None of them mentioned Wallender's kidnapping, but Husseini would know their reason for coming. Omar Yussef wondered why the general's guards had disappeared in the moments before the ambush. What did Husseini know about the kidnapping?

Omar Yussef pushed his legs off the side of the bed. He removed his bandage in front of the bathroom mirror. A lump rose from the end of his jaw to the tip of his eyebrow, black and red and purple. His upper neck was emerald green. He ruffled the white hair above his ear; the skin beneath was the color of pine needles. The wiry gray tufts inside his ear were sticky with drying blood. He stared at his pupils. One seemed bigger than the other – he thought that was a sign of concussion. Well, he was having enough difficulty thinking straight; what more proof did he need that he was concussed? He got into the shower and let the briny water run over his stiff back.

At nine-thirty, Omar Yussef put on a clean, short-sleeved shirt and transferred the notepaper on which he'd written Nadia's web address to the breast pocket, along with the Saladin Brigades leaflet and the black Mont Blanc fountain pen he usually kept in his jacket. He walked unsteadily down the hotel stairs with Cree and Sami. From behind her computer at the reception desk, Meisoun smiled flirtatiously at Sami, gave Omar Yussef a sympathetic look, and wished him health. He thought of asking her to call up Nadia's website, but there was no time for that now. It worried him that he could consider such a trifle when Wallender's life might be at stake. He touched the bruise on his head and wondered if it truly had affected his judgment. He thanked Meisoun for her good wishes.

The moment he stepped into the dust cloud, thicker yet than it had been the day before, he knew this would not be the day of health the receptionist had wished for him. Sami crossed the beach road and clapped a big handshake on the officer in the guard hut outside General Husseini's house. The other guards, their mouths wrapped with checkered keffiyehs against the dusty air, regarded Omar Yussef and Cree with narrow, suspicious eyes. Sami gestured for them to follow him.

The officer led them into the building, still holding Sami's hand.

Husseini's home was laid out like an apartment block. The lower floors were home to the General's sons and their families. He kept his wife on the sixth floor and saw her as often as anyone would who had been married thirty years and had to climb six flights of stairs to get there. The third floor was where he entertained.

When Omar Yussef caught up to the others at the door of Husseini's reception room, Cree was staring out of the window, swaying, blowing air through pursed lips like an athlete building concentration before a race. The officer's hand was poised to knock on the door. He smiled at Omar Yussef, who nodded for him to proceed. The schoolteacher inhaled as much air as he could, but the dust in the staircase was almost as thick as it had been outside. A guard opened the shiny rose-wood door.

'Enter, and may Allah grant you a safe entry into Paradise,' the tall officer said, before returning to his post downstairs.

General Husseini's reception room was the width of the building and occupied almost its whole length. It wasn't the kind of place you could pick up on a police officer's salary; this was the fruit of years of corruption. Four sets of lounge furniture each sectioned off a different area of the room in a neat square, so that a large party could divide into smaller conversational groups. The sofas and armchairs in each set were in different pastels, with gaudy whirling patterns like a cheap sweater. The far wall sparkled with crystal glasses and decanters in a glass cabinet. A long dinner table and a dozen bentwood chairs stood along the far side of the room. Above the table, there was a chandelier that looked like it had been made in the same work-shop as the louche number in Professor Maki's dining room. Omar Yussef noticed with an appre-hensive stirring in his stomach that the table was, indeed, set for breakfast.

The guard brought them to the table and resumed his place at the door. A youth in olive fatigues asked if they wanted coffee or tea. He was bony and, high on his cheeks, there was the kind of purple acne that works deep beneath the skin. His uniform was unmarked by any insignia of rank, even the lowest. He retreated with their order through a door that led to a short passage.

Three men appeared in the passage. Omar Yussef could see only their silhouettes, but he guessed that the short one in the middle was General Husseini. He spoke into a cellular phone and walked with the slow, absent paces of a man who'd forgotten that he could talk just as well sitting down. Husseini reached the big room. The two men with him took up their posts on either side of the door. They were tall, but only one of them, a shaven-headed, heavy man who breathed through his mouth, watched the new arrivals like a bodyguard. The other folded his delicate hands over a clipboard and rested his chin on his chest. He was evidently Husseini's *aide de camp*.

Husseini waved to acknowledge that he would soon finish on the phone. He was doing more listening than talking and he stared intently into the dust storm, as though whatever the man on the other end of the line was telling him about might emerge from the cloud in front of the window. He was shorter than Omar Yussef, who was himself not quite five feet seven. He wore an olive battle shirt, which must have been specially tailored to accommodate his rotund belly, and pants that were tucked into tall, maroon parachutist's boots. His fingers were stubby, thick and hairy and his skin was the color of a baked potato. He turned from the window, flipped the cellphone shut, stroked his trim gray mustache thoughtfully, then opened his arms wide in greeting. He had a broad, avaricious smile and eyes like pebbles in the rain.

General Husseini kissed Sami five times, puckering his thick lips and closing his eyes with pleasure. In between each kiss, he uttered a greeting. Sami introduced Cree and Omar Yussef. Husseini shook Cree's hand and pulled it low, so the Scotsman knew to bend for the kisses. When the kisses were over, Husseini kept Cree's hand low. He chuckled and, with his free hand, brushed some dried blood from Cree's ginger mustache. The Scot looked deeply embarrassed. Omar Yussef was glad he'd taken the opportunity to shower, instead of drinking through the night.

'Don't worry, I heard about your troubles from the brother Sami,' Husseini said. His reedy voice was quiet, cloying and cajoling, as though he were calming a nervous animal.

Omar Yussef wondered how close the brother Sami was to this man. He thought of the Husseini Manicure as the general took his hand and delivered three kisses. Husseini's lips left a wet dab on Omar Yussef's right cheek. The general caressed his guest's bruised temple, gently, moaning with his tenor of reassuring sweet-talk. He led Omar Yussef by the hand to the table and pulled out a chair for him. The coffee boy brought the drinks and Husseini nodded to him curtly, signaling it was time for the food.

'The brother Sami tells me you're a respected man in Bethlehem, Abu Ramiz.' Husseini smiled.

Omar Yussef nodded, modestly.

'Do you know my local commander there?' the general asked.

'Major Qawasmeh?'

'He's a colonel. But, yes, Qawasmeh is his name.'

'I haven't met him.' Omar Yussef knew this was a warning, a reminder that Husseini's power reached beyond Gaza to Bethlehem and that Omar Yussef's family could be threatened there.

'He's a good man. A strong man.' Husseini sat forward in his chair and bounced a little in excitement. 'I like strong men. They don't drop any of the things I ask them to lift. Unless I tell them to do so.' The general laughed. The low wheedling voice surrendered to a high-pitched squawk, like a parrot disturbed from its perch. 'And so long as they aren't strong enough to lift me.' He slapped his fat stomach and reached out a hand for Sami to give him five.

The coffee boy brought a platter big enough to hold a small child. It was loaded with *hummus* and ground lamb. With a rolling sensation in his stomach, Omar Yussef realized that the *hummus* and meat was mixed with tiny gobs of lamb fat

134

that were almost invisible in the chickpea paste. Cree held his hand to his mouth; Omar Yussef could tell that the Scot had been treated to this particular dish at some previous breakfast and was now regretting the whisky.

General Husseini stood next to the coffee boy and scooped copious portions of the meaty *hummus* onto his guests' plates with a wide, flat spoon. As Omar Yussef ate, he fought to maintain an expression of pleasure on his face.

'Mister Cree, I apologize on behalf of all Gazans for the scandalous assault against you and your colleagues,' Husseini said.

Cree's mouth was full of *hummus*. It looked like it might take some time for him to swallow, so he just nodded gravely.

'We also have seen the outrageous accusations of the Saladin Brigades against my Military Intelligence in this leaflet they released after the kidnapping.' Husseini scowled and waved his hands dismissively. 'I want to assure you, we shall not rest until we have freed your friend, *our* friend—'

'Magnus Wallender,' Sami whispered.

'Our friend Wallender.'

Omar Yussef swallowed a bite of the breakfast. He thought he'd better talk, to get his mind off the food and his stomach. 'Mister Cree would very much like to talk to Bassam Odwan.'

'A deadly criminal. I cannot allow it.'

'The United Nations wishes to aid your investigation in any way that it can.'

'Odwan didn't kidnap your UN man.'

'But his friends did.'

'So you should talk to his friends, not to him.'

'Perhaps he can help us reach his friends.'

'Do you think we haven't asked him the same questions?' Husseini smiled broadly around the table.

'He may find Mister Cree a more neutral figure.'

'How can anyone be neutral in a question of murder? This Odwan fellow killed one of my best officers in cold blood.'

Cree cleared his throat. 'There's a team arriving later this afternoon from the United Nations office in Jerusalem. They'll negotiate for the hostage, of course, at a very high level. But they consider it important that no time is wasted while they're en route to Gaza. They asked me to secure a meeting with Odwan.'

Omar Yussef hadn't heard about the negotiators. It must have been decided during Cree's phone call, while Omar Yussef slept. It was another card for him to play with Husseini. 'The UN negotiators know that you're the most trusted of Palestinian security chiefs among the foreign diplomats stationed in Tel Aviv,' Omar Yussef said.

Husseini looked interested.

'This is a great opportunity for you to boost that position still further,' Omar Yussef said.

Cree managed to get some more *hummus* down. 'We're coordinating the response to the hostage situation with the American ambassador, because the Americans have the best contacts on the ground with your security forces. Their ambassador's most interested to hear your ideas,' he said.

Husseini closed his gray eyes and nodded slowly. 'I am a good friend of the ambassador.' The pleasure on his face suggested that the general was visualizing a convivial supper with the ambassador at his residence overlooking the beach in Herzliya Pituach. Omar Yussef wondered if Husseini coveted that connection for the kickbacks it would bring or for the power of the ambassador's favorite to brutalize and kill his enemies with impunity.

'The ambassador values you as a friend and wishes you to have all the aid you need to conduct your operations,' Cree said.

All the aid, Omar Yussef thought. *In a suitcase or wired to a Swiss bank.*

Husseini bowed. 'I shall call to let him know the progress of our investigation into this important case.'

'He'll be waiting for your call, eagerly.'

'And the Swedes?'

Omar Yussef almost smiled. Husseini had the Americans and the UN promising him backhanders and the prestige of their connections, but he didn't hesitate to squeeze a little more.

'The Swedish ambassador has communicated to my superiors that he, too, wants your assistance very much,' Cree said. 'He's prepared to cover the costs of any operation you undertake to secure the release of Mister Wallender.'

Husseini took a pickle from a sideplate and crunched it. 'Odwan is held at the *Saraya*, our central jail. It's an easy matter for you to see him. I only request that you should not be taken in by this man. You are intelligent fellows, but you are not police officers. It takes years of police work to face a deadly criminal and not to fall for his tricks. Don't believe anything he says.'

'We can meet him? Thank you,' Cree said.

'What's your understanding of the events that led to Lieutenant Fathi Salah's death?' Omar Yussef asked.

Husseini cleaned his plate with a wedge of pita and gave a pensive belch. 'Lieutenant Salah went to arrest this Odwan for his smuggling activities. We can't allow weapons to come under the Egyptian border unchecked, as has sometimes been the situation in Rafah. When Lieutenant Salah confronted Odwan, the criminal resisted and killed Salah.'

'How was Odwan eventually arrested?'

'He gave himself up, when my men went to his family home an hour after the incident.'

'Why did he give himself up?'

'He's a coward.'

'If he was prepared to kill Salah to avoid arrest,' Omar Yussef said, 'why would he give himself up only an hour later?'

'He was confronted with overwhelming force. I told my commanders not to take any chances. I went to Rafah to take personal control of the operation.

I ordered all my forces to the scene, even from Khan Yunis and Deir el-Balah.' Husseini gave the parrot squawk once more. 'If someone had raided the jail here in Gaza City that night, they would have found it guarded by no one except this coffee boy.'

The pimply boy shuffled from foot to foot, glaring. He looked at Husseini as though he'd love to be the only guard at the prison, with the general as the sole inmate.

'I made sure the Saladin Brigades couldn't oppose the operation, because I brought such a big force. We surrounded the house of the Odwan family. They're very poor and live in a rotten part of the refugee camp in Rafah. Really, Odwan is scum. I shouted through a bullhorn that I would destroy every house in the camp, if I had to, but I would find Bassam Odwan and arrest him. Then he came out.'

Husseini seemed to enjoy bragging about the operation. Omar Yussef decided to demonstrate his appreciation of the General's police work. 'You were very thorough and effective, *Pasha*,' he said. 'If I may, I'd like to ask you about last night. Did you hear anything during the kidnapping?'

Husseini shrugged. 'Why would I?'

'It occurred below your window. Wallender was coming back to the Sands Hotel across the road, when he was taken.'

'I live a quiet life. I'm in bed early. I'm not up at all hours like these Westerners.' Husseini smiled at Cree.

It's time to needle him a little, Omar Yussef thought. 'You may have been asleep, but you had extra guards on duty last night. What did they see?'

Husseini brushed that off. 'In honor of my foreign friend Mister Cree, I would like to offer you a pleasure denied to most in Gaza.' The pebble eyes glittered mischievously. Husseini snapped his fingers twice and the coffee boy took one of the decanters from the cabinet. The liquid swilling around in its wide bottom looked like brandy and Omar Yussef heard Cree breathing hard again. Evidently the *hummus* wasn't sitting too well with the night's whisky intake and mixing brandy wouldn't do his stomach any favors. The Scot was pale. The blood seemed to have drained even from his swollen, bruised lips.

The general took the stopper from the decanter and inhaled the brandy's aroma deeply. The coffee boy brought glasses.

'This is a little vice of mine,' Husseini said. He laughed. 'I don't mean the brandy. Rather, I'm referring to the bottle. It's leaded crystal, Bohemian. I love the weight of it, so heavy and yet so delicate. I have collected many of them, as you see.' He gestured toward the sparkling wall of bowls and bottles, candlesticks and vases, all glimmering with reflected light from the chandelier. 'I developed a taste for Bohemian crystal when I was a student in Prague thirty years ago. I completed a Master's Degree in Economics, but you don't need an advanced qualification to understand the value of these little trinkets. In Prague, they're so cheap as to be almost disposable. This decanter costs less than one hundred and fifty dollars.'

That might be almost three months salary for the coffee boy. Omar Yussef looked at the stopper of the decanter in Husseini's thick hand. It was cut with hundreds of tiny, hard edges.

Omar Yussef asked Husseini not to pour for him. Cree hesitated, but he took the brandy and sipped it in silence. Sami lit a cigarette and rolled the brandy in his glass. Husseini put two doubles away before the small talk was over. The porcelain carriage clock on the dining table showed ten-thirty.

'Now I will call the American ambassador to update him,' Husseini said, as he showed them to the door, 'and you will go to jail.' As Omar Yussef reached the bottom of the staircase, he could still hear Husseini laughing.

CHAPTER 13

To Omar Yussef's dismay, Cree insisted on taking the wheel of the Suburban, protesting that Nasser's erratic driving would make him nauseous in his current condition. The Scot had to concentrate just to hold a straight line on the way to Gaza's central jail and military headquarters.

The Saraya's twelve-foot perimeter wall was a prime canvas for political graffiti artists. Its whitewash was daubed in green, red and black with exhortations to Allah, the president and his predecessor, the people, the land and the martyrs. Omar Yussef wondered when Bassam Odwan would join the list.

The guards lifted a red and white bar from across the entrance and directed Cree to the side of the main building, a three-story, dirty-gray block. At the end of a line of camouflaged trucks, a Military Intelligence officer awaited them. He recognized Sami. 'How're you doing, *ya zalameh?*' he said, raising his hand and bringing it down to make a loud, slapping shake. Omar Yussef wondered again about Sami's connections. Everywhere he went, these security people were his friends. This one even called him *man*.

The officer held Sami's arm, leading him into the jail and up the dingy stairwell. Omar Yussef and Cree trailed, breathing heavily. The air was dense with the dust that hung over Gaza City and the thick smell of enclosed men, of sweat and laundry, of stewing meat and cigarettes.

The officer led them through the jail like a cheerful tour guide, eager to share his knowledge of a place few saw and even fewer wished to see. 'This floor is where the officers have their quarters. At the end of that corridor is the bureau of the commander of the National Security Forces.'

They climbed another two flights of stairs. A guard at the top stood and rattled his Kalashnikov over his shoulder, as they approached. His keys clattered in a heavy metal door painted a soapy blue, and he locked it behind them.

The block was thirty yards long with five cells on each side of the walkway. From the first cell came the rustle of men rising in prayer and the words of the prayer leader, answered in unison with a deep, mumbled crescendo. The wind brought the dusty air along the corridor from an unglazed, barred window at the opposite end. Two guards in camouflage fatigues and red berets leaned against the door of the first cell, smoking and resting their elbows on their assault rifles.

'The prisoners aren't locked in at the moment,'

the officer informed Cree. 'It's time for midday prayers, so they've congregated in cell number one. This fellow leading the prayers, you see, is a big sheikh on the outside. This is the most exclusive mosque in Gaza City.'

Cree peered into the cell through a metal grille cut along the corridor at head height. 'Reckon it is,' he said.

'Odwan is at the end of the corridor.' The officer beckoned. 'He's in solitary confinement.'

'Even more exclusive,' Cree whispered to Omar Yussef.

The officer unlocked a solid iron door. Omar Yussef stepped into a small, unlit room with a stainless steel sink, some empty buckets and mops. It stank of dirty washcloths. At the other side of the room, a grille was cut in another metal door. Omar Yussef looked through it.

'That's the murderer Odwan,' the officer said.

Bassam Odwan stood with his head lowered and his open palms held before him. He knelt and prostrated himself on a cheap mat, touching his forehead to the gaudy synthetic weave. Omar Yussef hadn't prayed in years. He watched Odwan go down.

The prisoner had his back to the door as he prayed. Holes in his thin, dirty white T-shirt exposed his bulky back. His shoulders sloped from a thick neck and the muscles of his upper back undulated as he brought his hands up to cover his face in prayer. His was a broad, rounded, peasant muscularity.

Odwan made his final prostration and rolled his prayer mat.

'His prayers are over,' Omar Yussef said.

The guard unlocked the door. Odwan didn't turn. The officer called to him in a voice that had lost the tour-guide liveliness. 'Hey, Odwan. You have visitors.'

Odwan placed the rolled prayer mat on its end in the corner of the room. He turned. From the front, his body looked thicker still. His chest was wide and heavy and his belly was deep and strong against the T-shirt. He wore baggy army pants and his feet were dirty and shoeless. His black beard was thick and his lips were big and red and wet. His hair was black and layered to a straight fringe halfway down his forehead. The edge of the hair rose over a dark brown welt at the center of his brow, abraded by years of being lowered to the prayer mat. The weal looked like a massive wart. Omar Yussef estimated Odwan was a little less than thirty years old.

Odwan took in Omar Yussef quickly and mildly. His eyes twitched with suspicion when Cree ducked through the door and he regarded Sami with even greater distrust. Sami smiled and leaned against the wall. The officer shut the door behind them.

Omar Yussef approached Odwan and shook his hand. The man's grip was light, but it swallowed Omar Yussef's fingers. It was a worker's hand, strengthened and made large and clumsy by generations of simple toil. With a sudden relief that surprised him, Omar Yussef noted that Odwan hadn't endured the Husseini Manicure. He introduced himself and Cree.

'As with your family and in your home,' Odwan said. He looked around the cell and smiled at the absurdity of the traditional greeting. His smile was disarming and simple, reminding Omar Yussef of the innocent grin of the mentally handicapped, but the eyes were tough and astute.

The cell was empty but for a thin sleeping mat against the wall and a bucket for slops. Odwan had his prayer mat and a plastic bottle of water, its label worn away by reuse. A single window, too high to see through, was bolted shut and the air in the cell was oppressively hot. Sweat stood out on Odwan's face and soon Omar Yussef felt his own perspiration in the armpits of his shirt. Cree and Omar Yussef sat on the sleeping mat. Odwan crossed his legs in the center of the cell and kept his eyes on Sami, who squatted by the door.

'Who's he?' Odwan asked. His voice was hoarse. Omar Yussef thought of the tortures that Eyad Masharawi had undergone and wondered if Odwan had sandpapered his vocal chords screaming in pain.

'He's Sami Jaffari, a deportee from Bethlehem. He's helping us in our investigation.'

'What investigation, uncle?'

'At first, we thought we were investigating the

case of one of our schoolteachers who was jailed by Colonel al-Fara.'

Odwan dropped his thick lips open and frowned, hard.

'But since last night our investigation has changed course. The Saladin Brigades kidnapped our colleague, a Swede who runs the UNRWA schools in Gaza and the West Bank. In return for his release, they want you to be freed.'

'If Allah wills it.'

'Bassam, we need to find our friend.'

'Was there a leaflet?'

Omar Yussef nodded. 'The Saladin Brigades distributed a leaflet saying they carried out the kidnapping.'

Odwan looked at Omar Yussef's bruised head and Cree's swollen nose. 'I'm sorry if they hurt you. Did they, uncle?'

'It's okay. How can we get to our friend?'

'You'd have to see Abu Jamal.'

Omar Yussef shrugged.

'He's the head of the Saladin Brigades in Rafah,' Odwan said.

'How can we reach him?'

'I don't think he'd see you, unless you could convince him that you might do a deal for me.'

'What sort of deal?'

'What do you think? To get me out of here.'

'But General Husseini won't release you.'

Now it was Odwan's turn to shrug.

Omar Yussef checked his frustration. He needed

to cover some basics of the case with Odwan. 'What happened when Lieutenant Salah tried to arrest you?'

'Are you looking for your friend or investigating me?'

'Perhaps we can find out what really went on, and then we can convince General Husseini that you're innocent.'

'I *am* innocent.' Odwan raised his voice and coughed hoarsely.

'We can help you prove it.'

'Do you think proof is part of the equation? They didn't need proof to put me in this hole. Or to hang me by my wrists in front of an air-conditioning unit all day yesterday.'

'Bassam, the only way for us to free our friend is to prove that you didn't kill Salah. If the United Nations knows you're innocent, General Husseini will have to accept that. Particularly if we can present him with the real guilty person.'

Odwan closed his eyes and squeezed his big hands together. 'Brother Abu—?'

'Abu Ramiz.'

'Abu Ramiz, I believe life and death are in the hands of Allah. If I have to die, no one can save me from death.'

'Justice, too, is in the hands of Allah.'

'Not in Gaza.' Odwan laughed loudly and slapped Omar Yussef's knee.

He's simple, but not stupid, Omar Yussef thought.

He decided to anger Odwan into telling his story. 'Why did you kill Lieutenant Salah?'

'I didn't kill him. I told you.'

'If you were innocent, you'd tell us what happened. What're you hiding?'

'You think I'm trying to protect someone?'

'What reason do you have to remain silent? If you believe you're due to die, then may Allah be merciful upon you. But I want to save my friend.'

Odwan didn't move. Omar Yussef tried to keep the desperation from his face. He tried a line which sounded hopeless even as he said it. 'Who knows, if my friend is saved with the help of a Muslim, perhaps he will submit to Islam?'

'Convert?' Odwan laughed, as best he could without coughing again. 'Do you think he'll apply for a Palestinian passport, too?'

Omar Yussef was angry with himself. He had gauged Odwan wrongly; the man wasn't as simple as he had thought. His frustration got the better of him and he held out his arm to Cree. 'Help me up. This bastard isn't going to do anything for us. Let's go.'

Odwan put his big hand on Omar Yussef's shoulder. 'Wait, uncle, wait. Calm down, please. Take a drink.' He held out the bottle of cloudy water.

Omar Yussef was touched by this sad display of hospitality. He poured some of the water into his mouth. It tasted of lead. 'Thank you.'

Odwan shifted his crossed legs and rubbed his

back, grimacing. 'I went to meet Salah. He was selling something.'

'What?'

'Something he stole from us.'

'From the Saladin Brigades?'

'Uncle, you don't want to get involved in this.'

Omar Yussef leaned forward. 'Believe me, I'm involved already. I must know.'

Odwan glanced at Cree. 'How do I know this foreigner isn't a spy?'

'Because he doesn't speak Arabic,' Omar Yussef said. 'Anyway, all the spies in Gaza are Palestinian.'

Odwan's eyes flicked to Sami, relaxed by the door. Then he grinned. 'I'm glad you came, uncle. May Allah give strength to your friend from Sweden and lead him home.'

Omar Yussef nodded and raised his eyebrows expectantly.

Odwan sighed. 'We had arranged to receive a prototype missile. It was smuggled through one of the tunnels under the Egyptian border. Salah was selling this missile.'

'But there are missiles already in Gaza. The *Qassam* missiles.'

'We wanted to improve on the *Qassam*. To build a more reliable missile with a longer range.'

'What difference does it make to bring in a single missile?'

'The *Qassam* was based on a prototype North Korean missile that was smuggled through the tunnels a few years ago with the help of Hizballah in Lebanon. The engineers here used that proto-type to build hundreds of our own missiles. We intended to do the same thing again, only better.'

'So this stolen missile was to be replicated to create a new arsenal of advanced missiles?'

'Abu Jamal was going to call it the *Saladin I.* Sounds good, doesn't it?' Odwan seemed as proud as if the name had been his own invention.

Omar Yussef nodded his encouragement.

'Someone stole the missile as it was coming through the tunnels,' Odwan said. 'They must have paid a traitor inside the Brigades to tell them about the plan. They ambushed our guys just after we brought it through. They killed two of them and stole the missile.'

'Lieutenant Salah stole it?'

Odwan rolled his tongue in his cheek. 'The day after it was stolen, Salah contacted Abu Jamal and told him he had the prototype. Abu Jamal ordered me to meet Salah to make sure he was telling the truth. If he was, Abu Jamal would give him the money.'

'Why would you pay him for something he stole?'

'The important thing was to get the missile immediately. We could settle our score with Salah later.'

'How much did Salah want?'

'Twenty thousand dollars – it's a lot in Rafah. So I met Salah on the edge of the refugee camp, late at night. It was a quiet spot; there were buildings

151

around us, but they were bombed-out and empty. I left my car and walked toward Salah's jeep.'

'He was alone?'

'Just him. I asked him to show me the crate with the missile. He said it was hidden somewhere else. We argued about that, because Abu Jamal didn't want to hand over the money, unless I'd actually seen the missile. I walked toward my car to phone Abu Jamal. Salah followed me, talking nonsense. Then, there was a shot from somewhere. It hit Salah up here.' Odwan tapped his chest and it made a deep thump.

'What did you do?'

'I went straight to my car and got out of there. There were more shots from one of the bombed-out buildings. Someone was trying to kill me, too.'

'How many attackers were firing at you?'

'Just one. The reports all came from the same spot and I heard only one gun.'

'What did you do after you left?'

'I phoned Abu Jamal. He sent people to the scene. The security forces were already there. I went home and, when they came to arrest me, I gave myself up.'

Odwan was quiet. Omar Yussef tried to hide his excitement. If Odwan was telling the truth, he wasn't the killer. General Husseini might be persuaded to free him, if they could only prove it. But that also meant there was a killer on the loose who'd do everything he could to prevent Omar Yussef identifying him.

Odwan shook his head. 'It didn't make sense.'

'What didn't?'

'Every time I asked him where he'd hidden the missile, Salah kept saying something in a foreign language. I think it was English. Do you speak English, uncle?'

Omar Yussef nodded.

'What does *price* mean?' Odwan said.

'It means the cost of something.'

'I thought so. When I asked where the missile was, he kept saying something about the *price*, and I'd say, "Okay, you'll get your money, but speak Arabic and tell me where the missile is." Then he'd say something about the price again. I feel sorry about it now, but at the time I admit I became angry, because I thought he had lost his nerve under pressure.'

'Did he say anything else in English, or just the word *price*?'

'He said *high noon price*.'

'*High noon price?*'

'Something like that. "You'll get it," he said, "at *high noon price*." What does that mean, uncle?'

'The cost when the sun is high at noontime. Or the cost at noon is expensive.'

'You see, it doesn't make sense. It was midnight, not noon, and I already knew the price. It made me furious with him.' Odwan shot his fist into his palm in frustration. 'But after the poor man was shot, I started to think about it. He really was trying to tell me something. He seemed desperate when he followed me to the car, still repeating this crazy English phrase. But someone wanted to kill him – perhaps he knew that.'

Omar Yussef pictured the blabbering Salah, frantically trying to convey a message to Odwan, and the simple gunman, too hard-bitten to understand. 'What happened to the missile? Did Abu Jamal do a deal to buy it later?'

'I don't know. You'd have to ask Abu Jamal. I haven't heard anything since they arrested me.'

'Why did you give yourself up?'

'I could have escaped.' Odwan looked about and lowered his voice. 'There's a tunnel under my family's house that leads across to Egypt. It's supposed to be only for ferrying goods, cigarettes and baby formula and that sort of stuff. You have to haul everything through on a little cart that runs on metal tracks using a pulley at each end. It would have been a horrible squeeze for a man of my size, but I could get through there, just about.'

'Why didn't you?'

'They would have arrested my entire family. I have thirteen brothers and sisters, and a mother and father. If I ran, everyone would believe I had killed Salah and the police would've destroyed my parents' house.' Odwan looked down at his big hands.

The prisoner sounded like a child in one of Omar Yussef's classes, guilty about the lie he had spun to cover his own cowardice. Omar Yussef recognized the hesitations that undermined the falsehood.

Odwan looked up at Omar Yussef and saw that

his deception had failed. 'In my heart, Abu Ramiz, I just couldn't go through the tunnel,' he said. 'To my shame, I started to run away, despite the risk of reprisals against my family. I knew the police would torture me. I even climbed down to where the tunnel begins, but it was so narrow and long and dark that I feared I might become trapped. I was scared that I would die of suffocation down there.'

Omar Yussef took the Saladin Brigades leaflet from his breast pocket and showed it to Odwan. 'Perhaps this will give you hope, Bassam.'

Odwan read the leaflet and gave it back. 'Allah is my hope, Abu Ramiz.'

Omar Yussef put the leaflet back in his shirt pocket. 'May Allah grant you grace,' he said, standing stiffly.

'Go in peace,' Odwan said.

They walked in silence out of the cellblock. The inmates lay on their bunks and watched them with glassy eyes through the head-high grille in the wall.

On the stairs, Omar Yussef summarized his conversation with Odwan for Cree, who had only picked up some of the Arabic.

'High noon price?' Cree said. 'Is that to do with the film, or something? You know, Gary Cooper. No, it can't be. It's bloody weird, Abu Ramiz.'

Their escort kissed Sami five times. He raised his hand and gave Omar Yussef a slap on the palm. 'May Allah grant you grace, *ya zalameh*,' he said.

Omar Yussef could still feel the firm grip of Odwan's massive hand. 'Don't call me *man*,' he snapped. 'Prisons make me unfriendly.'

The officer shrugged. He turned to Cree and saluted. The Scotsman saluted back and gave Omar Yussef a shame-faced wiggle of his eyebrows. 'Old habit,' he said, as the officer sauntered toward the prison.

'I'm going to try to verify all this with the Saladin Brigades here in Gaza City,' Sami said, lighting a cigarette.

'The circumstances of the shooting, you mean?'

'Maybe they'll also tell me if they were expecting delivery of this prototype missile. Write down my mobile number, in case you find anything new.'

Omar Yussef took out the Saladin Brigades leaflet, unclipped his Mont Blanc from his shirt pocket and scribbled Sami's number across the back of it.

Sami walked around the barrier at the entrance of the Saraya and hailed a junky old taxi.

The dirt caught in Omar Yussef's throat and whipped against his temple, darting each grain of sand onto his bruise like the jab of a needle. He wanted to rest, but he knew that the day would be a long one. He looked up into the sky, obscured and orange with dust. *High noon price.* What did it mean? It was as veiled as the sun itself behind the Gaza sandstorm.

'Do you feel okay to drive?' he asked Cree.

'To tell you the truth, I'm not a hundred percent,' Cree said, touching his damaged nose gingerly. 'But this is really getting interesting.'

Omar Yussef smiled grimly. 'Let's go to Rafah,' he said.

CHAPTER 14

They were through the southern districts of Gaza City and were crossing the sandy reaches where an abandoned Israeli settlement had been ploughed over, when Omar Yussef sensed the UN Suburban listing toward the side of the Saladin Road. With a sudden hollow rumbling like the flapping of massive wings, the wheels rolled onto the rocks and lumpy earth at the edge of the field. Omar Yussef grabbed Cree's arm and jerked the wheel to the left. The Scotsman reared his head and pulled sharply back into the road, blinking out of his momentary slumber. He drove on slowly, past a decaying cluster of single-story refugee homes, with the punchy, wide eyes of a man struggling to follow a country lane through an impenetrable fog.

'You should take a break, James. We both had a tough night. Perhaps we should have had a doctor look at our wounds.'

'A doctor *did* look at our wounds.'

'He was a doctor who sits on the Revolutionary Council. I mean a real doctor.'

The wind squalled spirals of orange dirt out of the rows of cabbages and tomatoes on either side

157

of the road and whipped them onto the wind-screen. Cree curled his long spine forward until his chin was almost on the wheel, staring into the whirling dust. 'Don't worry. We're nearly there.'

'Rafah? We're only halfway there.'

'Not what I meant. Something I want to show you just here.' Cree turned off the main road and stopped under a tall date palm. He blew a few times, hard through his mouth, lifted his eyes wide open with his forefingers and rolled his shoulders.

'What's this?' Omar Yussef asked.

Cree winked a bleary eye, got out of the car and stretched his back.

Omar Yussef pushed his door shut behind him. The musty smell of chickens rode on the hot, thick air. A small, plain, two-story farmhouse of poured-concrete crouched beneath the date palm and behind a cinder-block wall. A hedge of neatly cut evergreen shrubs ran from the house to the corner of the main road. The gusting wind lifted an edge of corrugated tin from the roof of the farm's outhouse and dropped it with a repetitive slap. Behind the wall of the farmhouse, Omar Yussef heard the light voices of small children playing.

'This is part of Zuweida village,' Cree said. He was looking south into a broad cabbage field. 'Over there, somewhere in that dust is Deir el-Balah. You can usually see the date palms lining the main road of the town. Can't make out a bloody thing now, but it's there anyway.'

The wind was stronger out here than in Gaza

City, where the buildings blocked it. Omar Yussef screwed up his eyes against the sandy flurries that ruffled the cabbage leaves in the field. 'James, if you aren't feeling well, I can drive. I admit I'm a poor driver, but we should get moving. We have to speak to these gunmen in Rafah about Magnus and find out about the missile.'

Cree tilted his head to listen. 'He ought to fix that bloody roof. You hear the bugger banging away?' He turned. 'Like I said, something I have to show you here.' He walked unsteadily to the door in the wall at the side of the farmhouse. He rapped on the wood and peered over the top of the concrete wall. The children's voices stopped. A man's footsteps approached across the yard and the door opened.

'Greetings, Suleiman,' Cree said.

The man returned the greeting and shook Cree's hand.

'This is Mister Suleiman Jouda. He runs the place,' Cree said to Omar Yussef.

Jouda was short and slim and in his early thirties. His hair was neatly brushed back in a moderately tall bouffant and was as black as his thick mustache. Two dark children stood on either side of a pink tricycle, their pudgy feet bare on the mud floor of the yard, staring at Cree with their fingers in their mouths. Jouda led the way through the yard to a neat gate at the back of the farm-house. When he opened it, a shock of green hit Omar Yussef.

The wide lawn was greener and more lush than any patch of earth elsewhere in the Gaza Strip. The evergreen hedge extended around the entire lawn, each of its four sides about two hundred yards long. The hedge cut the wind and even the dust was unable to smother the brightness of the grass. Set back from the center of the lawn was a four-foot obelisk of granite on a square plinth of equal height. All around the field, neat rows of graves, carved from white sandstone, were gathered into small, square groups.

Cree strode toward the center of the field. Omar Yussef followed him. To the left of the path, the earth had been disturbed around several of the graves and Omar Yussef saw signs of hurried repairs to a few headstones, but Cree went right past them. Jouda kept a respectful distance.

'You're a history man, Abu Ramiz,' Cree said. 'You see where we are?'

'It's a British military cemetery.'

'Right you are. From World War One. The British consulate pays Mister Jouda's wage so that he'll take care of the place. It's bonny, isn't it?'

'Frankly, it's the only place in Gaza that I would call *bonny*. It really doesn't look like Gaza.'

'I agree. Seems you have to die to get any peace in Gaza.' Cree smiled with a distant, bitter squint. 'And you had to die in a war long ago to enjoy your peace in a beautiful place where someone cares for you.'

'A forgotten theater of that war, too.'

Cree rolled his tongue round his mouth. 'I haven't forgotten.'

Omar Yussef considered that. He was a history teacher, but he wasn't the only one who remembered the past. 'I spoke about the British campaign in the First World War with Professor Maki last night at dinner. He told me the British attacked Gaza three times before they took it and moved on to Jerusalem.'

Cree nodded. 'Look at the dates on the graves. See this fellow? He died in April 1917. But that one in the next row passed away in November.'

'The battles were here in this village?'

'By the time they established this cemetery in March of 1917, the fighting had moved north to Gaza City. If you died in action, they'd bury you more or less where you fell. But the wounded came to the Deir el-Balah field hospital and, if they didn't survive, they buried them here.'

Omar Yussef scanned the wide lawn. 'How many are there?'

'Seven hundred and fifty graves. Some of them over in that corner are Indians. There're seven Jewish soldiers here, too. But most of them are just pale, pasty, old-fashioned Brits like me.' Cree looked at Omar Yussef and frowned. 'Christ, can you imagine growing up in Britain, where it's gray and wet and bloody cold but at least it's home, and finding yourself forced to fight to the death for this alien, weird piece of land?'

'Unfortunately, James, there's always been

someone fighting for this stretch of land. Usually with no real knowledge of it or claim to it. The Jews were here millennia ago and the Arabs have been here more than a thousand years, but everyone else who fought for this place was a stranger, drawn by greed or hatred or God. The Crusaders, Napoleon, the Turks, all were alien to this place.'

Cree walked slowly along the line of graves. Omar Yussef looked at his watch. It was one o'clock. He wanted to get the information he needed in Rafah and be back in Gaza City before darkness closed in; he didn't fancy taking the Saladin Road through the dust cloud in even worse visibility with Cree driving the way he was. He followed Cree's steps impatiently, wondering if the Scot was stalling, trying to walk off his night of drinking and his concussion before he had to continue the drive.

Cree knelt in front of one of the graves. Omar Yussef came to his shoulder and read the inscription: *Private James Cree. 4 Battalion Queen's Edinburgh Rifles. 21 years. 5/11/17.*

'My great-grandfather. I was named after him. Married, got his wife pregnant with my Grandpa Billy, off to war. Not much of a life, eh?'

'How did he die?'

'Don't know. The records on private soldiers were kept in London and they were mostly destroyed by German bombs during the Second World War. There really is nothing left of his life.'

162

'Except your name.'

'Aye, there's that.' Cree's eyes had been red from the dust in the air and the blow to his face, but now the thought of his great-grandfather burned them. He wiped a tear with his knuckle and sniffed. 'This land means something to me, Abu Ramiz. I owe it to my great-grandfather that those who live in Gaza shouldn't die by the kind of violence that must have claimed his life. And the lives of the Turks who fought against him.' He smiled with one side of his mouth.

Omar Yussef put his hand to his chin. The drive to Rafah could wait a little longer.

'I went into the army when I was a young man,' Cree said. 'The Edinburgh Rifles had been amalgamated into the Royal Scots, so I joined them. I thought that would make me closer to him.'

'Not too close, thankfully.'

'As far as I know, no one specifically tried to kill me.' Cree smiled, absently. 'Thank God, I never had to kill anyone, either. Anyhow, because I knew so little about this fellow under our feet, I built a conversation in my head with the man I thought he'd have been. He told me that I was going about it all wrong. He was a conscript. He didn't choose a life in uniform, and he didn't want to fight. I left the army and went to work with the United Nations. I knew I'd see people at their worst, but I hoped I'd see them sometimes at their best.'

'How did it turn out?'

'I'll let you know after we find Magnus.'

Omar Yussef put his hand on the top of the gravestone. It was roughened to the consistency of sandpaper by ninety years of dust storms like the one that whipped into the hedge now. 'Man's inhumanity to man makes countless thousands mourn,' he said.

'"Man Was Made To Mourn." Robbie Burns. I thought you were just a history man, Abu Ramiz.'

'Sometimes the things historians ought to say are said better by writers of literature.'

The two men held each others gaze, firmly. Cree nodded and stood. He glanced toward the eastern side of the graveyard. He noticed the damaged headstones and the disturbed earth that Omar Yussef had seen as they entered.

'What happened here?' he said.

'Vandals came a few nights ago,' the caretaker said. 'I didn't hear them, Mister Cree, because I was asleep. They entered through the hedge over there in the corner farthest from my house. They dug up the grass around a couple of the graves and broke some of the headstones.'

'Has this happened before?' Omar Yussef said.

'Never. But people are very angry about the British army's part in the occupation of Iraq. They pasted some leaflets on the gravestones and they marked one of them with paint, with vicious comments.'

Omar Yussef walked to the vandalized section of the cemetery. The turf over a few of the graves had been lifted away, as though its lushness was an offense against the arid tombs of Gaza's Palestinian dead, and the earth beneath had been strewn around. Three of the stones had been smashed in half. The caretaker had balanced the remains of the headstones on the shattered stumps. Next to the broken stones, cheaply printed copies of newspaper photos were pasted onto three other headstones. The photos showed a British soldier urinating on an Iraqi prisoner. Omar Yussef had read about the photo, after it turned out that it was a fake. The dead of this graveyard were paying for the phony scoop.

'I haven't taken the posters off yet, because I'm waiting for advice on a way to do it without damaging the stone,' the caretaker said. He scratched his neck, nervously. 'This one had a slogan painted on it. I used turpentine to take it off, but I think it may have damaged the stone, so I decided to seek expert advice before I try to fix the others.'

Omar Yussef glanced at the single stone that had been daubed in paint. 'It's not damaged, Suleiman. The stones were all a little dirty. When you cleaned this one, you thought you'd stained it. In fact, you took away the layers of ingrained dirt. It'll look just as it always did, once the sun and wind have weathered it for a year or two.'

'Thank you, *ustaz*. I was quite worried. The dead have slept here for so many years, I feel as though these people who desecrated the graves wanted to kill them a second time.'

'Fortunately, that's not possible.'

The caretaker gave Omar Yussef a doubtful glance. *The man feels close to these dead foreigners, guarding them and tending to them as he does*, Omar Yussef thought. *He feels the injustice of this desecration very deeply.*

'Still, it's very upsetting,' Omar Yussef said. He put his hand on the caretaker's shoulder and received a grateful look.

Cree went alone toward his namesake's grave again. He ran a hand along the face of it, tracing the name where it was carved into the stone. He stood and moved purposefully toward the entrance. As he passed Omar Yussef, his eyes were clear and tough and his stride was firm. 'Thanks for stopping with me, Abu Ramiz. I had to gather myself. I'm ready to go on now.'

Omar Yussef stepped onto the path, away from the disturbed turf and the vandalized graves. He bent to flick the dirt from his loafers with his handkerchief. He looked around the graveyard as he straightened, stretching his stiff back. He remembered Nadia's story about the god Atum, whose weeping made mankind. Man was made to mourn all right. The only way to dry Atum's tears was for them to turn to dust.

CHAPTER 15

On Rafah's main street, Omar Yussef leaned out of the UN Suburban's window to ask directions to the Salah home. He breathed a hot gust of dirt and cleared his throat, as he beckoned to a young man sheltering in the doorway of a hardware store. The man crossed the sidewalk slowly, hands in the pockets of his jeans and shoulders hunched under the red-checkered keffiyeh he had wrapped around his neck as a muffler. He glanced past Omar Yussef to Cree, who stared ahead.

'Where is the house of Lieutenant Fathi Salah?' Omar Yussef said.

'The martyr Salah?'

Omar Yussef thought he detected a smile around the ends of the man's mouth. 'That's right.'

'It's near the border at the far end of town.' The young man leaned his head inside Omar Yussef's window as he gave his directions, avoiding the swirling dirt.

Cree groaned in concert with the growling gears of the Suburban, as he ground the car down a sandy lane and came to a halt behind the house where Fathi Salah had lived. He tugged on the handbrake, cut the engine and let his grip on the steering wheel relax for the first time in half an hour. 'I bet you thought we wouldn't make it, eh?' he said.

'Since when did a blow to the head and a mere sandstorm halt the Royal Scots?' Omar Yussef said.

'All right, so I'm a former military man who's too pig ignorant to know when to quit. What's your excuse for persisting?'

'I'm a Palestinian. I'm accustomed to eating crap.'

The Salah house stood alone across a small expanse of ground, a two-story block in unfinished concrete. On the roof, rusting rebar protruded from the supporting pillars like tufts of unruly hair, waiting for the addition of another floor. The silvery matte leaves of a few olive trees waved above the garden wall. In the lee of the wall, the black canvas awning of the family's mourning tent whipped in the wind. It was two days since the funeral of Lieutenant Salah and the tent was empty, except for one old man.

Omar Yussef struggled toward the tent, his shoes filling with sand that scratched through his light cotton socks. The wind was hot after the cool of the car and he narrowed his eyes. Under the awning, the wind dropped, but he still tasted dirt on his tongue as he greeted the old man. Cree came up beside him, ducking under the edge of the tent.

The old man sat, neat and small, on one of the dirty white plastic garden chairs lined around the edges of the awning. He covered his face with the tail of his *keffiyeh*, wrapping it below his eyes to protect his nose and mouth from the dust. His eyes were brown and mournful and his handshake was limp. He stepped to the garden gate and called a name that was lost in the wind. While the man's back was to him, Omar Yussef removed his shoes and tipped their sandy contents outside the tent. The old man rearranged his long, grubby white *jalabiya* and lifted it a little from the hips so that he could sit comfortably.

At the center of the tent, a small square of stones hedged a pile of burning coals and wood. The wood smoke made the dusty air acrid. A copper coffee pot, ornate and blackened, rested among the coals.

Along the garden wall behind the old man, posters announced the heroic death of Lieutenant Fathi Salah. A photo of the officer's darkly threatening face was juxtaposed with an image of the Dome of the Rock in Jerusalem. Fathi Salah was extolled as a martyr in a brief, devout panegyric across the top of the sheet. The corner of one of the posters flapped in the wind, a frenzied tenor counterpoint to the rumbling bass of the awning.

A teenage boy emerged from the garden and poured coffee from the blackened pot into tiny plastic cups and handed them to Omar Yussef and Cree. Omar Yussef enjoyed the brief hit of bitterness, clearing the dirt in his mouth. He turned to the old man and offered his wish that Allah should show mercy to the deceased.

The old man nodded and mumbled acceptance, removing the *keffiyeh* politely from his face.

'We're looking for the father of Lieutenant Fathi Salah,' Omar Yussef said.

'I'm his father.'

'Your name, dear sir?'

'Zaki Salah. Abu Fathi.'

Omar Yussef repeated his wish for the protection of the deceased and once more it was accepted.

'Brother Abu Fathi, we're here to discover the truth about your son's death. We hope in that way to free our friend who has been kidnapped by the Saladin Brigades. He will be freed, if Bassam Odwan is released. We want to be sure of the circumstances of your son Fathi's death.'

'It's well known,' Zaki Salah whispered.

'Odwan denies that he killed Fathi.'

'That's a lie. It has been investigated.'

'What did the investigators discover?'

'Exactly the story that was in the newspapers. Fathi was ordered to arrest the criminal Odwan. During the arrest, Odwan shot Fathi and fled. Fathi died instantly. Soon after, Odwan was arrested. Now he will face the death penalty, as is appropriate for a cold-blooded killer.' Zaki Salah's eyes were angry and wet.

Omar Yussef watched those eyes. He didn't want to push the bereaved man, but he felt the pressure of time. 'Odwan says he went to meet Fathi, because Fathi wanted to sell something to the Saladin Brigades.'

'How do you know what Odwan says?'

'We went to see him.'

170

'At the jail?'

Omar Yussef nodded. Zaki Salah shook his head. The old man's lips were a thin, bitter line. He stood. 'Come with me.'

Omar Yussef put his coffee cup on the chair next to him. Cree rose.

'Just you, *ustaz*,' Zaki Salah said.

Cree sat, with a look of relief.

Zaki Salah led Omar Yussef through the garden. The wind slapped the olive branches against the wall. As they entered the house, the dirt in the air was overcome by the warm, rich scent of *foule*. The smell of the vinegary fava-bean mash made him wish to be in his own home, with appetizing aromas drifting to him as Maryam prepared lunch.

Salah shuffled down the corridor, his sandals slapping the cheap tiles. He was probably no older than Omar Yussef, but he moved even slower and was slightly bent at the waist.

In the sitting room, Zaki Salah stood before three degree certificates mounted on the wall in gaudy gold and silver frames. He lifted a dark, wrinkled finger and pointed at the first of them.

'This is the degree my son Fathi obtained from al-Azhar University. He studied political science,' Zaki Salah said. 'Why would a man with a university degree and a good position in the security forces make shady deals in the night with a criminal like Odwan?'

Omar Yussef stepped closer to the wall and adjusted the bent frame of his glasses. He read the other two degree certificates. The first was a Bachelor's in political science awarded to someone named Yasser Salah; the second, a law degree earned by the same man. Both were inscribed with the crest of al-Azhar University, the dome and minarets of a mosque set against an open book. 'Who is Yasser Salah?' he asked.

'My other son. He's an officer, too.'

'In which security force?'

'Yasser's in the Preventive Security.' Zaki Salah tapped the frame of the last certificate on the wall. 'After he obtained his second degree, he was promoted to captain.'

'Congratulations.' Omar Yussef paused. 'Abu Fathi, the Saladin Brigades has demanded Odwan's release.'

'It's against all laws of justice.'

'But the Saladin Brigades are very powerful.'

'My son was part of the security forces. They're very powerful, too.'

'Do you believe General Husseini will execute Odwan, even if it brings him into conflict with the Brigades?'

'I demand the death penalty. If Husseini is weak and releases him, I will kill Odwan.'

'You?'

'My family. My son Yasser will take the responsibility. As a security officer, he's qualified. Odwan is a murderer. If the government is too weak to give us justice, then you know our customs and laws as well as anyone else and you understand what I must

172

do.' Zaki Salah's voice was a bloodless monotone, as though fatal revenge were an everyday event. 'When Odwan killed Fathi, he killed a whole family. Fathi had a daughter who was only three months old. If Odwan is released, I will kill him, and if I can't kill him, my son will kill him. Even if we have to wait longer, my grandson will kill someone from the Odwan family.'

Omar Yussef closed his eyes and breathed deeply. He hated the old tribal laws. They were made for a place where there was no government and where no one could be seen through the sandstorm except the man who came to menace you. Zaki Salah could have spoken these words a thousand years ago, and he might also harbor the desire for vengeance a thousand years.

'General Husseini has to weigh traditional family justice against the possibility that a foreigner could be at risk,' Omar Yussef said.

'Who cares about the foreigner? What makes him so important? If Husseini releases Odwan, he's not a Muslim. My revenge is what Islam requires. The killer must be killed. I can't give up on my son's blood.' Zaki Salah brushed his hands together as though he were washing them. His voice was angry and pleading. 'You have to explain that to the foreigners.'

Omar Yussef imagined Magnus Wallender dead and wondered who would avenge his blood. He closed his eyes and fought away the image. 'Abu Fathi, was your son ever involved in smuggling?'

'He was never involved in crime.'

'Does that include weapons smuggling? Or do you think of that as resistance work, not crime?'

Zaki Salah looked surly. 'He was always very busy fighting against the smugglers. At work, it was his duty. But then he would come home and the smuggling would be at his door, so even here he was forced to confront the criminals. We're very close to the Egyptian border.'

'Are we? How close?'

'If it weren't for the dust storm, you would have seen it behind the house, when you arrived. It's a hundred paces to the border fence from where we are now at the back of the house.' Zaki went to the window and drew back the curtain. 'There it is, you see?'

Omar Yussef peered into the thick dust outside. There was a garden behind the house, and a poorly built garage at the edge of the garden. Beyond the garage stood a thirty-foot fence of dark metal, rippled like the tin on a cheap roof. That was the Egyptian border.

'This area is thick with tunnels. Smugglers dig them under that fence,' Zaki Salah said.

A young man emerged from the garage and bolted the door with a padlock. He hunched across the garden in the wind. Omar Yussef heard him enter the house, coughing.

The savory smell of the *foule* came into the sitting room and hung around them at the window. 'You had better go back out to the mourning tent, so the women can set up for lunch,' Zaki Salah said to Omar Yussef. 'I would be honored if you would stay to eat with us.'

Omar Yussef's bruised temple pulsed in protest at the mention of food. 'You honor me,' he said, 'but I must continue to investigate this case. My friend may not have much time, unless I can discover the truth. Perhaps your son Yasser will be able to help me, as a member of the security forces and with his knowledge of the investigation.'

'I'll send him to sit with you.'

Omar Yussef went out to the tent. Cree sat in the same spot. He wiggled his shoulders and rolled his neck and smiled at Omar Yussef. The blackened coffee pot stood on the bricks that fringed the hot coals. Cree smiled apologetically. 'I'm afraid I already emptied that little bugger there,' he said. 'It took some doing with these tiny cups, but it was a case of extreme need.'

'To your double health,' Omar Yussef said.

The young man who had crossed the garden at the back of the house came to the edge of the dusty carpets on the floor of the mourning area. He stared at Omar Yussef.

'You're Yasser?' Omar Yussef asked.

The young man nodded.

'Allah will be merciful on your brother. Please sit with me. Your father believes you can help us.'

The young man hesitated. He sat opposite Omar Yussef and settled himself forward, leaning his elbows on his knees. He looked Omar Yussef up and down with hard, tight, angry brown eyes. The angle of his head showed his prominent widow's peak as a point so sharp that it looked like the blade of an axe. He drew his thick eyebrows down toward the bridge of his nose, where they quivered like the hair trigger of a pistol ready to be sprung. His nose was straight and pointed, and his teeth were jagged, broken and bared beneath his mustache. Every feature on his face looked like a weapon, and Yasser Salah seemed ready to use them.

'Yasser, what is the *Saladin I*?'

Yasser Salah's face sharpened still further. The weapons were cocked for action. He was silent.

'Do you know about the *Saladin I*?' Omar Yussef said.

'What is it?'

'I asked you.'

'It sounds like you know. So why ask me?'

'It's a prototype for a new stock of missiles to be made here in the Gaza Strip. Your brother was trying to sell it to the Saladin Brigades, when he was shot.'

Yasser Salah scratched his forehead. Omar Yussef wondered if the man might cut his finger on the point of his widow's peak.

'He was arresting Odwan,' Yasser said.

'That's not what Odwan says.'

'He killed my brother like a coward; now he's making cowardly excuses.'

'Perhaps he's telling the truth.'

Yasser Salah shook his head. Omar Yussef felt the young man's contempt as strongly as if he'd come over and slapped his face. 'You work for the United Nations?' Yasser gestured toward the Suburban, painted with the large black identifying letters of the UN.

Omar Yussef nodded.

'What do you know about the Saladin Brigades? What do you know about life in Rafah? This is the forgotten place of Palestine. Everything here is worse than anywhere else. More martyrs during the intifada than any other place. More invasions by the Israelis. You have no idea about life here, or how my brother worked for the people.' Yasser Salah prefaced every sentence with an impatient exhalation that sounded like a man stretching a stiff muscle.

'When did you first hear about your brother's death?'

'Immediately. I was called to the scene.'

'Why?'

'I was on duty that night. I'm an officer in the Preventive Security.'

'Your brother Fathi was alone at the time of the attempted arrest?'

'No, he was with a squad of his officers.'

'Really?' Omar Yussef thought of the lonely scene Bassam Odwan had painted of his late-night meeting with Fathi Salah. 'What did you see at the scene?'

'My brother's body under a white sheet. His comrades in a cordon nearby. Tire tracks from a car that looked like it had left quickly.'

'Where was this?'

'On the edge of the refugee camp. Near the border.'

'Why did Fathi go to such a quiet place to arrest Odwan? Why didn't he arrest him at home, as his comrades did a couple of hours later?'

'I don't know the details of the operation. Perhaps he arranged to meet him, but really intended to arrest him.'

'He lured him to a meeting so that he could arrest him?'

'It could be.' Yasser Salah cleared his throat with a wet grumble, went to the edge of the tent and spat onto the sand. He picked up the coffee pot and clicked his tongue when he found it empty. He lit a cigarette.

'As an officer in the security forces, did you hear about a new weapon being smuggled into Rafah?' Omar Yussef said.

'The Israelis have all the weapons. We have nothing. The Israelis have sonic booms that make Palestinian women miscarry. When they abandoned their settlements near here, they filled them with radiation to make all of Rafah sick. They have tanks that fire sound rays to turn your bowels to liquid.'

'We have the *Qassam* rockets.'

'They're nothing. They have to land on your head to kill you, more or less.'

'So they need to be improved?'

'Yes, but it would be difficult to do.'

'Why?'

Yasser Salah held Omar Yussef's gaze and was silent.

'Difficult, because you would need to bring a new prototype into the Gaza Strip, under the eyes of the Israelis,' Omar Yussef said. 'Isn't that right?'

'There're lots of tunnels under the Egyptian border, but most of them are too small to bring in a missile,' Yasser said. 'That's why it would be difficult.'

'Anyone who possessed that new missile, though, would be able to demand a high price from a group like the Saladin Brigades, which could use it to manufacture improved missiles. Right?'

Salah's eyes were narrow, but he relaxed them and raised his eyebrows with a shrug.

'The Saladin Brigades want Odwan released,' Omar Yussef said. 'They kidnapped one of our foreign staff as a hostage.'

'They're criminals.'

'If Odwan is innocent, our friend could be released.'

Yasser lifted his chin and sneered. 'If Odwan is freed, I'll kill him, anyway.'

'You don't worry about angering the Saladin Brigades by killing him?'

'I'm not afraid to die. It's my duty to avenge my brother. This is tribal justice and it's what I believe in.'

Omar Yussef watched Yasser Salah closely. He had seen this certainty in the eyes of his students over the years, violent and absolute. He held convictions of his own with equal depth, but he hoped he hadn't arrived at them through blind faith in tradition or at the expense of others.

Cree cleared his throat. 'Abu Ramiz, we have to be heading to the checkpoint to pick up the hostage negotiators. They're arriving at four-thirty.'

Omar Yussef nodded and stood.

'I warn you not to trust the Saladin Brigades,' Yasser Salah said. 'They're killers and criminals.' He picked up the coffee pot once more, remembered that it was empty and dropped it angrily beside the fire.

Omar Yussef struggled to the Suburban, his shoes filling with sand once more.

Cree started the engine. 'It's almost three o'clock. Why don't I drop you back in Gaza City and head on to the checkpoint to pick up the negotiators? I'll take them to the hotel afterward, so you can brief them. You can wait for me there and rest your aching head.'

Omar Yussef nodded. The Suburban labored slowly through the deep sand and past the side of the Salah house. He looked at the flimsy cinderblock garage at the back of the walled garden. It was wide and deep enough for four cars, two abreast. There ought to have been tire tracks leading through the sand from the garage to the road that ran parallel to the border, but there were none. *Perhaps the dust storm filled them in*, Omar Yussef thought. *But even in a storm like this, that would take days. Maybe it's not used for cars.*

CHAPTER 16

The Saladin Road carried them back to Gaza City. Hunched in the passenger seat, Omar Yussef contemplated the events of the last twenty-four hours. He swung out of his reverie only when Cree swerved to avoid a pedestrian drifting heedlessly into the traffic. Cree cursed, and Omar Yussef smiled, patted the Scot's long forearm and went back to his thoughts.

Saladin came along this road to liberate Palestine from the Crusaders. No liberators rode it now. Just brutal gunmen and corrupt policemen and government functionaries who cared only for their status as VIPs. No liberators, unless you counted Omar Yussef and James Cree.

A donkey cart laden with watermelons pulled out of a dirt road and Cree swerved once more. 'For Christ's sake,' he said, rubbing his forehead.

Omar Yussef traveled the same road as the great warrior Saladin. He would free Magnus Wallender and Eyad Masharawi. He closed his eyes and tried to visualize the moment when he would shake their hands to celebrate their release.

He felt a sudden panic. The men's hands were

mutilated by the Husseini Manicure and their blood poured over him. He forced open his eyes. Both of them could be under torture at this very moment and he was sitting in a car, helpless. He groaned.

'You all right?' Cree asked.

Omar Yussef hadn't realized that his groan was audible. 'Just my head.'

'Still a bit of a bump, isn't there?'

'I feel like I've been kicked by a donkey.' Omar Yussef thought about the British cemetery and the way Cree had talked to him there about his past. 'James, your link to all these things happening in Gaza is your great-grandfather,' he said. 'I, too, have a reason for taking this more personally than you might expect.'

Cree kept his eyes on the road, but lifted his chin. 'Yeah?'

'Like Eyad Masharawi, I was once jailed for political reasons.'

Cree grinned. 'You bad old boy. When was that?'

'It was when I was very young, during the 1960s.'

'The Israelis?'

'No, the Jordanians.' It was years since he had talked about that time and Omar Yussef was surprised that it brought a feeling of relief. 'I used to be involved in Bethlehem politics, quite a radical in fact. Some of my opponents framed me.'

'Framed you for what?'

Omar Yussef hesitated. 'Murder.'

'Bloody hell.'

'Very few people who're still alive know this. I've never told anyone about it, except my wife. And now, you. After it happened, I went to Damascus University and took a leading part in student politics. But when I came back to Bethlehem, I admit I was scared. So I laid low. I taught at my school and lived quietly. Jail was so awful, I knew I couldn't let them send me there again.' Omar Yussef dropped his voice. He seemed to be speaking to himself. 'Just recently, though, my anger at the way our people are governed began to outweigh my fear. That's why I won't rest until Masharawi and Magnus are free.'

'I know you won't.' Cree put his big hand on Omar Yussef's shoulder and smiled.

The Scotsman dropped Omar Yussef at the Sands Hotel and pulled away, north toward the crossing with Israel. It was almost four o'clock. Before the UN team arrived, Omar Yussef would have time to drink a cup of tea and clean away the muck that had laid itself over him in the Salah family's mourning tent.

Omar Yussef closed the smoked glass door of the hotel behind him. He rubbed his eyes and coughed. The coughing took hold and he bent forward.

From the reception desk, the pretty clerk beckoned. '*Ustaz*, come here and drink some water,' she said.

He emptied the glass. 'Thank you, Miss Meisoun.'

'Were you out stealing a camel to bring to my father?'

Omar Yussef thought it was good of her to flirt with him when he was covered in dust, bruised all over one side of his head, and purple in the face from coughing. 'I plan to liberate all Gaza, like the Emir Saladin, and I shall make you my Emira to sit beside me at great banquets,' he said.

She pretended to pout. 'If you were an emir, you wouldn't need a small woman like me. You could pay the dowry for a wife with big hips who would bring you many children.'

'Perhaps I would have the traditional four wives: three with big hips, and you to be my favorite.' Omar Yussef laughed in his guttural way. He coughed again and, as he did so, he tapped his hand against his chest. He felt the papers in his shirt's breast pocket and pulled out the notepaper on which he had written the address of the website Nadia had made for him. 'Meisoun, is it possible for you to type these letters into your computer, please?'

'Of course, *ustaz*.' Meisoun turned the computer monitor at a right-angle to the desk, so Omar Yussef could see it. She typed *www.pa4d.ps*. The screen went momentarily white, then a dark blue. Design elements popped up one by one across the screen until Omar Yussef was staring at his website.

Across the top of the screen, in yellow letters, ran the title: *Palestine Agency for Detection*. Below it, a quotation: '*Wherever there is injustice and bother, I am your man*' – Agent O. On the left side of the screen, framed by a soft, oval border, was a

184

photograph of a man's face: he was in his mid-fifties, balding and white-haired, with a white mustache and gold-rimmed glasses and a cheerful smile for the camera because it was held by his favorite grandchild.

'Isn't that you, *ustaz*?' Meisoun asked.

'It seems to be.'

At the center of the screen, yellow text was laid over a red background: *I am Agent O, Palestine's secret bringer of justice on behalf of the Palestine Agency for Detection. I am well dressed and sober and keenly understand the almost unfathomable workings of the Palestinian mind. I solved the case of the Collaborator of Bethlehem, even though the solution eluded our security forces. From my clandestine base in Dehaisha camp, I confront all wickedness with a good humor and a high sense of decency and honor. If you need help against the forces of darkness, contact me at agento@pa4d.ps.*

'You're very famous, perhaps?' Meisoun said.

'Infamous, I think,' he said. 'Meisoun, please don't show anyone that computer – I mean, the thing that's on it now, you know, whatever it's called.'

'Certainly, Agent O. Your dark secret is safe with me.'

Omar Yussef forced a smile and went into the quiet breakfast room. He ordered tea and sat by the window. The waves broke heavily against the beach in the dusty wind.

He imagined Nadia writing the text for the site

185

and smiled. She saw him as a hero, even a liber-
ator, like Saladin. He wanted to leave Gaza and
go to her now. He would tell her detective stories.
It would be more pleasant than being an actual
detective, and less risky.

He was sipping his mint tea with a smile, when
Khamis Zeydan rushed into the breakfast room.
His face was dark and tight. He leaned on Omar
Yussef's table and brought his face close to
whisper in his friend's ear.

'Your friend Cree has been attacked. A roadside
bomb, a massive one, near the Israeli checkpoint.'

Omar Yussef spilled his tea on the white table
cloth. 'Is he okay?'

'I don't know. Sami got the call a few moments
ago from one of his security guys.'

Omar Yussef stood. 'I have to get to James.'

Sami drove fast along Omar al-Mukhtar Street
in a shiny, black Jeep Cherokee. Khamis Zeydan
rode in the front while Omar Yussef sat in the
back with his palms flat on either side of him,
braced against the swerving trajectory of the
vehicle. His mind raced. He could feel his heart
speeding faster than the wheels of the jeep. The
bruise on his temple sent electrifying pain into
his eyes and around the back of his brain. *Perhaps
it wasn't a bomb, only a car crash*, he thought. *James
was very tired and woozy, not really up to driving.
He may have simply gone off the road.* The jeep
swung onto the Saladin Road, overtaking cement
trucks and donkey carts, sounding a long blast

on the horn whenever a child stepped off the curb to cross.

Beyond the warehouses and rough refugee apartment blocks at the northern edge of Gaza City, they passed into scabrous flats of dusty olive trees. Omar Yussef wondered if there had been a mistake. They were almost at the checkpoint. Perhaps Cree had made it there after all.

A crowd blocked the road ahead. Sami slowed. Even with the windows closed against the dust, Omar Yussef heard the rushing clamor of angry voices. Shots came hollow and popping, and the crowd retreated. Sami pulled over. Khamis Zeydan opened the glove compartment and pulled out a pistol. He got out of the car and shoved the weapon inside his belt. Omar Yussef followed him.

The thick dust raked his eyes. There was a bitter scent of burning fuel on the air. He squinted at the crowd of youths, charging and drawing back with each volley of shots. A clipped patter punctuated their rushes, the sound of stones against metal. Beyond the youths, a handful of Military Intelligence men went back and forth, shoving some of the boys away and shooting in the air. Beyond their red berets, Omar Yussef could see flames.

He followed Khamis Zeydan toward an officer who stood aside from the crowd with a walkie-talkie.

'What happened here?' the police chief asked.

'Who're you?'

'Brigadier Khamis Zeydan of the National Police, also of the Revolutionary Council.'

'Greetings, sir. It was a roadside bomb. The UN vehicle was blown from that side of the road, where you see the big crater, to this bank on the other side. You can see it there, past the crowd of youths, where the flames are.'

The officer continued to talk, but Omar Yussef didn't hear. He walked toward the wreckage. He felt Khamis Zeydan's good hand against his shoulder, but he shook it away. He sensed something darkening in his mind, something that he knew was hate.

He pushed through the youths. They jostled him and he struggled to keep his balance, grabbing their arms so that he wouldn't fall. He saw them smiling, exulting before the burning wreckage.

The UN Suburban was upside down. Black smoke and flames billowed from the engine, and the passenger cab was crushed almost flat. *James is in there*, he thought. *I have to get him out.* Omar Yussef pushed to the front of the group of youths. A boy of about fourteen wound up to hurl a stone at the car. Omar Yussef grabbed the boy's arm, pulled the stone from his hand and threw it to the ground. He wrenched the boy around and leaned close to him.

'Shame on you,' he growled.

The boy's expression was ecstatic, but his frenzy disappeared as Omar Yussef looked at him. His jaw dropped and he tried to back away.

'Shame on you, you son of a whore,' Omar Yussef said, squeezing the boy's wrist, feeling his muscles shake all the way up his own arm with the effort of holding the kid and from the adrenaline deep within.

The boy pulled away from Omar Yussef and ducked into the crowd. The Military Intelligence men fired another volley into the air and the youths dropped back. It gave Omar Yussef a brief break in the stones and he scuttled toward the UN car. One of the policemen shouted to him, but he didn't hear the words above the terrible roar of the fire. He held his hand to his eyes against the heat of the flames. The wind shifted and sent the oil-smoke all around him. He dropped to his knees and stared under the black cloud at the driver's seat. He couldn't see James.

He crawled toward the car, only a few yards away now. The black oil-smoke closed around him again. There was sweat in his eyes and his throat burned. He sensed sudden quiet all around and he felt his eyes narrow until they were ebony slits and every line on his face was filled with the shadow of hatred.

He stood and took a pace toward the car. He felt someone grab him and pull him away. He resisted. An arm came around his chest, but he put his weight against it. Stones were in the air once more. One of them hit his shoulder and broke the silence inside his head. He heard the snorting flames of the burning car now and the cheering of the youths beyond the smoke and the voice of Khamis Zeydan. 'James isn't in there. May Allah be thanked, he's at the hospital. Come on, let's get out of here.'

Omar Yussef didn't move. 'Give me your gun.' He pulled Khamis Zeydan close, by the lapel of his jacket. 'I'll kill them. I'll kill them all.'

Khamis Zeydan's eyes were hard with recognition of the hatred that overwhelmed Omar Yussef. He dragged his friend forcefully, but with tenderness and understanding, away from the wreckage. The stones fell about them and they left the UN car and the crowd of youths.

'There's no ambulance here, you see?' Khamis Zeydan said. 'It already came and took him to Shifa, to the hospital. I'll take you there to find him.'

Omar Yussef stumbled toward the Jeep, leaning on Khamis Zeydan's shoulder, wheezing and retching. Sami watched him, blankly. He climbed into the car. He thought of James Cree, squatting before the grave of his great-grandfather in the British War Cemetery, and he loathed the cruel history of Gaza. He smelled the smoke from the wrecked UN car on his clothes and skin. He saw his face in the rearview mirror. The shadows were deep.

CHAPTER 17

The hot, evening wind rattled the palm fronds in Shifa Hospital's broad quadrangle as Omar Yussef stepped out of the Jeep. Khamis Zeydan hurried through the main entrance, where the fluorescent tubes were lit early against the heavy, dust-storm twilight. Omar Yussef came through the door and inhaled a deep lungful of air. It was without dust or oil smoke, but still unsatisfying; it bore an undertone of body odor and corrupt bowels cloaked by antiseptic floorwash. He rubbed his eyes, flicked the gritty gum from the tear ducts, and cleaned the lenses of his glasses with his handkerchief.

Khamis Zeydan returned from the front desk, lighting a cigarette.

'Is he in the Intensive Care Unit?' Omar Yussef asked. He replaced his uneven glasses and saw the heaviness in Khamis Zeydan's expression.

'He's at the morgue,' his friend said.

Omar Yussef's knees shook. He stumbled against the wall. His shoulder took his weight on the tender spot where it had been hit by the stone as he struggled to get to Cree's burning vehicle,

191

and he gasped in pain. He felt feeble, and growing weaker.

'The nurse asked if you would identify the body.'

He searched for the hardness and strength he had felt at the wreckage of the UN car. 'Let's go to the morgue,' he said.

Khamis Zeydan led him into the dusty air and across the grass of the quadrangle, burnt yellow by the sun. The morgue was in the southeastern corner of the square, a single-story, sandstone block with its entrance up a small flight of steps. A nurse directed them to the pathologist's office. 'Abu Fawzi will be with you shortly,' she said.

The office was large, piled with files and painted the same soapy green color as surgical scrubs. Omar Yussef read the labels on the tall, black binders on the bookshelf: *Firearm Injury, Explosive, Head Injury, Strangulation/Hanging, Sexual Offense, Poisoning*. All the files were thick with cases. He tapped the *Explosive* binder with his forefinger and let his hand rest against it, thinking of James Cree, whose case would soon be filed within it.

He remembered confessing to Cree about being jailed as a youth and the way the Scotsman had smiled and laid his hand on his shoulder. It seemed almost as though the mention of the word *murder* had been enough to bring it about. *When it comes from my mouth, at least*, he thought. 'Those kids,' he said. 'It's inhuman for them to stone the wreckage of the car.'

Khamis Zeydan sat in a rickety chair in front of

the pathologist's desk. He stubbed out his cigarette in an ashtray that balanced on a pile of manila folders, measured the stability of his chair by its creaking as he leaned back, and lit another Rothman's. 'Everything that represents authority is an object of hate for them,' he said. 'They don't think about the poor bastard inside the car. To them, it's a blow at everything that keeps their lives shitty.'

Omar Yussef touched his grimy fingers to his mustache. They smelled of the smoke from Cree's car. *When* you're *a victim, there's no room in your life for other people's suffering*, he thought.

He recalled the shocked face of the boy by the burning car, when he had grabbed him and taken away the stone he was about to throw. He would have liked to slap that face. *It's the people who did this to James for whom I must reserve my anger, not that stupid kid*, he told himself. *And for the people who still hold Magnus*. He felt sorry for what he had said to Khamis Zeydan about wanting to kill them all.

A man in light green scrubs entered through the office's second door, which was marked *Surgery*. Behind him, Omar Yussef saw light glimmering off stainless steel freezers. He closed the door and greeted them. 'I'm Doctor Maher Najjar, the hospital pathologist. In fact, the *only* pathologist in the Gaza Strip.'

'You must be a very busy man,' Khamis Zeydan said.

'I have six trainees. It's an expanding profession,' the pathologist said.

Najjar was broad and bulky under his scrubs. A surgical cap rested on the back of his bald head and his face mask was pulled halfway down his gray beard. Omar Yussef looked for signs on his face that would mark him as the man who saw every corpse in the Gaza Strip, opened them up and queried them, called death by what it was.

'Are you a colleague of the deceased gentleman from the United Nations?' the doctor asked Khamis Zeydan.

'No, I'm accompanying my friend Abu Ramiz. He's been working with the UN man.'

Najjar turned to Omar Yussef, gravely. 'Allah will be merciful upon him, the departed one.' He shook Omar Yussef's hand and placed his palm over his heart. 'Would you like some tea to steady your nerves before we identify the body?'

Omar Yussef shook his head. Najjar took his arm and led him into the bright light beyond the *Surgery* door. The walls were banked with stainless steel freezers. A red circle on a white background affixed to the first freezer indicated that they had been donated by the Japanese government. Najjar led Omar Yussef to the four mortuary tables at the center of the room. The first table was empty. There was a hole at its center to drain blood to a gutter in the floor tiles. The other three tables were occupied, each by a body covered in a cream plastic sheet. The body closest to Omar Yussef was very tall. He could have told Najjar that this was Cree without lifting the sheet, and he was glad the Scot was intact enough after the explosion that he could still recognize him by his height.

'I'm sorry for the number of bodies. These are unusual cases. I must think hard about them.' Najjar seemed to choose his words carefully. 'Usually the bodies that come in here aren't so complicated: either they are domestic accidents, or car crashes, or some member of the resistance killed by the Israelis. These two in the back require more thought.' He held Omar Yussef's shoulders and guided him to the side of the table which held the long body.

Omar Yussef nodded. Najjar lifted the corner of the sheet.

Cree's face was red and black, as though it had been skinned. At the nape of his neck, his hair was scarlet with blood and the rest was burned away. His lips were gone and his teeth were bared and ghastly. Traces of his mustache feathered the remnants of his nose. His puffy face had tightened as it burned. He looked like a slightly damp mummy from an Egyptian museum. Omar Yussef nodded and Najjar replaced the plastic sheet on the body.

'There's some paperwork, but first I will bring that tea, after all.' The doctor left Omar Yussef with Khamis Zeydan.

Omar Yussef looked at Cree's body, covered now. He wondered if they would bury him with his great-grandfather in the British War Cemetery.

Probably the UN would ship his corpse home. He imagined the cold ground where they might lay him in Edinburgh. He noticed Khamis Zeydan cradling his prosthetic limb in the palm of his good hand. The policeman pulled tight on the black leather glove he wore to disguise the false hand. 'Have you ever seen a body look this way?' Omar Yussef asked, gesturing toward Cree's table.

'I'm sorry to say that I have,' Khamis Zeydan said. 'It's my misfortune that, if you lifted the sheets on the other two tables, I'd probably have seen dead men who looked just like those, as well.'

Omar Yussef wondered what horrors his friend had experienced in his decades roaming the Middle East and Europe for the PLO. He imagined the rough field-surgery where Khamis Zeydan had been treated for the loss of his hand to a grenade in Lebanon.

The nurse brought two plastic cups of tea. Omar Yussef breathed the heat from the steaming water. The temperature gauge on the Japanese fridge read three degrees Celsius. *That must be the temperature at which they store the bodies*, he thought, with a sudden urge to feel as warm as he could be. He sipped at his tea and felt it scald his throat.

As he leaned against the empty dissecting table, he imagined it might soon bear his dead weight. He wondered if Najjar would describe his death as routine, or if his would be a complicated case that required a lot of thought on the part of the pathologist.

Najjar entered with a clipboard. He asked for Cree's details, so far as Omar Yussef knew them, and gave the board to him for his signature. 'Will you ask the United Nations office to contact my nurse? She will get the full details and next of kin from them,' the doctor said.

Omar Yussef nodded. 'Did he suffer?'

'Abu Ramiz, the compassionate response to that question is always "no," but in this case I can honestly say that it's the correct answer. He died instantly. The shock waves from the explosion killed him, rather than the flames.'

Omar Yussef felt his anger straining through his chest. He wasn't angry at the doctor, but someone had to get it. 'How about this one?' Omar Yussef said, pointing at the next corpse. 'Or this last one over here? Did they suffer?' He let his cup tilt and the tea burned his finger.

'I said that my response was always 'no.' But that's just a matter of sensitivity toward the relative or friend who identifies the body,' Najjar said, calmly, watching Omar Yussef and measuring the schoolteacher's emotion. 'I'm free to answer you truthfully in the case of those other two. This one in the middle, well, I can't tell for sure, but I suspect he died a long and lingering death from infection. The third one I can assess with absolute certainty: he suffered terribly.'

Omar Yussef looked at the two bodies. He remembered the black binders on the pathologist's shelf. *So many ways to die. So much suffering,*

197

so much to be feared. So many people ready to take another's life.

'I'm sorry for speaking angrily, doctor,' he said. 'It's only that I came to Gaza three days ago, and since then one of my colleagues has been kidnapped, another is in jail under torture, and now this one has been killed. It's too much for an old history teacher.'

Najjar reached for the clipboard and, as he briefly checked the details, took the opportunity to turn the talk away from Cree's body. 'A kidnapping? Of whom?'

'A Swede named Wallender. He was kidnapped by the Saladin Brigades last night. They're demanding the release of one of their men from jail in return for his freedom.'

'These things happen frequently in Gaza, Abu Ramiz. The government always gives in. Don't worry. They'll free this Saladin Brigades man and your friend will be released.' The doctor countersigned the form on the clipboard. 'It won't be a pleasant process for you or for him, but you can be calm about the outcome.'

'I'm not so sure. The Saladin Brigades man killed a Military Intelligence officer. General Husseini seems determined to give him the death penalty.'

Doctor Najjar froze.

'Doctor?' Omar Yussef frowned.

'He killed a Military Intelligence officer?'

'Yes, the one who was buried two days ago. Lieutenant Fathi Salah.'

Najjar glanced at the dissecting tables before him. His eyes leaped back and forth between Cree's corpse and the body on the furthest table. 'Bassam Odwan,' he said.

Omar Yussef and Khamis Zeydan suddenly straightened.

The doctor went to the door and shut it. 'Do you know what Bassam Odwan looks like?'

'I saw him in jail this morning,' Omar Yussef said.

'Is this him?' Najjar pulled the sheet partially back from the last table.

Bassam Odwan's wide shoulders were naked. His face was pale and his thick lips protruded purple from his black beard. His hair was shaved above the ears and the skin there was yellow and blue and singed.

Omar Yussef turned to Khamis Zeydan. 'It's Odwan.'

Najjar covered Odwan's face, but Omar Yussef pulled the sheet away, revealing the man's entire body. He recoiled, with the sheet still in his hand.

Odwan's heavy, muscular torso was so bruised he seemed to be wearing a camouflage T-shirt. His genitals were partially shaved and cut. His finger-tips had been sliced off and there were bloody scabs where his nails should have been. *The Husseini Manicure*. A stink of burned flesh and feces emanated from the body.

Khamis Zeydan took the sheet from Omar Yussef's hand and covered the corpse. He glanced at Omar Yussef and his expression was desolate and angry. 'I assume there'll be no paperwork in this case, doctor,' he said.

Najjar nodded. 'There won't even be an official autopsy,' he said. 'The prison guards brought him here not long before your friend from the United Nations arrived. The prison doctor said he died of a sudden heart attack. I wasn't even sure it was Odwan, because they've brought bodies here under false names before, when there's been a death in the prison.'

'Do they bring many people dead from the jail?' Omar Yussef said.

'There seem to be a lot of heart attacks in the jail,' the doctor said, with a quiet, conspiratorial edge.

Omar Yussef felt a jolt of tension pulsing through his own heart. *With Odwan dead, the Saladin Brigades will kill Magnus in revenge*, he thought. *Now I have even less time than I expected.* 'What has been done to this man, doctor?'

Najjar looked hard at Omar Yussef, before he spoke. 'He has been given electric shocks on his temples and genitals. He has been beaten. You can see what has happened to his hands, of course. I can't tell you if these things killed him, but I doubt it. I would have to examine his brain, for example, to see if it hemorrhaged when he was beaten. The inside of his mouth and his upper esophagus is badly cut, which is something I can't quite figure out. It's as though he swallowed razor blades.'

Najjar lifted the lids of Odwan's eyes. Omar Yussef let out a little gasp as the dark, blank eyeball gazed at him. 'You see just here, there're burst blood vessels, tiny ones in this membrane where the eyelid is joined to the eyeball,' the doctor said. 'That's a sign of asphyxia.'

'He choked to death?' Khamis Zeydan asked.

Omar Yussef recalled Odwan's shudder of fear as he had confessed that he gave himself up to Husseini's men for fear of suffocating in the tunnel under the Egyptian border.

'Not on a piece of kebab. Remember the lacerations in his mouth,' the doctor said. 'I'd have to do an autopsy to be certain. Until I've seen if there's an obstruction further down in the trachea, it's really hard to say for sure that someone died of choking.'

'When will you have the results of your autopsy?' Omar Yussef asked.

'I remind you that I have been ordered not to perform an autopsy. The verdict of the prison doctor is sufficient for the authorities.'

'A heart attack?'

'It's something to tell the man's relatives. The body should be buried today, of course, but I've been ordered to keep it here until the authorities decide to tell the family that he has died. Of a heart attack.'

'No one will believe it,' Omar Yussef said.

'No one is asked to believe. They're asked only to be quiet. As quiet as Odwan's body, here.'

'Quiet?' Omar Yussef said. 'When I look at his body, I feel as though I can hear him screaming.'

'The poor one, may Allah be merciful upon him,' Khamis Zeydan said.

Omar Yussef tapped the end of the second dissecting table and turned to Khamis Zeydan. 'Everyone I meet in Gaza is tortured or killed. If I didn't see you standing before me, I'd assume you were lying under the sheet on this table,' he said.

'Thankfully we met long before you came to Gaza. Otherwise I would be in extreme danger,' Khamis Zeydan said.

Doctor Najjar stroked his beard. 'As a history teacher, Abu Ramiz, you will be interested in that body. It's not really a body; it's just bones.' He took the sheet away. On the table, a skeleton lay, yellow and dusty. Thick wedges of dry earth were attached to the joints of the shoulder and knee. 'This fellow came to me two days ago, all in pieces. The police brought him in a plastic trash bag. I put him back in order. I'm not sure what to do with him really. I'm waiting for the religious clerks at the *waqf* to decide where to rebury him.'

Omar Yussef recalled the story from the bottom of the newspaper's front page, below the coverage of Lieutenant Fathi Salah's funeral. 'This is the body that was discovered by a farmer in Deir el-Balah?'

'Yes, in the corner of his field. He reported it to the police and they brought him to me.'

'Him?'

'Yes, him. The pelvis is heavier and thicker than a woman's. Also the opening of the pubis is triangular, whereas a woman's has four sides.'

'Are you supposed to identify him?'

'That would be almost impossible. It's an old skeleton. There's no soft tissue left, which means he's been buried at least five years. But the bones aren't yet crumbly, which is how they get after a hundred years in the grave.'

'So he's been dead between five years and one hundred years.'

'It's very difficult to be more accurate than that. I could test to be sure that it wasn't more than a hundred years by cutting through a bone.' The doctor laid his hand sideways like a saw on the skeleton's long thigh bone. 'Under ultraviolet light, there'd be very little fluorescence in a bone more than a century old. It's not as pressing, of course, as the cases of Odwan and your friend.'

'Perhaps this one's old enough to have died a nice peaceful death in his home,' Omar Yussef said.

'The skeleton is old, but I didn't say that he was an old man when he died. In any case, you forget, Abu Ramiz, this is Gaza. The odds are against a peaceful death.' Doctor Najjar pointed to the ribcage of the skeleton. 'Look at the third rib on the right-hand side.'

The rib was snapped jaggedly halfway along its length. 'Here's the end of that rib,' Najjar said, holding up a few inches of bone. 'But it doesn't fit together with the rib from which it was broken.'

'What does that mean?' Omar Yussef said.

'It didn't just snap. It was shattered. If we had opened up this fellow's grave, rather than finding him tossed in the corner of a field, we would probably have seen many tiny fragments of this rib. I believe this is a gunshot wound. The bullet struck the rib and shattered it.' The doctor sighed as he put the fragment of rib on the metal table next to the skeleton. 'It would have been a terrible injury. Shards of bone from the impact would have created multiple lacerations in the lung behind it.'

'So he died from a shot through the lung?'

'The puncture of a bullet, even right through the lung, wouldn't kill you. But the massive destruction of tissue by all those tiny fragments of bone would have been impossible to repair. If this was a poor man with no access to proper healthcare, or if he was living in Gaza a long time ago – let's say, early in our range of five to one hundred years – the infection from those many little wounds would have killed him.'

'And now he suffers the indignity of having his bones strewn in a farmer's field.'

'No indignity should surprise us in Gaza, Abu Ramiz.'

Omar Yussef took in the three tables with their awful freight. The way death finally took a man seemed always to be a grisly surprise in a place like this. To be alive was to know the constant threat of death and the macabre reality of its arrival. But even beyond that moment there was no peace, not even when your bones were almost crumbled to dust.

'I'm staying at the Sands Hotel,' Omar Yussef said to Najjar. 'If you have questions about the deceased one, James Cree, I hope you'll call me.'

Najjar looked firmly at Omar Yussef. His eyes were frank and his jaw was clenched beneath his beard. He glanced at Odwan's table. 'I'll be busy all night in this autopsy room. You'll hear from me.'

In the morgue's entrance, Khamis Zeydan lit a cigarette. 'You're running out of time,' he said.

'Now that Odwan is dead, will they really kill Magnus?' Omar Yussef leaned against the handrail of the steps.

Khamis Zeydan's silence was his answer. He smiled grimly. 'James Cree and Bassam Odwan, dead in the same room. You certainly came to the right morgue.'

Omar Yussef waved to Sami, who pulled the Cherokee through the deepening darkness to the foot of the steps. 'What do you mean?' he said. 'Doctor Najjar said it's the only morgue in Gaza.'

'Then I should rephrase,' Khamis Zeydan said. 'You were the right man to come to the morgue.'

CHAPTER 18

As Sami sped through the twilight, Khamis Zeydan turned in the front seat and looked hard at Omar Yussef in the back of the car.

Omar Yussef frowned and lifted his chin. 'What?' he said. 'What are you looking at?'

His friend stared. 'I have to go to the president's residence now. The Revolutionary Council is meeting.'

'If you decide to start the revolution, let me know. Otherwise, you can all go to hell.'

'I'll be sure to put that on the agenda. Look, I don't want to leave you alone. I'm worried about you. Sami will stay with you.'

'Sami's *your* bodyguard, not mine.'

Khamis Zeydan raised his eyes and sighed.

Omar Yussef stared out the window, as they slowed in the heavy traffic around Palestine Square. The more crowded the streets became, the lonelier he felt. He had to acknowledge that he didn't want to be alone, with his head full of the horror of the bodies in the morgue. 'Take me to Salwa Masharawi's house. I'll spend a couple of hours there, while you're starting the revolution. It's a good family. It'll help me calm down after all this.'

When they reached the sandy lane to the Masharawi house, Khamis Zeydan grabbed one of the two cellphones from Sami's belt. 'Take this,' he said, tossing it into Omar Yussef's lap. 'If I need to find you, I'll call you on that.'

'I don't like cellphones,' Omar Yussef said. 'They make you sick.' He tapped the unbruised side of his head and tried to push the phone back into Khamis Zeydan's hand.

'It can't give you brain cancer unless you actually have some brains,' Khamis Zeydan said. 'By Allah, it's just for keeping in touch while things are dangerous. Put it in your pocket and forget about it.'

'What if I get a call for Sami?'

'Tell them he couldn't afford a prettier secretary and have them call him on his other phone.'

'His other phone? Is that the number I wrote down earlier?' Omar Yussef remembered the digits scribbled across the back of the Saladin Brigades leaflet in his breast pocket.

'No, that's the number of the phone you're holding,' Sami said. 'My other number is written on the label stuck to the back of that phone, Abu Ramiz.'

Omar Yussef waved as the Jeep reversed out of the lane. He felt exhausted. It was all he could do to lift his arm. He let it flop to his side and watched the taillights turn out of sight.

The alley was dark. A blue fluorescence glimmered from the house beyond the olive grove. Naji's doves were silent. The spray-painted Dome of the Rock was indistinct on the whitewashed wall. Omar Yussef rested his forehead against the rough cinderblock. He closed his eyes and saw the burned corpse of James Cree, Odwan's tortured body, the dusty old skeleton in the morgue. He thought of Magnus's voice, his inquisitive Scandinavian accent, his laughter. Omar Yussef's breath was heavy. He heard someone whimper and he realized it was him. He reached a finger behind the bent frames of his glasses and wiped away a tear.

At the door of the Masharawi home, Naji greeted him with a shy smile. Salwa came from the salon at the back of the house. She looked expectantly at Omar Yussef. Then as he shambled into the light her face fell.

'Don't worry, my daughter,' he said. 'I'm not here with bad news about your husband.'

'Abu Ramiz, you look . . .'

'Like a donkey's backside after too much whipping?'

Naji giggled and Salwa covered her mouth with her hand, smiling. 'Welcome, Abu Ramiz. Come and sit with us.' She led him to the salon and Naji went to the kitchen to make coffee.

Umm Rateb rose from an armchair as Omar Yussef entered the room. She pointed a remote control at the television to mute the volume. 'Abu

Ramiz, I'm happy to see you. Please sit down.'
She gestured to the armchair. 'Salwa and I were
watching the news to see if there's any report of
Abu Naji.'

Omar Yussef sat and the two women went to the
couch. Sami's cellphone dug into his hip. He
adjusted his posture so that his weight wasn't on
it. *I hate these stupid things,* he thought. *I'll probably get bowel cancer from sitting on it like this. I
wonder if even the phones are more lethal in Gaza.*

Salwa smiled at her guest. 'Who has been beating
this donkey, Abu Ramiz?'

'Only other donkeys,' he said. He touched the
bruise on his temple. It seemed like ages since
Magnus was kidnapped. 'My Swedish colleague
was taken by the Saladin Brigades. As a hostage.'

Umm Rateb took Salwa's hand. 'Abu Ramiz, did
they kidnap him because he wanted to free Salwa's
husband?'

Omar Yussef had no proof of a connection, but
he remembered once more what Khamis Zeydan
had said about each crime being linked to many
others in Gaza. Even so, he didn't want to add to
the two women's worries. 'I expect it's something
else. They want one of their men released by the
authorities in return for Magnus's freedom.'

'If Allah wills it, he will be freed soon,' Umm
Rateb said.

The desperation he had felt in the alley left Omar
Yussef. With these two women, he experienced a
little of the calm and warmth he knew at home.

He missed his wife, and he felt guilty about spending time with another woman to whom he was attracted. But he needed to get out of the lonely, violent worlds of hotels and jails, and Salwa Masharawi's living room now seemed like the most relaxed place on earth.

Naji brought coffee. Omar Yussef thanked him. The boy was about to leave the room when he stopped in front of the television. '*Ustaz*, isn't that your friend, the foreigner?'

Omar Yussef turned to the screen. The channel was broadcasting a fuzzy video clip. A man in a blue shirt sat upright in a plain room before a poster of the Dome of the Rock. His hair was a gray-blonde quiff and his chin was stubbled with a short beard. His glasses slipped down his nose and he lifted his head to slide them back into place, evidently because his hands were bound behind his back. It was Magnus Wallender.

'Turn up the volume, quickly,' Omar Yussef said.

'You have the remote control on the arm of your chair,' said Umm Rateb.

Omar Yussef picked up the remote. He stared hopelessly at the colored buttons. 'Naji,' he said, thrusting it at the boy.

Naji pointed the remote at the television and Magnus's voice burst into the room. The poor recording quality and the echoing, empty room where he sat blurred his words. Omar Yussef moved to the edge of his armchair. Only then did he notice the masked gunman in the corner of the

210

frame. He wore camouflage fatigues and a black stocking cap pulled over his face with two holes cut for his eyes. He directed the barrel of his Kalashnikov toward Magnus.

'—the governments of the European Union to secure the release of the brother Bassam Odwan, who is a struggler for the rights and freedom of the Palestinian people.' Magnus paused and glanced sideways at the gunman. The barrel of the Kalashnikov twitched, directing the Swede's gaze back to the camera. He spoke in a hoarse drone, squinting through his tortoise-shell spectacles to read the message, which appeared to be held by someone next to the camera. 'If the brother Odwan is not released, the Saladin Brigades declare that something bad will happen to me in two days.'

Magnus stopped. His jaw fell open.

The coffee cup shook in Omar Yussef's hand. He put it on a side table. He thought of Odwan's tortured corpse in the morgue. When the Saladin Brigades found out about that, Magnus would be killed. Perhaps this tape was more than a few hours old. They might even know by now. Magnus might already be dead.

The gunman pushed Magnus to his knees and stood over him. He raised his rifle and shouted *Allahu akbar*. With his other hand, he grabbed Magnus's hair and pulled his head back. The gesture exposed the Swede's sunburned neck. Omar Yussef blinked hard, gasping as he imagined the gunman severing his friend's head from that neck.

The video clip ended and a news anchor with a loud tie went into a story about delays at the border crossing between Rafah and Egypt caused by Israeli operations against smugglers' tunnels. Salwa gave Naji a glance and he muted the television once more.

James is dead, because of this stinking place, Omar Yussef thought. *I can't let it happen to Magnus, too.* He stared at his hands. He was sure the liver spots had grown. His fists shook, even when he pressed them tight together. He was too weak and old to help his friend, too frail to help anyone. He felt ashamed of his self-pity, of his tears in the alley outside Salwa's house and the homely contentment he had experienced sitting with the two women. 'I just don't know what to do,' he said.

'Don't worry. You'll save him, I'm sure, Abu Ramiz,' Salwa said.

'Just as you will free Salwa's husband.' Umm Rateb held her friend's hands in both of hers.

Professor Masharawi, I'd forgotten about him, Omar Yussef thought. He looked at the two women. Salwa's face was lost and stricken. He felt a wave of protective, fatherly affection for her and took a deep breath to keep from shedding a tear. 'You're right, Umm Rateb,' he said. 'I won't rest until both men are here to eat at Salwa's table.'

Salwa looked up. 'Wait, did you have dinner, Abu Ramiz?'

When she asked him, he knew it was why he had come. He wanted to sit with a family and eat food made with love, not for profit. But that had been weakness, he told himself. *You don't have time to sit here, even if it feels good. You can't pretend you didn't just see that video of Magnus.*

'I already ate,' Omar Yussef lied. 'Now I must go to my hotel. I need to speak to some UN people. Don't worry about your husband.'

Umm Rateb followed him to the front door. In the shadows at the front step Omar Yussef smelled her rosewater soap. 'These men who took your friend, Abu Ramiz, they make me sick,' she said. 'They're not Muslims.'

'I'm afraid they are, Umm Rateb.'

'Not Muslims as they should be.'

'No, not as they should be.'

Omar Yussef shuffled through the sand to the main road to find a taxi.

CHAPTER 19

Meisoun gave Omar Yussef a phone message on a slip of paper when he arrived at the Sands Hotel. 'It was a lady named Nirnberger,' she said. 'She spoke very fast in English, so I didn't understand the other details, *ustaz*. I hope I wrote the number correctly. Perhaps she too is a secret agent.' Her friendly smile made him feel weak. He wanted to collapse onto the reception desk and tell her the disturbing story of his day. He decided to call his wife, instead, as soon as he had dealt with the message.

As he mounted the stairs, he caught the scent of grilled chicken wafting from the breakfast room. 'Meisoun, that *shish tawouk* smells good. Please have the kitchen send some up to my room, and a plate of *hummus*.' He felt a stab of guilt that he could be consumed by the commonplace sensation of hunger so soon after seeing Cree's corpse.

'Of course. To your health, *ustaz*,' she said.

The corridor outside his room was quiet. The hotel's occupants were with Khamis Zeydan at the president's office for the Revolutionary Council meeting. Omar Yussef listened to his slow feet on the carpet. It seemed a foolish thought, but he felt that death remained on his trail, no more than a few paces behind, as it had been throughout his days in Gaza. He heard its footfalls in the silence as he walked, dropping with a hiss like words of warning.

Omar Yussef's room was hot and stuffy. He searched near the door for the switch Sami had used to shut off the air-conditioning, so that he could reactivate it. He found a digital gauge, a small dial and tiny, colored icons of a red sun and a blue snowflake. He fiddled with the dial, elicited some electronic bleeps, and waited, but nothing happened. He undid the buttons of his shirt, went to the telephone and dialed the number on Meisoun's note. The line connected to a cellphone surrounded by the low, rushing sound of a speeding car's interior.

'This is Nancy,' said a voice in the car in English.

It was a hands-free phone, like the one Omar Yussef's son Ramiz had in his car. It gave him an uneasy feeling of talking into nothingness. 'Missus Nirnberger?' Omar Yussef said.

'*Miz* Nirnberger.'

Omar Yussef wondered what that meant. 'This is Omar Yussef speaking.'

'Mister Yussef, thank you for calling me back.' Nancy Nirnberger sounded American to Omar Yussef. She spoke with a deliberate excitement, as though it were delightful to receive a call, and whose call could be more unexpected and agreeable than one from the principal of the UN girls' school in Dehaisha camp? 'I'm heading up the negotiating team that was on its way to the checkpoint when James was hit.'

Omar Yussef nodded at the phone. Then he remembered that she couldn't see him. 'Yes, of course,' he said.

'We've talked through the situation with our guys in Jerusalem and New York, and we're inclined to think that it's too risky for foreign nationals to be in the Gaza Strip right now. In light of what happened to James. So we turned around at the checkpoint and we're en route to Jerusalem again. As we speak, all other foreign employees at our Gaza City office are on their way out of the Strip.' Then, as if she were holding up a new dress for him to admire, Nirnberger added: 'What do you think?'

I think it's too risky for me, too, even if I'm not a foreigner who's worth keeping out of harm's way. 'I agree that it's very dangerous.'

'We'll coordinate negotiations for Magnus's release from the office in Jerusalem. We feel that from there we'll be able to manage contacts with senior government and security guys on the Palestinian side. But we need for you to remain on the ground in Gaza to provide situation assessments and to make material contacts.'

'To make what?'

'To meet the guys who have Magnus, if they want to set a meeting.'

Omar Yussef gripped the receiver tightly. 'I see.'

'None of the local hires in our Gaza City office are as close to this as you, so you're the man on this one, Mister Yussef.' Nirnberger's tone reminded Omar Yussef of the American politicians he had seen in television interviews. He imagined her with her head held to the side, nodding archly, a knowing smile slightly suppressed, as though she had heard all the secrets. 'Is there anything you need, in the meantime? Just name it.'

'The hospital would like James's details so they can notify the next of kin and transport the body.'

'Taken care of, Mister Yussef. Already done. We haven't just been sitting around. Don't worry. We're behind you.'

You certainly are. 'Did James have close family?'

'I don't know, really. I didn't personally handle that.'

'He had a great-grandfather who's buried in the British War Cemetery here in Deir el-Balah. I know the grave meant a lot to him. Perhaps his family would like him to be buried there, because of his personal bond with the place.'

Nirnberger dropped the bonhomie. She sounded as though she were speaking without moving her jaw. 'Well, we can put that to them, but I think it'd be a mistake to set up a new tomb that might be the focus of anti-UN demonstrations down there.' She cleared her throat and reverted to her cheery tone. 'So there's a British cemetery in Gaza, huh? What's up with that?'

'I beg your pardon?'

'Who'd have thought there'd be a bunch of dead Brits buried way the heck down in Gaza?'

'Gaza has a special relationship with the dead.' Omar Yussef's grip grew tighter still. 'I will keep you informed of what I learn here, Missus Nirnberger.'

She let the missus go this time. 'Don't worry. We're going to get Magnus out of there.'

'If Allah wills it.'

'You bet.'

The hotel room was dark. Omar Yussef flicked the switch on the nightstand lamp. He rubbed his shoulder where the stone had hit him in the riot at Cree's burning car. He gave a rasping laugh when he realized that the shoulder hurt so much he'd almost forgotten the wide bruise on the side of his head. The idea of food had made him nauseous all day, but now he was famished. He put the *shish tawouk* out of his mind; it only made him more ravenous to think of it being prepared downstairs. He dialed his home. Once again, Nadia answered.

'Hello, Nadia. What's happening there? Everything all right?'

'Grandpa, did you see the website?'

'I was only able to have a very quick look at it.'

'What did you think?'

Nadia's voice was reedy with excitement. Omar Yussef wondered how much he could tell her about the reality of what her *Agent O* had gone through since she last saw him. He feared that the filth surrounding him like the dust on the air would harm her. 'I liked the website,' he said. 'The lady who showed it to me on the computer was very impressed, except that now she thinks I'm a spy.'

Nadia laughed.

'When I come home, I want you to show me how you do the design,' Omar Yussef said, 'and how you put it into the computer so that it comes out in a computer on this end, too.'

'It's easy, Grandpa.'

'Only because you're very clever. Is Grandma there?'

When Maryam came to the phone, a child was whimpering in the background. 'It's Dahoud,' she said. 'He misses you. He saw something about Gaza on the news and he's been crying all evening. He said he wouldn't go to bed "until uncle calls."'

Maryam and Omar Yussef had adopted Dahoud and his sister Miral at the turn of the year, after the violence of Bethlehem took their parents. The boy's concern for him touched Omar Yussef. The poor little fellow had already lost a beloved father and no doubt feared the death of the man who had stepped into his place. 'Tell him I'm fine, he can go to bed now, and I'll see him soon.'

'When will that be, Omar?'

'I don't know.' He cleared his throat and tried to sound nonchalant. 'You saw the news?'

'No, I told you, Dahoud saw it. But I can't get

any sense out of him. Why? What happened?' Maryam's voice was edgy and loud, as though she had dived suddenly into the phone.

Omar Yussef hesitated. 'Well, Magnus was kidnapped by the Saladin Brigades and another UN fellow who was working with me was blown up in his car—'

Maryam gave a high-pitched gasp. 'By Allah, Omar, you have to get out of there.'

'I have to see to Magnus's release, Maryam. The UN won't send anyone else. They're scared to have a foreigner here.'

'Don't they have local Gazan staff?'

'I assume they're keeping their heads down.'

'So should you. Are you to be sacrificed?'

'Maryam, I can handle this.' He could imagine her shaking her head at the other end of the line.

'You're not so tough, Omar. Just because you stood up to the gangs in Bethlehem last year, doesn't mean you can do the same thing in a strange town. Gaza is a terrible place.'

'I can take care of myself. And Abu Adel is here too. He won't let me do anything risky.'

'Abu Adel may be police chief in Bethlehem, but in Gaza he's nothing. They'll kill him as though they were squashing an insect. And he can be just as rash as you, Omar.'

'Who are *they*, Maryam?'

'Whoever it was who kidnapped Magnus and blew up this other man.'

'It might not be the same group.'

'That only doubles the threat.'

Omar Yussef never liked to argue with Maryam. Usually, her perspective was more simplistic than his, and he would grow angry when she failed to understand the subtleties that were evident to him. This time, he knew she was right, and just as surely he knew he had no choice but to defy her logic. 'Maryam, I need you to be calm. I don't want you to upset Dahoud any more than he already is, or Nadia and the other children. Now, go to Dahoud and tell him not to worry. And Maryam—'

'What?'

'If you don't put on a convincing show, Nadia will see through you. So you'd better really persuade yourself that your poor husband will be all right.'

'I can handle Nadia.'

'She's a lot more difficult to bamboozle than the gunmen of Gaza, my darling. So don't take it lightly.'

There was a knock at the door. 'Maryam, room service is here with my dinner. You see, you were so flustered that you didn't check if I was eating properly.'

'I'm derelict in my duty as a wife,' Maryam said. 'Come home where you'll be safe – from dangerous men and bad hotel cooks.'

Omar Yussef hung up with a few endearments.

He picked at his grilled chicken and dabbed some flat bread into the plate of *hummus*. He wondered what Magnus was eating, in whichever filthy little room the Saladin Brigades had hidden him. His mind gravitated to the corpses in the morgue at Shifa Hospital, no matter how he tried to focus on his food. His stomach ached for nourishment, but it turned at the thought of the dead men laid out on the dissecting tables. His head was heavy; the bruise on his temple had come back to life and was pulsing and jabbing at his brain. He opened the minibar. There was a large bottle of mineral water, some rosewater colas and canned fruit juices. He smiled bleakly at the empty racks in the small refrigerator, designed for miniature whiskies and vodkas. *Allah be thanked that the Islamists of Gaza put so little temptation in my way,* he thought.

He sat at the foot of his bed until the chicken was cold, slowly working through the plastic bottle of water. It halted the nausea and soothed the pumping sensation in his temple. He considered sleeping, but he couldn't slow his thoughts. Instead, he listened to the wind, loud against the picture windows, and the pattering of the dust it blew against the panes.

It was almost midnight when there was a knock at the door. Omar Yussef froze. A pause, then a second knock.

'Abu Ramiz?'

It was Sami's voice. Omar Yussef opened the door. The young man stood confidently in the corridor, smoking. His black T-shirt was tight across his muscular torso and he had a thumb tucked casually into the belt of his jeans. He looked Omar Yussef up and down, evidently finding his raggedness amusing, and smiled. He put his hand on Omar Yussef's arm. 'How're you feeling, Abu Ramiz?'

'Rough, Sami. Where's Abu Adel?'

'He's down the corridor gossiping with some of the other Revolutionary Council members in his room.'

'The meeting is over?'

'The Council? Yes, for now. Those bastards never really finish talking, though.'

'Come in.'

Sami sat at the desk and glanced at the chicken.

'Be my guest,' Omar Yussef said.

Sami picked up the chicken pieces in his fingers and ate them languidly. 'Thank you, Abu Ramiz. It's the best *shish tawouk* I've had in an age. I haven't eaten very well since I was deported from Bethlehem.'

'You miss your mother's cooking?'

'It's the best.'

'I know, I've tasted it.'

'Of course you have. My father speaks highly of you, and naturally I know your reputation around town as a man of integrity.'

'When will the Israelis let you come home, Sami?'

The young man turned a cube of chicken in his fingers, regarding it meditatively, like a connoisseur with an expensive cigar. 'When my home is burned to the ground and demolished by my neighbors.' He chewed the chicken and looked at Omar Yussef. 'Not before then.'

'Do you have any news of Magnus?'

Sami shook his head. 'I'm trying to find out who killed James. I believe that will lead us to Magnus.'

'Remember you told me about the Husseini Manicure? That's what had happened to Odwan before he died. I thought of telling you about it, when you were driving us back from the morgue, but I just couldn't stand to speak of it.'

Sami ate another piece of chicken. He licked his fingers and nodded with understanding at Omar Yussef.

'The Saladin Brigades might murder Magnus in revenge for Odwan's death,' Omar Yussef said. 'Can we find him before they discover that their comrade has been killed?'

Sami shook his head. 'No chance. If they don't already know Odwan's dead, they'll have found out before dawn. They have men inside the jail with hidden cellphones. They know everything that goes on in the Saraya and all the other prisons and military bases. But I don't think they'll kill Magnus.'

'They have to show a response, to avenge Odwan.'

'I don't get the sense that they're ready to escalate things as far as killing more foreigners. They'll choose something else. Something domestic that will send a message to the top people in Gaza, but that won't bring the entire outside world down on them.' Sami held the plate of *hummus* in his palm and ran his bread around the edge of the chickpea paste, brooding.

'How did the Revolutionary Council meeting go?'

'Abu Adel says it was tumultuous. And dangerous.'

'Dangerous?' Omar Yussef remembered what Khamis Zeydan had said about the growing confrontation between the security chiefs.

'General Husseini accused Colonel al-Fara of corruption. He called for an official investigation of al-Fara.'

'But General Husseini is corrupt, too, isn't he?'

'Yes, but these Councils are strange. If someone accuses you of something, you can't just turn around and say, "By Allah, you're as corrupt as me." It makes you look like a stupid kid whose only defense is to turn the charge back on the accuser and, more importantly, you're admitting the truth of the accusation.'

'So what did Colonel al-Fara do?'

'Abu Adel says al-Fara was silent. But everyone else was in uproar.'

If al-Fara was silent, Omar Yussef calculated it was a perilous sign. In that silence, the Colonel would have been plotting his revenge.

Omar Yussef remembered the comical exuberance, the heavy paunch and the wet, pebble-gray eyes of General Husseini, the man who probably had asphyxiated Bassam Odwan. Across the table at the Council, he imagined the lank, black hair and mustache of Colonel al-Fara, the bony hand

225

collecting sputum in a tissue and the cigarette smoke flaring from his nostrils. Al-Fara, the torturer of Eyad Masharawi. The meeting of the Council had set the two men up for a final confrontation. With what new evil would they move to their endgames?

'Who will lose this battle between Husseini and al-Fara?'

'The first one to show weakness,' Sami said. 'You know the proverb: *When the cow falls down, many knives come out.* Each of them has enemies who'll be eager to cut off a piece of the carcass, as soon as it's vulnerable.'

'Did anyone mention the bomb that killed James?'

'At the Revolutionary Council? No, it didn't come up. Everyone was focused on the fight between Husseini and al-Fara.'

Omar Yussef took a strawberry-banana juice from the minibar and handed Sami a rosewater coke. He poured the thick, syrupy liquid into a glass for himself. It was the nearest thing to food he could keep down. He wanted to sleep, but there was still one thing he needed to talk about.

'Sami, that story Odwan told us about the *Qassam* rockets. Is it correct?'

'That they brought a single prototype to Gaza through the Rafah tunnels and manufactured masses of them here?'

Omar Yussef nodded.

'Yes, it was a North Korean missile transported

through Iran,' Sami said. 'Now everyone's trying to secure an even bigger weapon. The group that uses it successfully against Israel will gain a lot of prestige on the street and be able to impose its will on the president.'

'The Saladin Brigades?'

Sami shrugged. 'The more trouble the Saladin Brigades make, the more the president needs to keep them on his side. If you want money from the president, step one is to make a lot of trouble in Gaza and to kill some Israelis from time to time. Ultimately, the president will pay you to keep a lid on it.'

Omar Yussef put his forefinger to his chin and frowned. 'We know the Saladin Brigades don't have this new prototype missile, because it was stolen from them after they smuggled it into Rafah. So who *does* have it? That's what we need to find out. Perhaps we can present the Brigades with the missile in return for Magnus's freedom.'

Sami looked serious as he finished the last of the *hummus*. 'You'd better think that through, Abu Ramiz. Whoever has the missile won't be handing it over to you, and the nastiest men in Gaza will be trying to find it and take it away from them, too.'

Omar Yussef realized that, even if he found the missile, he could never give it to the Saladin Brigades. No matter who possessed this missile, they would use it to kill, to draw down the Israeli army on the refugee camps, and to dominate the corrupt politics of Gaza. If he found it, he would have to destroy it. But then how was he going to bargain for Magnus's life?

He groaned and put his hand to the bruise on his temple. 'The UN negotiators aren't coming. They turned back at the checkpoint. They think it's too dangerous here. We're alone, Sami.'

'We're better off without them. Those people think they have all the answers, but they don't know how to listen. They're useless to us. They're a shekel-worth of shit.'

Omar Yussef looked at the young man, surprised at his vehemence.

'I'll try to arrange a meeting with the Saladin Brigades people here in Gaza, so you can ask them about what happened to James,' Sami said. He wiped his hands on a napkin, pulled a packet of cigarettes from his back pocket, and stood. He smiled apologetically. 'I know you don't like me to smoke in here, Abu Ramiz, so I'll say good-night. You need to sleep.'

CHAPTER 20

Omar Yussef dreamed of death. He sweated through the explosion that killed James Cree, shaken by the shuddering blast and swathed in the flames, jarred by the twisted metal of the UN Suburban, broken by the stones the local boys hurled. He choked through the last breaths of Bassam Odwan's life, even as the blood pumped from his severed fingertips. He recoiled as an antique rifle discharged its bullet into his rib, fragments of bone tearing his lungs. The shot came again and again, each time thrusting him into the mattress. Death wasn't following him any more. It was sharing his bed, not like a wife, but like an illicit lover, jealous and angry, giving him no sleep.

The telephone rang. The rifle bullets ripped his ribcage and the phone rang on. He rolled to the nightstand and picked up the receiver. He couldn't speak; he gasped into the phone.

'Abu Ramiz, is that you?'

Another gasp. The shots continued. He whimpered.

'Is everything okay? This is Doctor Najjar, from the morgue. Is that gunfire?'

Omar Yussef looked around. *I'm in my hotel room,* he thought, but it was a vague realization.

'What's that noise, Abu Ramiz?' the doctor asked.

'I was being shot.'

'Abu Ramiz?' The doctor was alarmed.

Omar Yussef put the receiver on the pillow and wiped the sweat from his face with the end of the sheet. There *was* gunfire. He looked at the red light of the digital clock on the nightstand: 6:00 a.m. He picked up the phone again. 'Yes, that's gunfire outside. I don't know anything about it. I was having a bad dream.'

'I'm sorry to call you so early, but I've been at work all night and I'm going home now. I wanted you to know what I discovered, as soon as possible.'

Omar Yussef cleared his throat and pushed himself up onto his elbow, trying hard to leave his nightmare behind. 'Thank you.'

'This must remain between you and me, Abu Ramiz. As you know, the official cause of Bassam Odwan's death is that he suffered a sudden heart attack in his jail cell. However, my initial suspicion that he died of asphyxia was correct. A blockage in his airway suffocated him.'

Omar Yussef sat upright on the edge of his bed. 'Odwan choked on his food?'

'It wasn't food. You remember that the inside of his mouth and the upper part of his throat were covered in tiny cuts? Further down in the trachea, blocking the air, I found some sort of glass.'

'Glass?'

'Actually, it's something I've never seen in Gaza. But once, when I was in a hotel bar in Jordan, I saw something like it. I think it's the stopper from one of those crystal bottles that people use to store alcohol.'

Omar Yussef thought of General Husseini's collection of Bohemian crystal. 'A decanter?'

'Is that what they're called? It's been carved into many tiny flat surfaces, so that it reflects the light like a precious stone. But between each of the surfaces it's almost as hard and sharp as the cutting edge of a diamond. It was big and, as it was forced down his throat, it caused the lacerations. Then it choked him.' The doctor paused. 'That shooting sounds very close, Abu Ramiz.'

Omar Yussef stood and moved toward the window to draw back the curtain. The phone cord wouldn't stretch far enough. The gunfire outside was a deafening, bass volley with the light chimes of shattering glass laid over it. 'I can't see just now. The curtains are closed,' he said, raising his voice to be heard over the gunbattle. 'Was Odwan's body brought to you directly from jail?'

'Military Intelligence brought him. He could've arrived from anywhere.'

Omar Yussef listened to the shooting. It seemed to be concentrated on General Husseini's house across the street. *From anywhere. Even from there*, he thought. He thanked the doctor and hung up.

He crept along the wall and lifted the curtain.

A dozen jeeps were drawn up on the street outside the hotel, a mixture of camouflage and flat, dun paintwork. The men taking cover behind the jeeps were dressed like the Saladin Brigades squad that had kidnapped Wallender: stocking caps pulled down to disguise their features, camouflage jackets and black T-shirts, military pants and heavy work-boots. They fired Kalashnikovs and M-16s at Husseini's home.

The windows on every floor of General Husseini's building were shot out. Omar Yussef squinted into the dusty dawn light. Muzzle flashes from the third floor of the Husseini home jolted through the dirty, gray air.

There was a knock at the door. Omar Yussef pulled on his trousers and answered it. Khamis Zeydan pushed past him, his shirt open over the gray hair on his chest, the white fringes on his bald head sticking up still from the pillow.

'What the hell is this?' Khamis Zeydan said. He coughed and it was as though he had sprayed an atomizer filled with Scotch around the room.

Omar Yussef's nostrils flared at the whisky on his friend's breath and he thought that perhaps he wasn't the only one whose nightmares had been disturbed by the shooting. 'Did you come straight from dawn prayers?'

Khamis Zeydan rubbed his face. 'May Allah forgive you, it's too early for sarcasm.'

'Something's happening at Husseini's place,' Omar Yussef said.

'Son of a whore. I can't see it from my side of the hotel.'

'The management gave the Revolutionary Council people the nice sea view.'

'But you get the view of the fireworks.' Khamis Zeydan lifted the end of the curtain. 'Fuck your mother,' he said, with a tone of wonder.

Omar Yussef peered outside from the other end of the curtain. 'What's going on?'

'It looks like the Revolutionary Council convened for a special session.'

'You think this is something between Husseini and al-Fara?'

'Maybe. Or perhaps the Saladin Brigades decided to show Husseini that they know who killed Bassam Odwan.' Khamis Zeydan grinned. 'Could be a joint maneuver: the Saladin Brigades and Colonel al-Fara's men.'

From behind one of the jeeps, a camouflaged gunman brought out a shoulder-launched missile. 'By Allah,' Khamis Zeydan said, his eyes wide.

'What's that?'

'A LAW anti-tank missile.'

The missile took off from the man's shoulder with a sound like a demon's inhalation and smashed into the third floor, where Omar Yussef had breakfasted the previous day with General Husseini.

The firing from within Husseini's building halted. Even the gunmen on the street stopped to marvel at the destruction. Some of them stood up, their assault rifles held in one hand, pointed to the ground. Omar Yussef saw them laughing at one of their colleagues who had covered his ears against the blast. Another gave a high-five to the missile man. When they resumed their volley, it was cover for a squad of six who ran low across the street and into the entrance. They stepped over a body in military fatigues and a red beret and they went up the stairs. Omar Yussef hadn't noticed that anyone had been hit. He stared at the body and willed it to move. He wondered if he ought to call Doctor Najjar and tell him not to go home just yet; he would be needed soon at the morgue.

The smoke cleared around the third floor, where the missile had hit. Only a small hole, the size of a man's head, showed in the wall, but there were flames inside. Omar Yussef figured the sofas and armchairs must have ignited. Movement was visible in the room. Some shots sounded, and men came down the stairs quickly.

General Moussa Husseini appeared at the foot of the stairs. He was naked except for a pair of baggy white underpants. His big stomach was covered with thick white hair and his legs looked too skinny to support his fat torso. His bald, dark forehead was laced with streams of blood. One of the gunmen shoved him from behind. He slipped on the pool of gore seeping from his dead guard and tripped over the corpse's legs, tumbling down the steps. The gunmen followed, kicking him. He scrambled on his knees into the street.

'It can't be,' Khamis Zeydan said.

Husseini's face was contorted, weeping. One of the gunmen stood behind him, lifted his Kalashnikov and shot him through the neck.

It was a sudden, single shot. Omar Yussef inhaled quickly.

The same gunman emptied his magazine into Husseini's body. The attackers walked briskly to their jeeps and pulled away. Some went down the beach road, while a couple turned up Omar al-Mukhtar Street toward the center of town. General Husseini lay on his face in the road.

Omar Yussef put his forehead against the window and closed his eyes. Khamis Zeydan laid his hand on Omar Yussef's shoulder. He tilted his head toward the street. 'Come on,' he said.

'Do you think it's safe?' Omar Yussef asked.

Khamis Zeydan shrugged. 'Safe or not, unless you want to settle for the official version, we'd better go and check things out.' He hit his shoulder on the wardrobe as he made unsteadily for the door and, when he cursed, he left a cloud of whisky vapor that made Omar Yussef cough.

They were the first to climb the drive of the hotel and reach the scene. Omar Yussef's legs felt as though his thigh bones had been turned ninety degrees in his hip sockets – his feet rejected any straight line he commanded them to follow and his pelvis was full of pins and needles. His body was exhausted after the nightmares that had ruined his sleep. But whatever dreams had tormented him, they were surely better than being awake in Gaza.

Khamis Zeydan knelt by Husseini's body. The road was empty. 'Where are the police?' Omar Yussef said.

'Husseini must have forgotten to dial the emergency operator.' Khamis Zeydan raised a sarcastic eyebrow. He felt peremptorily for a pulse in Husseini's neck.

Omar Yussef looked down at the shattered back of the skull and the gashes in the rear of the plump torso where the gunman had fired on automatic. Excrement filled Husseini's baggy white underpants and the dust had already settled a gritty layer over the bullet wounds. 'How terrible.'

'At least he died with his fingertips intact,' Khamis Zeydan said.

Omar Yussef stared at his friend. 'Even the worst of men deserves to be respected in death,' he said.

'Take it easy. You know exactly what I'm saying. Let's have a look in his house.' They stepped over the dead guard at the entrance to the building and the blood pooling around him.

The door to the third floor salon was open. The foam in the couches smoldered, filling the room with choking smoke. There was a black blast mark on the center of the ceiling, where the crystal chandelier had been, and glass crunched underfoot.

'The missile came through the wall and struck the ceiling there,' Khamis Zeydan said. 'Anyone in this room would've been caught by shrapnel from the missile.'

'Or pieces of the chandelier.'

Behind the long dining table, Omar Yussef found the coffee boy on his back, his arms wide and a bullet through his bony, acned cheek. His eyes were open. He looked no more than a little dazed, but he was quite dead. Omar Yussef glanced down the corridor. Two more guards lay twisted and motionless.

The shelves of crystal along the far wall had collapsed. Husseini's collection of bottles and glasses and plates lay shattered across the marble tiles. Omar Yussef bent stiffly and picked up the neck of a smashed decanter.

'Just as all this was starting, Doctor Najjar called me from the morgue,' he said. 'He found the stopper from one of these in Bassam Odwan's throat. The prisoner choked on it.'

Khamis Zeydan sniffed a dark liquid at the bottom of another piece of partially smashed crystal. 'Brandy. Do you suppose Husseini asked Odwan over for a cozy drink?'

Khamis Zeydan went into the other rooms to look around. Omar Yussef weighed the neck of the decanter in his hand and rolled it against the soft part of his throat below his Adam's apple. Its cold touch on his sagging skin returned him to the choking moments of his nightmare. He shuddered and he put it on the table.

A siren approached along the beach road. Omar Yussef felt his pulse tick faster. *When you hear a siren*, he thought, *you can't help but think that they're coming for you.* A turquoise police jeep rolled to a halt near Husseini's body. Five policemen jumped from the back of the jeep and an officer joined them from the front seat. They stood in an indecisive huddle a few yards from the corpse. The officer approached Husseini and stood over him. He pushed back his blue beret and scratched his forehead.

Khamis Zeydan came to watch at Omar Yussef's shoulder. 'I look forward to an energetic investigation from the security forces,' he said, smiling.

'Don't you have a meeting to go to?'

'What's wrong with you?' Khamis Zeydan said, surprised by his friend's angry tone.

'You people on the Revolutionary Council, you kill one another and then you hold a meeting and you make peace until the next time you decide to murder each other,' Omar Yussef shouted. 'Meanwhile, it's ordinary people like that poor damned coffee boy on the floor over there who pay the price.'

'You think I like it that way?'

'You seem to do all right from this system, despite your cynicism about it.'

'What do you mean?' Khamis Zeydan put a cigarette in his mouth and reached into his pocket for his lighter.

'Who's paying for your nice hotel room? And your expensive dinners? And your apartment in Bethlehem? And the booze you reek of right now? And the stupid smokes that are killing you?' Omar Yussef slapped the cigarette from Khamis Zeydan's mouth.

The police commander on the road below looked up at the third floor window. He pointed and spoke to two of his men, who ran toward Husseini's building.

'The cigarettes? You're worried about my health?' Khamis Zeydan took another cigarette from his pocket and lit it. 'I didn't know you cared, my dear.'

'Don't make a joke of this.'

'Back home in Bethlehem, I admit you'd be right to worry about me,' Khamis Zeydan said. He gripped Omar Yussef's arm, his eyes wide and excited. 'But in Gaza you've got it all wrong. In Bethlehem I drink because of depression, loneliness, disgust with my life. In Gaza it's all action, and I have to admit that I thrive on it. The smoke-filled rooms, the dirty maneuvers, and the violence. In Gaza, I drink because it's part of the biggest buzz imaginable. Even this incident this morning gives me a kick.'

Omar Yussef pushed the police chief's hand away.

'It's true,' Khamis Zeydan said. 'Here I am, the man you call your friend. I'm not proud of it and I wouldn't tell anyone else, but Gaza feels like the good old days, back in Lebanon with the Old Man, before we messed everything up.'

'By Allah, what could be more messed up than Gaza?' Omar Yussef said.

'The truth is, we should've stayed underground forever. We can't govern.'

'This place is governed according to the rules of the Middle Ages.'

'Come on, history teacher. No lectures.'

There were footsteps on the staircase.

'Feuding emirs, unnamable fear you can taste in every particle of dust in this storm, and death,' Omar Yussef said. 'Death even for those like Husseini who're accustomed to wielding it.' Omar Yussef grabbed his friend's shoulders so that their faces were close. 'That's not history. That's the present.'

One of the policemen arrived in the doorway, panting. He leveled his Kalashnikov. Omar Yussef laughed with a rasping exhalation. He walked toward the door.

'Identify yourself,' the policeman said. He was slim and young and his thin mustache twitched.

Omar Yussef glared at him. 'I'm the Emir Saladin, that's who I am. Now get out of my way, I'm going to eat breakfast. There's a boy in that room who's dead because you were too busy eating *your* breakfast to do your job.'

The policeman stepped back and dropped the barrel of his rifle to his knees. A second policeman came up the stairs, breathing heavily. He looked with confusion at Omar Yussef and leaned against the banister to let him pass.

CHAPTER 21

Omar Yussef was into his second serving of scrambled eggs when Khamis Zeydan weaved across the breakfast room, his grim face fixed on the floor to avoid conversation with the Revolutionary Council delegates at the other tables. Though the politicians and their aides occupied almost every chair, the room was subdued in the wake of Husseini's execution. They fiddled with their napkins, nervous and darkly expectant, staring into their coffees with hunted expressions.

Omar Yussef drained his cup and wiped his lips on his napkin as the Bethlehem police chief reached his table.

'To your double health,' Khamis Zeydan said.

'I may have finally found my appetite, but I can't associate anything in Gaza, even the food, with health.' Omar Yussef cleared his throat and looked at his plate. 'I'm sorry for my outburst back there. After seeing the bodies of Husseini and the guards and the coffee boy, well, it was all too much for me.'

Khamis Zeydan waved his hand and chose to ignore the heart of Omar Yussef's earlier accusations. 'No, you were right. I ought to smoke less.'

He sat next to Omar Yussef, though he perched on the seat restlessly. He unfolded a sheet of paper from the inside pocket of his jacket. 'This is the Saladin Brigades leaflet about Husseini's death,' he whispered.

Omar Yussef raised his eyebrows and buttered his toast. 'They type fast, don't they?'

'It says that Husseini was killed by the Brigades, because he was a collaborator who killed "the struggler and brother Bassam Odwan after first administering tortures that were cruel and characteristic." That means the Husseini Manicure, doesn't it? How did they know about that?'

'I told Sami about it,' Omar Yussef said. 'He said they have spies in the prisons.'

'The leaflet accuses Husseini of working to undermine the resistance and arresting its most important fighters.' Khamis Zeydan placed the single sheet of paper on the table.

Omar Yussef glanced at the leaflet and ate a triangle of toast in three bites. As he chewed, he peeled a boiled egg with his fingers, cut it in two, salted it and ate one half. After a day and a night without food, he was ravenous.

'You're eating like a condemned man with his last meal,' Khamis Zeydan said. He waited for Omar Yussef to meet his eye. 'There's an emergency session of the Revolutionary Council in twenty minutes. To discuss the Husseini assassination and to see how the security forces should respond.' Khamis Zeydan looked about the breakfast room.

At the other tables, delegates were rising, brushing crumbs from their elegant suits and issuing murmured orders to their aides. 'What're you going to do?'

Omar Yussef swallowed. 'What does a condemned man usually do after his last meal?' He ate the second half of the egg.

'Don't be ridiculous,' Khamis Zeydan said. 'Ignore that remark. It was a joke. The British call it *gallows humor.*'

'Fortunately there's no hanging in Gaza. I expect to be beheaded when the time comes.' Omar Yussef tapped a forefinger against the two crossed scimitars of the Saladin Brigades' crest. He looked more closely at the leaflet.

'My point is this: after the Revolutionary Council meeting, there'll be some kind of response against the Saladin Brigades,' Khamis Zeydan said. 'A military response. Arrests. Maybe the Brigades'll fight back. It could get nasty on the streets today. We can't let it look like they're getting away with the assassination of one of our own, no matter that we all thought Husseini was a son of a bitch. Don't get caught in the crossfire, okay.'

Omar Yussef popped the top off a miniature pot of honey and drizzled it over a croissant. 'If self-protection was my main priority, I wouldn't even be in Gaza.'

Khamis Zeydan drew an impatient breath. 'The atmosphere today is very, very dangerous. You need to be careful.'

243

'You told me you love this dirt, this intrigue and deceit, this violence,' Omar Yussef said. 'But those pleasures are reserved for members of your select club? I want to join in the fun.'

'Don't be ridiculous. You know you hate all this. You damn near broke down yesterday when you couldn't keep the different security forces and the various gunmen straight in your head.'

'I took the advice you gave me then: I'm not trying to keep track of their organizations, only their intentions.' Omar Yussef bit into the croissant. 'They want to eat me alive.'

'That was only a turn of phrase.' Khamis Zeydan leaned close. 'They don't really care if you're alive.'

Omar Yussef smiled and waved the croissant. 'How long will this meeting of the Revolutionary Council go on?'

'Everyone will say how shocked they are and pretend that Husseini wasn't a bastard. That should take about two hours, I'd say. Then add a little time for someone, probably al-Fara, to say that such things can't be allowed in Gaza and to order the arrest of those responsible. Two hours fifteen.'

Omar Yussef nodded and bit the croissant. The honey ran into his mustache. He sucked it away with his lower lip.

'I have to go,' Khamis Zeydan said. 'Why don't you just walk on the beach and keep out of trouble?'

Omar Yussef looked out of the breakfast room

window at the dust in the wind along the narrow strand. 'It's a lovely day for it,' he said.

Khamis Zeydan sighed, rapped the table in exasperation with his gloved prosthesis and went to the door.

On the beach, a boy with his head and face hidden by a red and white *keffiyeh* laid out a net. The hot wind ruffled his ripped T-shirt. The first time Omar Yussef sat in this breakfast room, three boys had been fighting on that beach. He wondered if this was one of them and where the other two boys were. He hoped they were only keeping out of the dust storm.

He could go no further with his investigation of the Saladin Brigades and the fate of Odwan's stolen missile until he heard from Sami. If Sami arranged a meeting for him with the Saladin Brigades men, he would need to have something to give them in return for Wallender's freedom. The Brigades had wanted to exchange Odwan for Wallender; now Odwan was dead, they would demand something else, if Wallender was still alive. Sami was right: he couldn't offer them the missile. Even if he found it, he knew he would have to destroy it – or bring it to someone decent, who would disable it and wouldn't sell it back to the militias. He wouldn't give them a new toy for their murderous game.

With the Odwan end of the puzzle blocked, Omar Yussef turned to the plight of Professor Eyad Masharawi. Masharawi was held in a Preventive

Security jail. He didn't think the professor's case could really be connected to Wallender's kidnapping or Odwan's death. But he surmised that if he pursued the Masharawi case, any dirt he unearthed about the Preventive Security would at least interest the Saladin Brigades, particularly since the Revolutionary Council – now dominated by al-Fara – was about to set the security forces on them in revenge for the Husseini hit. In exchange for Wallender's release, he could offer the gunmen information they might use against the Preventive Security head.

He thought back to the efforts he and Magnus had made to free Masharawi. Before the Swede's kidnapping, he had dined with Professor Maki and discussed the case. He should investigate Maki's real reasons for calling down the security forces on a troublesome teacher. Omar Yussef recalled the degree certificates from al-Azhar hanging behind Colonel al-Fara's desk and on the wall of the Salah home in Rafah. He had suspected that al-Fara's degree was phony. Perhaps the Salah brothers' degrees also were fakes.

Omar Yussef pushed another croissant into his cheek and chewed, thoughtfully. He folded the Saladin Brigades leaflet and slipped it into his shirt pocket next to the other one. Professor Maki would be at the Revolutionary Council meeting that morning. Omar Yussef decided to go to the professor's office and ask his secretary to show him the files on the Salah brothers. If they had bought their degrees, it might be information worth offering the Saladin Brigades: some dirt on the dead lieutenant who had been held up as a hero and in revenge for whose death their man Odwan had been murdered.

At the front desk, he asked Meisoun to call him a taxi. 'Where to, *ustaz*?' she asked, as she dialed the cab company.

'I prefer not to say.'

She leaned forward, smiling. 'Do you have another girlfriend? My father is waiting for his camel. Are you going to disappoint him?'

He coughed. 'I'm on my way to steal the camel now, as promised.'

'I await you. But don't get caught. They'll put you in a special jail for camel thieves. There's a special jail for everyone in Gaza. Even for unfortunate lovers.'

Omar Yussef stroked his mustache awkwardly. It was still sticky with honey.

He paid the taxi driver at the gate of al-Azhar and walked past the posters of the suicide bombers into the main building.

Umm Rateb rose with an exclamation of pleasure when Omar Yussef reached the open door to Maki's suite of offices. 'Morning of joy, *ustaz* Abu Ramiz,' she cried.

'Morning of light, dear Umm Rateb.' Omar Yussef tried to take his eyes off the smile on her wide, sensual mouth.

'Sit and drink coffee.'

'Allah bless you, but I enjoyed a big breakfast only a short while ago.'

'To your double health, *ustaz*, in your very heart.'

'Thank you, thank you.' Omar Yussef glanced toward Maki's personal office.

'But Professor Maki is not here.' She gestured toward the blinds dropped over the window between her office and Maki's inner sanctum. 'He's at the Revolutionary Council. They're having a special meeting to discuss the assassination of General Husseini.'

'I know,' he said. 'I came about something else.' Umm Rateb looked blank. Then she smiled. 'What're you up to, Abu Ramiz?' She wagged a finger at him.

'I need to look at the files of a couple of students.'

'They're supposed to be private.' The finger continued to wag.

'It's okay. When I was here the other day, Professor Maki discussed certain issues with me and my colleagues from the United Nations. In fact, his very words were that we could ask Umm Rateb to bring the file of any student and we would be able to see their records, and so on.'

'I should really check with him.'

'He's in the Council meeting, as you said.'

Umm Rateb's smile subsided. She glanced at the empty desk where the other secretary had sat during Omar Yussef's last visit. 'You're lucky that my colleague Amina is not here this morning. She's a real stickler.' She went to the outer door and closed it. 'This has to do with Salwa's husband, *ustaz*? With Professor Eyad Masharawi?'

Omar Yussef nodded.

'Whose file do you want?'

'Fathi Salah and Yasser Salah.'

Umm Rateb nodded gravely. She went to the tall gray filing cabinets along the wall and pulled one of them open. She wrenched a file from the crush in the drawer and handed it to Omar Yussef. 'Read it at Professor Maki's desk,' she said, 'in case someone comes in. They won't see you behind his blinds.'

He laid the file on Maki's desk. It held the academic record of Lieutenant Fathi Salah. Fathi's high school grades were quite good, and Omar Yussef noted with approval that Fathi had earned top marks in history. Next was a transcript of the courses Fathi took at al-Azhar: grades from C up to A, a full transcript. He reached into his breast pocket and pulled out the Saladin Brigades leaflets. He put the newer one back and unfolded the first one. He laid it on the desk and, below where he had scrawled Sami's cellphone number, copied out Fathi Salah's transcript. He flipped through the file to a computer print-out from the accounts department. It listed dozens of payments, all small amounts, the last of which was shortly before Fathi's graduation. It had the look of a poor man struggling even to meet the meager financial requirements of a local university. Omar Yussef closed Fathi's file, went to the door of

Maki's inner office, and handed it back to Umm Rateb. She gave him another file in return.

It was Yasser Salah's record. The high school graduation certificate showed straight Bs. A transcript for his bachelor's degree – more straight Bs. Then his law degree transcript. *Surprise me,* Omar Yussef thought. 'Straight Bs,' he said aloud. The accounts department summary of Yasser's payments was missing. He wrote on the back of the Saladin Brigades leaflet: *Yasser Salah all Bs. No money.* He turned the sheet over and re-read the Brigades' demand for Odwan's freedom in exchange for Wallender's release. Could there really be a connection between the grades scribbled on the back of the page and this message printed on the front? He laid his notes on the desk and went to Umm Rateb, who stood next to the filing cabinets, waiting. He gave her the file and she slid the drawer shut.

They breathed in relief. Omar Yussef patted his breast pocket and remembered the leaflet on the desk. He took a step toward Maki's office to retrieve it. Then the door opened.

'Abu Ramiz, what a delightful surprise,' Adnan Maki said. As he entered, the university chief bit his bottom lip and opened his eyes wide, flirtatiously. 'Umm Rateb, has this cosmopolitan, glamorous West Banker lured you away from your religious morals?'

Omar Yussef and Umm Rateb took a step away from each other, as though they had been caught in an illicit clinch.

'Oh, don't worry,' Maki said. 'I'm quite sure you two are up to something naughty. And I thoroughly approve.' He laughed and caught Omar Yussef's hand. He fondled the back of it with his thumb and leered, the tip of his tongue touching his upper lip. His fingers were so light Omar Yussef had the sensation of being touched by a web of fish bones.

Maki dropped his leather briefcase on the black sofa so that he could embrace Omar Yussef. He gave him five kisses and touched the bruise on Omar Yussef's head. 'You've been in the wars, as they say in England.'

Gallows humor, Omar Yussef thought. 'Everyone's quoting the British to me today.' He coughed and it became a choke.

'Umm Rateb, bring water for our friend and then some coffee,' Maki said. 'Come into my office, Abu Ramiz.'

Omar Yussef continued coughing. He shook his head and sat on the black sofa in the outer office, holding Maki's hand and pulling him down next to him. He glanced at Umm Rateb and flicked his watery eyes toward Maki's office, hoping she would rescue the Brigades leaflet, but in her nervousness she was blind to his hints. 'Abu Ramiz, you stay just where you are,' she said. 'I'll bring you a glass of water. Abu Nabil, what did the Revolutionary Council decide?'

She's trying to make sure he doesn't wonder what I'm doing here, Omar Yussef thought. Umm Rateb brought the glass of water. *She doesn't know about that piece of paper on Maki's desk.*

'The meeting was much as expected, Umm Rateb,' Maki said. He opened his arms wide and, as Omar Yussef sipped the water, he slapped him on the back, making him cough again. 'Sorry, Abu Ramiz, but I feel in a fine mood this morning.'

It's not the stinking weather that made you so breezy. It must have been a good assassination, Omar Yussef thought.

'At the Council meeting, I spoke at length about the strong response that must be ordered,' Maki said. 'Colonel al-Fara agreed with me and said that he will join with the other security forces to apprehend the murderers of General Husseini. It was all very quick, as there was complete agreement with my statement among all the members. It was a proud moment for me.'

Omar Yussef had one last cough. 'Shall we go into your office to talk privately?' he said. Perhaps he could grab his notes before Maki saw them.

Maki picked up his briefcase and led Omar Yussef by his hand into the inner room. The leaflet, wrinkled and curling at the edges, lay on the blotter. Maki put his briefcase flat on the desk. Without noticing it, he had covered the leaflet. Omar Yussef stared. He leaned forward. The corner of the leaflet protruded from under the briefcase. If Maki left the room for a moment, he could snatch it back.

Umm Rateb brought two coffees on a tray. 'Now

that you're back early, Abu Nabil,' she said to Maki, 'your postponed schedule can be resumed?'

She's trying to save me, to get me out of here, Omar Yussef thought. *She's going to make me leave before I get the paper from his desk.* He tried to catch her eye.

'Yes, of course, back to work.' Maki smiled broadly. 'With a vengeance.'

'I'll inform your next appointment.' Umm Rateb winked at Omar Yussef. She leaned forward with the tray of coffees.

Omar Yussef smelled her soap. She put the coffee on the edge of the desk. Maki dragged his briefcase away from the tray to make room and, reaching for the coffees, carelessly laid the briefcase on the floor beside him. The leaflet went with it. *Which way up did it land?* Omar Yussef wondered. *Perhaps it fell straight into a wastepaper basket and I'm in the clear.* Either way, he couldn't retrieve the paper now.

Umm Rateb went to locate Maki's next appointment.

'May there always be coffee for you,' Omar Yussef mumbled.

'Blessings,' Maki said, acknowledging the formula of gratitude for hospitality. 'I heard about the problem of your Swedish friend. It was discussed briefly at the Revolutionary Council.'

'Briefly?'

'So many other pressing issues. Last night, Colonel al-Fara urged General Husseini, the departed one,

253

to release Odwan so that the Saladin Brigades would free your friend and colleague.'

'Well, Odwan's dead and so is General Husseini. Why doesn't Colonel al-Fara release someone himself?'

'Are you back on the subject of that liar, the awful Professor Masharawi?' Maki dropped the corners of his mouth and screwed up his wet, black eyes, as though he'd just accidentally sucked down the thick grounds at the bottom of his tiny coffee cup.

'That's why I'm here, after all.'

'Is it?' Maki said, quietly. He put his cup down. A new voice sounded in the outer office. 'My next appointment has arrived, Abu Ramiz. We shall have to continue our discussion another time. I have much to do before attending the funeral of the departed General Husseini.' He stood. 'I keep a rigorous schedule here. It's most un-Palestinian. But it's one of a number of characteristics I picked up during my travels.' Then he whispered: 'In the civilized world.' He giggled.

A bearded man came to the door holding a sheaf of papers and squeezing out a sycophantic grin at Maki's laughter. Maki turned to greet him. When Omar Yussef went out, he closed the door behind him.

Omar Yussef bent over Umm Rateb's desk. 'When Professor Maki leaves his room, see if there's a piece of paper with a Saladin Brigades announcement on it. It should be on the floor behind his desk. Like a fool, I made some notes on it and left it there.'

'I'll try to get it, Abu Ramiz.' She looked nervously toward Maki's door.

The blinds of Maki's office window lifted with a single, swift motion. Maki smiled, holding the draw cord, waving farewell through the glass to Omar Yussef.

'How is Salwa today?' Omar Yussef asked, nodding politely toward Maki.

'May Allah be thanked,' Umm Rateb said.

'As good as that, eh?'

'She's at home. I'm sure your company would be welcome.' Umm Rateb nodded at the files behind her desk. 'If you have discovered any news for her.'

Omar Yussef smiled, went to the door and down the corridor. He stepped out into the dust and hailed a taxi.

CHAPTER 22

Among the old olive trees in front of Salwa
Masharawi's house, Omar Yussef caught
the homely scent of hot bread on the air.
Salwa sat on a low stool in front of the clay oven
in the corner of the garden. She made to stand
when she saw him, but he gestured for her to
continue her work.

Salwa bent double, spreading her dough over
the rounded surface of an upturned frying pan.
She stoked the coals beneath the blackened metal
and the thin dough sizzled. She unrolled it and
flipped it over. The exposed side of the bread was
a buttery yellow, studded with crisp bulbs of bitter
charcoal and brown smears where air trapped in
the dough had burned.

Omar Yussef rested his foot on the low brick
wall around the cooking area. 'Lovely weather for
a barbeque,' he said, gesturing toward the dusty
air around them. 'Let's get the whole family out
here.'

Salwa's cheek twitched when he mentioned her
family and Omar Yussef regretted his joke. He
cleared his throat. 'My daughter, I came to tell

256

you that I've discovered something which will help your husband.'

The woman straightened on her stool and looked at Omar Yussef intently.

'I went to Professor Maki's office. I examined the records of two brothers from Rafah. I discovered that the academic transcript of the one who's an officer in Colonel al-Fara's Preventive Security clearly had been rigged.' Omar Yussef leaned closer to Salwa. 'His financial records also smelled bad.'

'How does this help Eyad?'

'Now the UN has proof of Eyad's accusation against the security forces, we can make a strong case that Eyad was arrested because he uncovered a real conspiracy.'

Salwa nodded, slowly. Omar Yussef had thought she would be happier with his discovery. The smell of charcoal came to them strongly. Salwa gasped and pulled the burning bread from the upturned pan. She stood with her hands on the small of her back and stretched. 'I apologize for this reception, Abu Ramiz. It's difficult for me to see the good in anything at the moment,' she said.

'That's understandable, my daughter.'

She bent to pick up the pile of flat bread she had already made. 'No, it's not. It doesn't help Eyad for me to be depressed. That's why I decided to make bread today. I needed to show myself that the world continues, in spite of what has happened.'

Omar Yussef followed her toward the house. 'That was very wise.'

'Until I burned the bread.'

In the kitchen, she put the bread by the sink and ran water to make coffee. 'It was good of you to come with this news, Abu Ramiz,' she said. 'I know you're busy. You're working hard for my husband and your friend, the foreigner.'

Omar Yussef leaned against the refrigerator. Salwa hadn't sent him to the sitting room, but had let him follow her into a place usually barred to male visitors. He felt the comfort of being with a woman in her kitchen and wondered that it could be such a solace even in a home turned inside out by fear like this one. He wished he were with Maryam and that he could reach out to rub his wife's shoulder blades as she liked him to do.

Salwa poured coffee and sugar into the pot and put it on the stove. Her shoulders jolted, but only when he heard her sob did Omar Yussef realize she was crying. He pulled his handkerchief from his trouser pocket and dangled it against her hand. She wiped her face and sniffed.

'Sometimes I think the only Palestinians who aren't crying are the dead,' Salwa said.

'I don't think Colonel al-Fara sheds many tears,' Omar Yussef said.

'I wish *he* were dead.' Salwa looked up at Omar Yussef and her face went limp, as though she had horrified herself.

'In this, as in everything else, you have my complete solidarity.' Omar Yussef smiled at Salwa until she rewarded him with a small giggle behind the handkerchief.

'You're very good to help my husband this way, Abu Ramiz,' she said.

'I know he would do the same for me. I was once unfortunate enough to be unjustly imprisoned in Bethlehem, a long time ago. I wouldn't leave an innocent man to suffer in such a place.'

Salwa lifted her eyebrows. Omar Yussef knew she was about to ask him why he had been jailed. The last time he spoke the word murder, it had been as though the very syllables were fatal to Cree. He wouldn't utter them to Salwa. 'It was a political dispute. It's in the past,' he said. 'Your husband is all I'm concerned about now.'

She held his gaze a moment, then smiled. 'I'm being very inhospitable. Please make yourself comfortable in the salon while I finish preparing the coffee, Abu Ramiz.'

Omar Yussef sat in the armchair where he had watched Magnus on television the previous night. He thought of his encounter with Professor Maki and his breath quickened. He rubbed his forehead and wondered whether Umm Rateb would recover his notes before the professor found them.

He heard a tune playing somewhere nearby. It was a thin, electronic version of a Bach cantata, accompanied by a low buzzing. Omar Yussef couldn't place it at first, but then he felt something vibrating in the pocket of his pants and realized it was Sami's cellphone. He clicked his tongue impatiently and frowned at the keypad of the phone. He assumed the green button was for accepting a call. He pressed it, held the phone a few inches from his ear and spoke. 'Who's this?'

'I want to talk to Abu Ramiz.' The voice on the phone was harsh and loud.

'Speaking.'

'Abu Ramiz from the UN?'

Omar Yussef nodded. He was wary of cellphones, but the voice put him doubly on guard. 'Who're you?'

'Someone wants to say hello.'

A new voice came over the line, wheezy and thick. It was Magnus Wallender. 'Abu Ramiz, how're you?'

Omar Yussef gripped the phone tight and pressed it hard to his ear. 'May Allah be thanked, Magnus. You're still alive.'

'If you say so.'

'Where are you?'

'I don't know, Abu Ramiz.' Magnus broke off and spoke away from the phone. The harsh voice responded with an order to 'read.'

'Abu Ramiz, I'm reading now: *The Saladin Brigades have avenged themselves on the traitor and collaborator Husseini, the murderer of the brother Bassam Odwan. But the Brigades warn that something bad . . .'* Wallender groaned and breathed deeply. *'Something bad will happen to the foreigner Wallender unless all UN personnel leave Gaza immediately.'*

'They *have* left.' Omar Yussef thought of his conversation with the American woman from the UN.

'Why have they left, Abu Ramiz?' Magnus sounded at once curious and lonely.

'Someone in Jerusalem decided it was too dangerous.' He thought of James Cree's burned corpse. 'Because of your kidnapping.'

'So there's no one here except you?'

'There're some locals. But they're keeping their heads down.'

Magnus relayed this to the other man. There was a rattling sound and the harsh voice barked down the line once more. 'You, too, must leave Gaza immediately, if you want your friend to be safe.'

'I'd need a special permit from the Israelis to pass through the checkpoint on such short notice.'

The voice hesitated, but it came back with scornful finality. 'That's crap. You're with the UN. Get a permit and get out of here.'

'Let me speak to Magnus again.'

The line went dead.

Omar Yussef cursed. Salwa entered with his coffee. She glanced at him with a stern, expectant face. The phone sounded again. Omar Yussef thrust his forefinger at the green button. 'Magnus?'

'What?' Khamis Zeydan's voice was surrounded by the murmur of conversation.

'The kidnappers just called me. I spoke to Magnus.'

'So he's alive.'

Omar Yussef stared into the thick blackness of

his coffee. 'How did they get Sami's number? How did they know I had this phone?'

He heard Khamis Zeydan growl with impatience.

'I've only had this phone since last night,' Omar Yussef said. 'Did they call Sami's other phone first?'

'You're suspicious of the wrong man, my friend,' Khamis Zeydan said.

'Just because someone calls you *my friend*, doesn't mean he is.'

Another growl. 'Remember what the Prophet's son-in-law said: *He who has a thousand friends has not a friend to spare*,' Khamis Zeydan said. 'You need Sami.'

'You're leaving out the second part of Ali's saying: *And he who has one enemy will meet him everywhere*.'

Omar Yussef heard a grating click and an inhalation, as Khamis Zeydan lit a cigarette. The police chief breathed out. 'I'm on my way to our hotel. We need to talk.'

'I'm at Salwa Masharawi's house.'

'I'll pick you up there, then.'

Omar Yussef looked at Salwa's eyes. They were red, but the tears were gone. He shook his head at the phone. 'Not yet. I'm going to stay here a little longer.'

'No, you're coming with me.' Khamis Zeydan was firm. 'I'm taking you to a funeral.'

CHAPTER 23

Sami rolled his Jeep toward the mahogany porch at the front of the presidential building. Military Intelligence men linked arms to restrain the crowd in the courtyard of the president's compound. The mob chanted 'Allah is most great' and jostled the soldiers, dislodging their red berets and shoving some of them against the car with low, hollow thuds that made Omar Yussef jump. A steady crackle of guns firing into the air penetrated the insulated calm of Sami's expensive car.

'There must be thousands of people here,' Omar Yussef said. 'I thought Husseini was unpopular.'

'He was a bastard,' said Khamis Zeydan. The police chief looked out at the crowd over his cigarette.

'Then what're these people so upset about?'

'You know what it's like when an Arab leader dies. No one liked him, but nonetheless he represented something good to them – stability, a pay check, support for the people of their village against another village. That's all this is.'

'They're angry. There could be a riot, after the funeral.'

'The funeral is already a riot. After the funeral? Someone'll have to die.'

Sami pulled up to the porch. An officer opened the door and saluted. Khamis Zeydan headed for the entrance. Omar Yussef squinted into the hot, dusty wind, over the mass of heads. It seemed as though the chanting, shouting crowd was pressing toward him alone, thrusting fists in the air and demanding vengeance. He was unsurprised that, at the last moment, the president had elected to stay in Ramallah and give the funeral a miss.

From along the beach road, a deep thump rumbled like the resonating soundwaves of a bomb in the seconds after detonation. It came again, a regular beat. A band joined it and Omar Yussef realized it was a bass drum, struck with a full swing of the shoulders. The band played Tchaikovsky's *Marche Slav* and the big drum sounded every second bar. They were bringing the body from Husseini's house. The crowd swelled behind the military cordon. Omar Yussef followed Khamis Zeydan into the presidential building.

At the top of a whitewashed staircase adorned with a few potted plants, Omar Yussef entered a conference room filled with smoke and mumbling clutches of well-dressed men. At the head of the long table, large portrait photos of the president and his predecessor hung on the wall. On either side of the photographs, the Palestinian flag was draped from poles the height of a short man. A Military Intelligence officer in a neat, plain

264

uniform and without his beret poured a small cup of bitter coffee for Omar Yussef from a plastic flask that was shaped to look like a traditional copper pot.

Khamis Zeydan beckoned from the window. He spoke quietly to Omar Yussef as he inhaled on his cigarette. His lips barely moved. 'Where did you go this morning?'

'What do you mean?'

'I only brought you to this funeral because I want to keep an eye on you. You can't be trusted to stay out of trouble.' His eyes flicked about the room. 'So tell me, after I went to the Revolutionary Council meeting and left you at breakfast, where did you go?'

'Why didn't you ask me this in the car on the way here?'

'This is not for Sami's ears. You were supposed to be going for a walk on the beach.'

'I neglected to bring my swimsuit to Gaza.'

Khamis Zeydan hissed cigarette smoke over Omar Yussef. 'You'll have to find one. They're shooting a calendar, like the American ones that have supermodels frolicking in the waves. This one's called Assassination Victims on the Gaza Shore. You're Miss August.'

'My favorite time of year. Anyway, I'm not scared of ruffling feathers. I want to free Magnus, even if no one else seems to remember him.'

'Haven't you heard? He's Miss September.'

'I'm not prepared to let that happen.' Omar Yussef

drew his shoulders back and raised his chin. He felt his jaw shivering with anger. 'And I was doing my best to prevent his death this morning.'

'I don't think so.' Khamis Zeydan's jaw tightened with every word. 'I think you were making a mistake this morning.'

'You know where I went?'

'I have a good idea. Look, Maki can't help you. You'll only get into deeper trouble if you pester him.'

'I have no other leads.'

'It's not a lead. It's a dead end, a brick wall that you're charging into, just because Magnus was kidnapped right after you had dinner with Maki.'

'That's not what I meant by a lead.'

'What other big conspiracies have you uncovered, then?' Khamis Zeydan blew smoke furiously, as though it might cloak him and Omar Yussef from the other party men.

'On the wall of Lieutenant Fathi Salah's family home, there are degree certificates from al-Azhar. For him and his brother Yasser, a Preventive Security officer.'

Khamis Zeydan shrugged. 'So what?'

'This morning I looked at their academic files in Maki's office,' Omar Yussef said.

'You did what? How?'

Omar Yussef waved his hand impatiently. 'Fathi's record was clean, a regular student who evidently worked hard to make all his tuition payments. But Yasser's was faked, and his father had told me he was recently promoted. It's just what Eyad Masharawi alleged: al-Fara's officers buy bogus degrees from Maki so they can get a promotion.'

'That's only a minor scandal.'

'Then why did they torture Masharawi for exposing it?'

'Because torture is a minor punishment in Gaza.'

'I think there's a link between the torture of Masharawi for exposing the fake degrees, and the stolen *Saladin I* missile.' Omar Yussef laced his fingers together and held them close to Khamis Zeydan's face. The two men were almost touching. 'If so, Magnus's kidnapping and James's murder are connected, too.'

'You said Lieutenant Fathi Salah's degree wasn't faked. But he's the one who was trading the missile and is now dead, not his brother Yasser. So you've got a guy with a degree who was selling a missile and another guy with a bogus degree who wasn't. How does that give you a connection? And what does it have to do with the killing of James Cree?'

'If I knew all that, I wouldn't be arguing about it with you. I'm still trying to figure it out, but I'm certain there's a connection.' Omar Yussef looked out of the smoked-glass window at the crowd below. He imagined them surging up the stairs to lynch him. He turned to his friend. 'What do you know about websites?'

'What're you talking about?'

'If someone made a website for me, would just

anyone be able to get inside the computer and look at it?'

Khamis Zeydan coughed out a short, scoffing laugh. '*Get inside* the computer? My brother, you're behind the times. Are you still cleaning your teeth with the bristly end of a *miswak* twig?'

The delegates jockeyed for position near the door. Professor Adnan Maki entered, his arm hooked through the well-tailored sleeve of Colonel Mahmoud al-Fara. Khamis Zeydan took a deep drag on his cigarette and crushed the butt under his shoe on the carpet. 'The undertaker has arrived,' he said.

Omar Yussef strained to see through the tobacco smoke. The crowd drew faintly toward Colonel al-Fara, like nervous children approaching a big dog. Al-Fara acknowledged the men he passed with a vicious, superior smile. He wore a light gray suit, a white shirt whose cuffs came an inch beyond the sleeves of the jacket to expose gold cufflinks, and a somber silk tie. His lank, black hair fell over his forehead and his mustache was gleaming and moist. He slouched through the room dispensing mirthless grins. He brought a tissue from his pocket and expectorated. The coffee boy put out a hand and al-Fara gave him the crumpled tissue without looking at him.

Maki caught sight of Omar Yussef. His smile wavered, then he lifted his hand and wiggled his fingers in greeting. Omar Yussef searched for a sign that Maki had noticed the Saladin Brigades leaflet and his handwritten notes on the floor of his office. The professor's sybaritic lips twitched as though blowing a kiss. He went with al-Fara out of the back of the conference room to a wide balcony. The other men followed.

The *Marche Slav* was close. The band's ponderous measures punctuated a new level of hysteria in the crowd at the front of the building. The musicians came to the open yard at the back of the presidential compound and marched across a broad yellow circle painted on the concrete as a helicopter landing pad. Two men carried the bass drum and another gave it the beat with a bulbous stick he held in two hands. Behind them, a jeep brought General Moussa Husseini's casket, wrapped in the Palestinian flag. Red-bereted troopers leaned out of the jeep, shielding the coffin, deflecting the thrashing arms of people in the crowd who managed to reach over the cordon of soldiers. The people threw their arms in the air and chanted that they would sacrifice for Husseini, whom they called a martyr.

'Do the idiots think he died for Allah?' Omar Yussef muttered. 'A martyr?'

Khamis Zeydan lifted an eyebrow at that. 'Jihad is a very flexible concept,' he said.

The jeep reached the clear space behind a double row of troops and, as the band stepped to the side, it circled to the corner of the yard. Two ranks of Military Intelligence troopers rested their rifle butts at ease against their heels, forming a lane to the grave. They came to attention.

The party men on the balcony trotted down the steps to the yard and crossed the yellow paint of the helicopter pad. An imam waited at the graveside, his hands crossed in front of him, wearing a long brown robe and a white turban wrapped around a scarlet fez. The imam lifted his chin from his chest and stroked his short gray beard, as Omar Yussef and Khamis Zeydan moved grimly toward the grave. The delegates dropped their cigarettes as they left the helicopter pad and stepped into the sand by the fence, where Husseini was to be laid to rest. The imam led them in the funeral prayer. The troopers in the back of the jeep lifted Husseini's body from the open coffin and brought him, wrapped in two white cloths, to the graveside. Omar Yussef considered the rituals of burial, the traditional washing of the corpse that was omitted for a martyr because the manner of his death purifies him. A martyr would be buried with blood on his face, where it sprayed from his wound, and dirt under his fingernails, where he clawed the ground in agony. He wondered what the men who wrapped Husseini in his shroud had done about the feces in the general's underpants.

When they handed Husseini down into the grave, his skin was tinted light green against the white sheet that circled his face. The corpse looked small, dropping out of sight, but a soldier inside the grave had to struggle as he maneuvered Husseini's tubby body onto its right side, so that it would rest facing Mecca. The imam's prayer urged those present to praise Allah and consider the reward to which the dead man went. Omar Yussef thought that Husseini had already received his reward for a violent, cruel life, and that it had been a machine-gun magazine emptied into his spine and his bowels voided into his underpants. Further weighing of eternal balances was unnecessary.

The prayers were barely done when the Revolutionary Council leaders turned back to the presidential building. Behind them, the two ranks of Military Intelligence men fired volleys over the grave. Maki made a joke and al-Fara gave an exhausted smile. He glanced toward the crowd and his languid slouch tensed. His expression switched to fear and then to anger.

The mob was breaking through the cordon at the side of the building. People rushed across the concrete with their fists raised, heading for the grave. Al-Fara turned to the armed funeral detail for protection, but the soldiers retreated behind the grave and made no move toward the party men.

The delegates of the Revolutionary Council hurried on old legs for the safety of the presidential building. A black Audi roared from the side of the paved lot. The back door opened and al-Fara jumped in. The crowd flowed toward it. A window dropped and one of al-Fara's guards aimed a pistol into the air. He fired off a few rounds and the car sped around the far side of the building.

The head of the crowd came to the grave and halted, pumping fists in the air and chanting to Allah. To reach the graveside, the mass of people at the back of the crowd looped quickly to the side. Their swing caught Omar Yussef as he fell behind the dignitaries escaping into the president's building. He saw Khamis Zeydan turn and shout to him, just as the crowd enveloped him.

The force of the swarm took him a few paces sideways, setting him off balance, and he couldn't counter its momentum. He fell onto his right knee. He put his hand to the ground to keep from falling further. Someone trod on his fingers. He cried out, but he dared not move the hand. If he went down, he'd be trampled to death. A man put his knee in Omar Yussef's shoulder and tumbled over him. The man came down on his back and rolled a few times as the mob kicked him into the hard surface of the president's helicopter pad.

The cries of the crowd were hoarse. Omar Yussef sensed its force, as though he were far down in a body of water or buried by a weight of earth. The screams of the trampled man punctuated the mob's chant. Dust was thick in the air and his eyes were full of it. Someone's fist connected with the side of his head and he took a knee in the small of his back. He felt a hand under his right arm, lifting and dragging him. He pushed his glasses into place on his nose and went with the hand that supported him. He blinked the dirt from his eyes and threw his arm around Sami Jaffari.

The young man pulled him across the flow of the crowd, bracing his legs against its momentum, shoving and elbowing those in their way. Omar Yussef saw the limbs of those in the crowd only as blurs, but he noted faces clearly. No one looked directly at him; everyone's eyes were unnaturally wide, unfocused, cast ahead to where they thought the grave was. *They've all gone mad*, he thought. Even when Sami pushed them hard, they didn't seem to see the two men in front of them. They ebbed roughly around the obstruction, swirling on toward Husseini's grave.

Omar Yussef came to an open area, but Sami didn't halt. He hurried him toward the corner of the building.

'Where's Abu Adel?' Omar Yussef asked. He looked around for Khamis Zeydan.

'He's inside.'

'I need to sit down. Let's go in there with him.'

Sami dragged Omar Yussef. The schoolteacher stumbled as he struggled to keep up with the younger man.

'Sami, I'm exhausted. Where are we going?'

'You're coming with me.'

'I need to sit down.'

Sami kept going, around the corner and away from the entrance to the presidential building. 'Not in there. Not with them.'

In a parking lot at the side of the presidential building, Sami ducked Omar Yussef's head with a hand on the back of his neck, shoving him into the passenger seat of his Jeep, slamming the door shut. He started the car and pulled around the front of the building so fast that the force pinned Omar Yussef to the leather. The crowd was thin at the gate, since it had mostly pressed into the helicopter pad. People jumped out of Sami's way as they heard his wheels screech toward them. The Jeep cut left and started north.

'Sami, what's going on?'

'I told you, you're coming with me.'

'Evidently. Are you kidnapping me?'

Sami stared at the narrow roads, taking them fast and working the gears on the powerful car. He leaned forward and opened the glove compartment. There were two pistols inside. Omar Yussef pushed himself back into the seat. Sami pulled out a rag that had been wrapped around a third pistol, flipped the compartment shut and tossed the rag in Omar Yussef's lap. 'I've noticed you like to look neat and tidy in company,' he said. 'Clean yourself up. You're going to meet someone.'

CHAPTER 24

S ami raced to the northern edge of Gaza City and into the sandy sidestreets of Jabalia refugee camp. From the murk of the dust storm, objects seemed to fly toward them as though borne on the air by a whirlwind. Children chased a goat into the road; blue dumpsters donated by the European Union loomed out of the dust; a donkey cart jogged erratically along a narrow lane. Sami negotiated all these obstacles without easing off the gas.

He pulled up at a corner near the northern edge of the camp. 'Get out,' he said.

A scrubby dune rose at the end of the block and, beyond its crest, the sands undulated a half mile to the fence marking the end of the Gaza Strip and the beginning of Israel. In the shade of a bare wall, a stocky man in the black T-shirt and dark green baggy pants of the militias rested against the hood of a white jeep. Omar Yussef sensed that he and Sami and their expensive car were being carefully measured.

Sami cut down an alley barely wide enough for his square shoulders. The ground was laid with concrete, set in a shallow V so that water would run down the middle in the rainy months. Now it was dry and the alley was choked with trash – packaging for cheap cookies, empty plastic bottles, the peelings of vegetables and fruit, and a small child's leather sandal caked in sand and dust.

Omar Yussef followed Sami down the alley, stumbling through the trash. They moved deep into the maze of single-story cinderblock hovels. He was astonished that Sami knew the place so well. At home in Dehaisha, every sad dwelling was familiar to him and he could recognize family resemblances even in children he didn't know. But here every corner seemed identical and all the children stared at him with silent, blank faces.

The quiet domestic sounds of mothers calling their children and of concrete floors being washed with heavy, wet cloths receded, as Sami edged into a new alley that opened onto the main street of the camp. Sami ducked past the buckets and brooms dangling from the ragged awning of a shop at the corner. He went quickly through the jammed lanes of traffic and into a falafel restaurant. Omar Yussef followed past the blackened fryer in the doorway, bubbling as it received a new batch of green chickpea balls. Sami nodded to a man chopping tomatoes at the counter and went three steps at a time up a makeshift staircase at the back.

The stairs led to a cheaply decorated dining area. The walls and floor were tiled in pink. The tables were black metal frames topped with fake squares of marble, peeling at the corners. The chairs were of chrome tubing with puffy cushions. The plastic packaging hadn't been removed from the cushions, but in places it was gashed and peeling.

A series of portraits and photographs along both walls depicted a young man in his early twenties with neat hair combed to the left and a thick beard, softly slick because it had never been shaved. Some of the photos showed a montage of the youth backed by the Dome of the Rock in Jerusalem and another had him in front of the Aqsa Mosque. A local artist had copied the photo in childishly clumsy oils. On the opposite wall, the same photo had been weaved into a cheap prayer mat.

Sami sat at a table by the window and studied the busy street below. He lit a cigarette.

Omar Yussef stood by the table and pulled out his handkerchief to mop the sweat and dust from his forehead and neck. Sami pointed to the seat opposite him. Omar Yussef shook his head. 'Before I sit down, tell me what's going on?' he said.

Sami looked at him and exhaled smoke slowly. 'I'm sorry I dragged you away from the funeral in such a hurry. But there's an order out to kill you,' he said.

Omar Yussef wondered fleetingly if Sami would be the one; there was something newly dark about the young man's eyes. But he doubted he would bring him to a place so public for the execution.

'I had to get you away from there. It's one of the men in the Revolutionary Council who issued the order,' Sami said. He took another drag and looked at his wristwatch. 'We might be here a while. Sit down and we'll eat something.'

Omar Yussef lowered himself onto the uncomfortable chair. His knees ached. The warm wind rattled the windows of the restaurant. 'Who is it? Who wants me killed?'

'I don't know yet. But it's dangerous for you to be around any of those party men.' Sami crushed his cigarette into a tinfoil ashtray. 'Let's eat something.'

A thin youth came to their table. His white T-shirt was stained around the belly where he had wiped his hands after chopping peppers. The shirt hung lank from his narrow shoulders and his face was bony and raddled. He reminded Omar Yussef of Husseini's dead coffee boy.

They ordered falafel, *hummus*, and a plate of pickles and olives. The youth had turned to go when Omar Yussef asked him the identity of the young man in the portraits on the wall.

'It's the owner's son,' the boy said. 'He was martyred in the operation at the pizza restaurant.'

Omar Yussef remembered hearing about that bomb. It went off in a pizzeria in Tel Aviv or one of the featureless towns nearby. A dozen people in the restaurant died.

'You're safe from such an attack here,' the waiter said. 'It's the only advantage of dining in Gaza.'

'You should wait for me to taste the food before telling me that.' Omar Yussef rasped a laugh.

The youth sniggered and went away with their order.

'You're remarkably cheerful,' Sami said.

'You think I don't take seriously the idea that there's an order to kill me? I'm in your hands. Tell me how to handle this.'

'You're onto something, Abu Ramiz. That's all I can tell you. Somehow the business with Eyad Masharawi touches on things much bigger than the freedom of one professor. I don't know how, but I'm trying to find out.'

'Let me come with you, as you track down the truth.'

Sami smiled and opened his arms wide. 'I already did.'

Omar Yussef looked around the empty restaurant. 'Who's meeting us here?'

'I found out who killed James.'

'By Allah!'

'They'll be here any moment now.'

Omar Yussef rose from his chair and slammed his hands on the tabletop. 'The bastards are coming here?'

'Cool it, Abu Ramiz. I don't think they're really the people you're after.'

'They killed a UN official. They killed James.'

'Because someone told them to. Or paid them. It's the one who gave the order that you want, not these guys. But you need to tease it out of them, carefully.'

'Bastards.' Omar Yussef brought his hands down on the table again.

'True. But bastards who realize that perhaps they got in too deep and now believe they might be able to cover their asses by helping me.' Sami reached out and gently pulled Omar Yussef down into his seat. 'And helping you.'

'Who are they?'

'Saladin Brigades men. From here in Gaza City. Remember, the Saladin Brigades are divided. The most powerful branch is down in Rafah, where the group was founded on the profits from smuggling arms and contraband under the Egyptian border. The Rafah gang needed an operation up in Gaza City, because it's the biggest market for goods and weapons. So they recruited some guys here to set up a wing of the Saladin Brigades.'

'The Rafah gang smuggles the stuff in; the Gaza City people sell it, right?'

'Yes, and everyone's happy. Except, after a while, the Rafah gang started to think the Gaza City bunch were keeping more than their fair share of the profits. The quarrel got nasty. They've patched things up, but there's still bad blood between the different wings of the group,' Sami said. 'More importantly, no one in the Gaza City gang is ever sure that Rafah isn't about to sell them out to the security forces. That makes them easy to manipulate.'

'By whom? Who's manipulating them?'

'That's what I hope they'll tell us. I'm expecting two of them to meet us here. They chose this restaurant. They know the owner.' Sami smiled sourly and gestured to the photos and pictures on the wall. 'The Saladin Brigades sent his son to blow himself up.'

'I suppose they get some kind of discount on their meal for that?' Omar Yussef said, with a laugh that was full of scorn.

Sami was silent, smoking, staring through the dusty air to the street below. Omar Yussef watched him. He was a good boy, a hard man, and he was all that stood between Omar Yussef and a lonely death in Gaza. Back in Bethlehem, Omar Yussef's clan was big, with ties to all the different security forces and militias. The gunmen would hesitate before killing him there. In Gaza, he was an alien and yet not a foreigner, so he could be made to disappear with fewer problems than Wallender or Cree, and no one with the power to do anything about it would care that he had vanished.

The waiter brought a small plate of olives and pickled slices of radish that had been dyed purple with beetroot juice. Omar Yussef looked at his watch. They had waited twenty minutes. He realized he was hungrier than he had thought. 'Where's our food?'

'It's coming,' the waiter mumbled.

It was another ten minutes before a plate of cold falafel and mediocre hummus arrived at the table.

Omar Yussef asked for a bottle of water and stared at the disappointing food. Sami picked up a falafel, rolled it in the hummus and took a bite. He put the second half back on his plate and lit another cigarette.

Omar Yussef ripped a corner of flat bread and tasted the hummus with it. The nausea of the previous day returned. Every tiny chip of chickpea in the purée seemed to cut into the roof of his mouth and the back of his throat like the crystal that had choked Odwan. He swigged a glass of water and rinsed it about his mouth until the nutty taste was gone. He covered his lips with his hand, so that Sami wouldn't see the quivering tension that tightened his lower face.

They had been at their post by the window an hour. Downstairs the noise of customers in the restaurant grew louder, but no one ascended to the dining room. The owner of the restaurant stamped up the stairs just before one o'clock. He was a sad-looking man with a drooping mustache and a spare frame that suggested he thought little more of his establishment's food than Omar Yussef did. He nodded to Sami, who snapped upright in his chair. The owner lifted a catch on a metal door in the back of the dining room. He took a step up the unlit staircase of bare concrete outside and whispered.

Two men came down the steps and into the restaurant. The first was tall, gaunt and mournful, with graying hair and a slouching curve to his back and neck. He looked around the room quickly, grimacing and touching his uneven front teeth with his tongue as though they pained him. Behind him came a smaller man in a blue baseball cap with skin almost as light as a European. He wore a rounded black beard and a black vest. Both carried M-16s across their chests, their right hands on the triggers, left hands low on the barrel ready to lift and fire. They came toward Sami and Omar Yussef, their heavy military boots resounding on the thin floor.

The restaurant owner went down the stairs.

Sami rose to greet the men. Omar Yussef held his hands tight to his sides, fighting the temptation to step forward and strike these murderers in their faces. Both men offered him their hands. He looked at the floor and gave them quick, light handshakes. The tall gunman's shake was weak, but the smaller man's hand was thick and hard against Omar Yussef's palm. The tall man pulled out two chairs at the table where Omar Yussef and Sami were sitting and placed them far enough away to be out of reach.

Sami introduced Omar Yussef as the colleague of the UN official who had been killed. The shorter gunman flicked his eyes toward Omar Yussef. The irises were dark brown, surrounded by malevolent sclera the color of milky coffee.

The tall gunman cleared his throat. 'I'm sorry, *ustaz*, for the death of your colleague. We acted upon instructions, but we were misled.' He coughed again. 'I'm Walid Bahloul from here in the camp. This is the brother Khaled al-Banna, who's also from the Saladin Brigades in Gaza City.'

The second man's eyes twitched, as though his name shouldn't have been disclosed.

'Why did you carry out this act against the UN?' Omar Yussef said. He concentrated on the taller gunman, Walid. His wet, gray eyes were less disconcerting and he seemed ready to talk.

'We really are sorry about the foreigner, *ustaz*,' Walid said. 'We thought there would just be a driver or some local staff in the car.'

'Local staff? A Palestinian? Someone like me?' *Remember what Sami said: cool it,* Omar Yussef thought.

'It wasn't an operation against the UN, in truth, *ustaz*,' Walid said. 'It was a signal to the security forces to release our departed brother Bassam Odwan, may Allah be merciful to him.'

'But you already kidnapped Magnus Wallender and were holding him in return for Odwan's freedom.'

'Who?'

'The Swede, also from the UN.'

'Him? That wasn't us, *ustaz*.'

'Who was it?'

Walid looked nervously at Khaled, whose eyes were firmly on Omar Yussef.

'The Swede was taken by someone from Rafah,' Walid said.

'The Saladin Brigades from Rafah?'

'I don't know. I think so.'

'But you aren't sure?'

'Communication is difficult.' Walid's smile was as weak as his handshake and he lifted his shoulders apologetically. 'We took action against the UN car and killed your colleague, because we thought it would be a gesture to the Saladin Brigades in Rafah. To show that we were willing to perform drastic acts in support of their man Bassam Odwan.'

'You saw the leaflet that the Saladin Brigades put out after the Swede's kidnapping? Demanding Odwan's release in return for the Swede?'

'Yes.'

Omar Yussef was angry with these men for killing James, but now they were lying to him, as well. He raised his finger and pointed at the tall man. 'You were just trying to show that if Rafah people invaded your turf in Gaza City to kidnap a foreigner, you could do a more spectacular job?'

Walid turned fully to Khaled. The second man didn't look at him, but he licked his thick lips in the midst of his black beard and sniffed. 'There's no need for excuses,' Khaled said. 'Walid is trying to make this sound nice, like we had fine motives. I don't care what you think of me, I only want to be sure that I don't end up carrying the can for this. So let's cut the bullshit. We were paid to blow up the UN car.'

'By whom? Someone in Gaza City?' Omar Yussef was thinking of the Revolutionary Council people at the funeral and the order to kill him.

'No, he's not from here. He's a real bastard.'

'You don't have real bastards in Gaza City?'

'We have people here with hard hearts and we have others here with shit for brains,' Khaled said. 'But this guy's the other way around. His head is hard and a dirty piece of shit throbs where his heart ought to be.'

Omar Yussef thought he might have liked Khaled, if the man hadn't also been Cree's killer. 'Who is he?'

Khaled breathed deeply and wrinkled his nose. 'Yasser Salah.'

'Yasser Salah paid you to kill the UN man?'

'He paid us to blow up the UN car.'

'What's the difference?'

'Whoever was in the UN car was supposed to die.'

'Meaning me, too?'

Khaled shrugged. 'He called us early yesterday afternoon. He said a UN car was on the way to the checkpoint. He told us he'd pay us to blow it up. He didn't give us the passenger list.'

'That was a short deadline.'

Walid smiled, proudly. 'We have the northern areas of the Saladin Road rigged with explosives permanently, in case the Israelis use it to invade Gaza again.'

Khaled hissed and raised his eyes briefly toward the ceiling. 'So now you know what you need to know. We're clear with you and you'll square it with the UN?'

'You think I'm a decision-maker at the UN?' Omar Yussef said.

'Don't fuck me about,' Khaled leaned forward. 'They won't know anything unless you want them to know it. We're not big fish, either; we've been exploited in all this. You figure out how to keep us in the clear, or you'll go the same way your colleague did.'

'I don't know the whole story yet.'

'Yes, you do.' Khaled pushed out his bearded chin.

'I do not.' Omar Yussef scratched his mustache and narrowed his eyes to hold Khaled's stare. 'Why did the Saladin Brigades kill General Husseini?'

Khaled broke the stare with a humorless laugh. 'The UN thing is your business. You're entitled to know about it. Husseini's another matter.'

'I think it's connected and I want to know the truth.'

'You don't think Gaza's better off without that bastard?' Khaled said.

'That's not my judgment to make. Why did you kill him?'

Khaled's face was stern once more. 'He killed our brother Bassam Odwan.'

'And he was coming after us,' Walid said. 'At the Revolutionary Council last night, General Husseini said he knew that the Saladin Brigades killed the UN man and he vowed to bring us in for it.'

Omar Yussef glanced at Sami. He was smoking

and watching the street, but he was listening. 'Who told you that? Colonel al-Fara?'

The gunmen weren't about to answer that. They both sniffed and coughed.

Omar Yussef touched the ends of his mustache, as though something unexpected had just occurred to him. 'Do you know about the *Saladin I*?'

'The what?' Khaled asked.

'Never mind. Do you have any of the old *Qassam* missiles?'

'*Qassam* missiles?' Khaled leaned forward. 'Is the *Saladin I* a missile, as well? What do you want to know about missiles for?'

'It may be important.'

Khaled pulled his upper lip high toward his nose, as he breathed in. 'We have some *Qassams*. We don't use them much – it pisses off the Revolutionary Council leaders.'

'Why?'

'When we fire the *Qassams* over the fence, the Israelis cancel all the VIP cards and the chiefs can't go to Tel Aviv to fuck their Russian whores. We've got a bunch of *Qassams* in a warehouse right here in the camp. You want to buy one?' Khaled pushed his chair back and stood. 'We're going. You'll make sure the UN doesn't come looking for anyone in Gaza City, right? Rafah's where all the strings have been pulled. It's them you want.'

Omar Yussef remembered what Odwan had told him about the key to Wallender's freedom being held by the head of the Saladin Brigades in Rafah. 'Okay, but you have to get me a meeting with Abu Jamal.'

There was a long silence. Sami picked up the remaining half of his falafel and tapped its crust against the edge of his plate. Khaled eyed the green center of the falafel angrily.

'Sami will hear from us about that,' Khaled said.

'This afternoon?'

'Go to Rafah. I'll be in touch with Sami on his cellphone and I'll tell you where to meet Abu Jamal.'

'We'll go there right away.'

Khaled swallowed hard. 'Don't be in a hurry. Abu Jamal isn't that easy to reach. Sami will hear from us.' He walked backward to the metal door. Walid mumbled a farewell and followed. Khaled leapt up the concrete steps three at a time and Walid trotted after him, pulling the door shut with a heavy clank.

'What they said about the Revolutionary Council isn't true, Sami. You told me yourself that no one mentioned James's murder at that meeting,' Omar Yussef said, excitedly.

'That's what Abu Adel told me.'

'He was present at the meeting. We can trust what he said.'

Sami smiled and shrugged. 'Of course.'

'Yasser Salah must have told these guys that Husseini had promised to arrest them, so that they'd assassinate Husseini. But why? Yasser Salah wanted Odwan killed for murdering his brother, and Husseini did exactly that: he killed Odwan in his prison cell.'

Sami gestured toward the door through which Khaled and Walid had left. 'Those two are pretty scared. They realize that this is something bigger than they expected. They also see that it reaches high up, and they don't know who they can trust, in the Saladin Brigades or the security forces.'

'But why would Yasser Salah want Husseini dead?'

Sami ate the second half of his falafel ball. As he swallowed, he lit another cigarette and dropped three five-shekel coins on the table. 'Let's go and ask Abu Jamal,' he said.

CHAPTER 25

When Omar Yussef and Sami returned to the Jeep, a layer of dust an eighth of an inch thick covered the black paint. Omar Yussef pulled the door shut behind him and blinked the dirt from his eyes. 'This storm is going to break tonight, Sami. It's thicker than it has been,' he said.

Sami glanced at him as he turned the key in the ignition. 'We might be in Rafah late and you're only wearing a shirt,' he said. 'I'll stop at the hotel for you to pick up a sweater on the way south.'

'If you're so worried about my health, perhaps you ought to get me a bullet-proof vest.'

'So you don't want to be a martyr?'

Omar Yussef gave a choking laugh. 'If the food in that restaurant didn't kill me, nothing can.'

Sami leaned forward over the wheel, swung the rear end of the car around and propelled the jeep back through the refugee camp.

Omar Yussef braced himself against the door and closed his eyes. A faceless man appeared behind his eyelids, dressed in the stocking cap and black vest of a gunman, prodding Omar Yussef with a

Kalashnikov. The gunman was gone when he opened his eyes. They stung from the dirt in the air. *These eyes have no rest,* he thought. *Open, they fill with the filth that floats around Gaza; when I shut them, they're prey to deadly nightmares.*

An order was out to kill him. Would it be a gunman in a stocking cap who pulled the trigger on him? Would it be quick? Humiliating, like the death of Moussa Husseini, in the street with his underpants full of crap? Terrifying and long, like Bassam Odwan's torture? Was he next, or was he only holding a number in a long line of victims? How much time did he have?

Sami took a right off the Saladin Road and up through the *souk* to Omar al-Mukhtar Street. He leaned on the horn when a service taxi stopped in the road to pick up a couple of women laden with bags of vegetables.

'This order to kill me, Sami,' Omar Yussef said. 'If it succeeds—'

'Don't be ridiculous, Abu Ramiz.' Sami hit the horn with three short bursts. 'Let's go,' he shouted, shaking his head.

'Just *if.* I would like you to be in touch with my family in Bethlehem.'

Sami smiled as he lit a cigarette. 'You want me to tell your wife you loved her?'

'Just say that I liked the website very much.'

Sami frowned. 'What website?'

'They'll know.'

The taxi moved off slowly, and Sami edged along

less than a yard behind its rear fender, waiting to overtake.

'Abu Adel says that sometimes it's a mistake to tell you what's really going on, because you overreact,' Sami said.

Omar Yussef wondered what else Khamis Zeydan had told Sami about him. 'You said there's an order out to kill me, so how am I overreacting?'

'There's always someone who wants to kill you, whoever you are, Abu Ramiz.'

'So now you're like Bassam Odwan, who believed he would die when Allah determined his time had come?'

'Well, was there anything Bassam Odwan could have done about that moment? Maybe it's better to accept that death is coming and that it's in the hands of someone else, whether that's Allah or General Husseini or those two guys we just met back in the camp. It might be unknown when and how death comes, but in Gaza there should be no surprise that it's on its way.'

'Is there someone who wants to kill *you*, Sami?'

'Only this fucking taxi driver.' Sami leaned on the horn again. He swung the car into the opposite lane and roared past the long yellow taxi, making a few pedestrians jump onto the sidewalk. 'Abu Ramiz, I'm not as old as you and I don't have your wisdom, but there're things that I've had to learn fast – things which perhaps you've never known, working in your classroom at the school.'

'You've had many hardships, my son, I know.'

'If there's one thing my life has taught me, it's that killing is easy and dying is easier. Suffering is hard.' Sami looked at Omar Yussef and, for a moment, his face rearranged itself into that of a much older man, deeply lined and sagging with the weight of troubling experience. Omar Yussef wondered if Sami would live to be that old.

As they rounded the traffic circle on the beach road, the dust storm was thicker than ever. The sea was barely visible beyond the Salaam Fish Restaurant. It was three o'clock in the afternoon, but Sami had the headlights on. He turned onto the beach road and rolled past the Deira Hotel toward the Sands. Omar Yussef stared into the gloom.

A jeep's red brake lights punctuated the dust cloud ahead. The back door flew open. A man dropped out of the jeep, stumbled and fell. Omar Yussef strained forward. The jeep was at the entrance to the driveway of the Sands Hotel.

'Sami?'

'I see it.'

Sami accelerated.

The man struggled to his feet, lifting himself without the use of his arms, which seemed to be cuffed or tied behind him. He took a few quick steps toward the perimeter wall of the Sands Hotel, halted and looked in both directions. Confused, he moved to his left, then to his right, and turned to face the jeep. He crouched, poised to run, but a short, hollow bellow of gunfire dropped him against the wall.

The jeep sped into the dust, its back door flying open. A man leaned out to pull it shut. He wore a stocking cap.

Omar Yussef's mouth was dry when Sami skidded the car to the side of the road. He lifted himself stiffly from the Cherokee.

The whitewashed perimeter wall of the Sands Hotel was smeared red where the man had been flung against it. Three narrow trails of blood daubed the stucco, where he had slipped to the floor. He sat with his legs out in front of him and his shoulders leaning to the right. Blood seeped into the sand around his thighs.

Omar Yussef came to the body. He wasn't sure. He lifted the man's head. The ear was splayed out at a right angle, just as the son's was. He felt the neck for a pulse, but Eyad Masharawi was dead.

Masharawi's head fell to the right, as though he were still shielding the strangely formed ear from sight the way he had disguised it in the photograph at his house. He had a few days' growth of beard, gray and black. His feet were bare and his blue shirt was stained with sweat and dirt and soaked with blood. All the buttons were missing, and his torso, punctured with three bullet wounds, was bruised and slack. Omar Yussef closed Masharawi's eyes with the edge of his palm.

'Get in the car, Abu Ramiz,' Sami said.

Omar Yussef felt Sami pulling him to his feet.

'What're you talking about? We have to report what we've seen.'

'To whom? The people who killed this man? Or the people who're about to kill you?'

Omar Yussef heard voices approaching on the driveway of the hotel. Khamis Zeydan came to the end of the drive. He held a pistol and there was fear in his face, which dissolved into a hard relief when he saw Omar Yussef. He turned back to the drive and shouted: 'Stay where you are, everyone. I'll handle this.' He came toward Omar Yussef. Dust was thick on his face and shirt; clearly he had been loitering outside the hotel, behind the wall, waiting for Omar Yussef to come back. 'You have to get out of here.'

'It's Eyad Masharawi,' Omar Yussef said.

Khamis Zeydan looked at the dead man, briefly, blinking away the dust. 'I'll see to it that his wife is informed.'

'It was a jeep. They pushed him out and—'

'Sami, get him out of here, in the name of Allah.'

'Why? Why do I have to go?'

'How many dead bodies do you have to see before you develop a better sense of self-preservation? I think Doctor Najjar liked you, but not so much that he wants to see you naked on the dissecting table in his pathology lab.' Khamis Zeydan drew close. 'My brother, go now.'

Omar Yussef climbed back into the jeep. As Sami started the car, Khamis Zeydan tucked his pistol into the holster in the back of his waistband and watched his old friend. When they reached the junction at the end of the Beach Road, Khamis Zeydan was a vague spot in the cloud of dust and the body of Eyad Masharawi had disappeared from view.

Sami turned south onto the Saladin Road toward Rafah. Omar Yussef imagined Salwa Masharawi watching the dust swirl through the olive grove in front of her house and listening to her children playing in the other rooms. He wondered if she had sensed her husband's death and what he would tell her about the way Eyad died.

He thought guiltily of the Saladin Brigades leaflet he had left in Professor Adnan Maki's office. If Maki had read the notes on the back, he might have connected it to Omar Yussef's interest in Masharawi and the selling of university degrees. He might have passed that along to Masharawi's captors. Omar Yussef slapped a fist into his palm. His own clumsy attempt to investigate may have killed Masharawi. But he couldn't believe the security agents would murder a man over something as minor as accusations of corruption at the university.

Sami's cellphone rang. He listened, spoke quietly, and hung up. 'That was Khaled. Abu Jamal will see us in Rafah in the next few hours.'

The wind was hard against the car's windows. Omar Yussef hadn't had the chance to pick up a sweater at the hotel, after all. He shivered.

CHAPTER 26

Bent under backpacks twice the size of their torsos, streams of schoolchildren slouched home to the ragged tin farmhouses along the seashore near Rafah. In the dunes, shredded plastic sheeting flapped against the metal frames of greenhouses left behind by the Israelis when they evacuated their settlements. Sami shook his head. 'It should be lovely down here. If only things were different.'

'I prefer the hills around Bethlehem,' Omar Yussef said. 'The rocks and the sharp slopes and the sunrise over the mountains beyond the Dead Sea.'

'The sun rises here, too, Abu Ramiz.'

Omar Yussef gestured at the pale darkness of the dust storm. 'If Allah wills it.'

The road veered inland away from the palm groves near the Egyptian border and dropped toward Rafah. The town lay like a pile of rocks strewn carelessly across the sand by a wrecking ball. The dark corrugated metal of the border fence slid past the town like a serpent, silent, muscular and venomous. The shot-up buildings on the edge of

Rafah looked like the grin of a streetfighter, teeth punched away, broken and blackened.

They drove along the southern rim of the town to the Saladin Gate. Sami pulled the car into the shade of an awning outside a shuttered grocery. A boy of about three stood on the roof of the store, throwing tiny stones at Omar Yussef as he stepped out of the car. He wagged his finger at the boy. Another stone tapped the hood of the car. The boy's chubby, tawny face was resentful and fierce and his legs were planted wide. *He's working on his arm for the battles to come*, Omar Yussef thought. He breathed slowly and got back in the car to wait for Abu Jamal's summons.

Sami toyed with his cellphone. The tapping of stones continued on the roof of the Jeep, a counterpoint to the constant impacts of the sand volleying out of the hot wind. Omar Yussef's head dipped forward and he closed his eyes. When he opened them, it was to the ringing of Sami's cellphone and a sense that the light had dimmed. Sami listened and murmured agreement into the phone as he started the car's engine. He hung up and took off along the town's main street.

'Was I asleep?' Omar Yussef asked, yawning. His mouth was dry.

'For about three hours.'

'We've been waiting that long? Why didn't you wake me?'

'You needed sleep, and I didn't need company.' Sami peered into the dust. The street was almost empty. The town was hiding from the dirt in the air. The few pedestrians were sinister shadows in the dust storm. Ghostly fluorescent light shivered from the shopfronts.

Sami spotted a stationery shop on a corner of the main road. 'That's the place,' he said. He pulled into a sidestreet. A blue metal door opened onto a dark stairwell. Omar Yussef saw the vague shape of a man's head and a hand beckoning to them. Sami leaned over, took the pistol out of his waistband and put it in the glove compartment.

'Won't we need that?' Omar Yussef said.

'By the time we needed it, we'd already be dead.' Sami smiled. 'Anyway, these guys would take the gun off me before they'd let me see Abu Jamal.'

In the stairwell, there was a handshake for each of them, but Omar Yussef's eyes couldn't adjust to the deeper darkness. The hand led him up a rough flight of stairs. The leather of his loafers made a sound like sanding wood on the bare concrete and he stumbled twice in the dark.

At the head of the stairs, they entered a long, narrow room. A pair of hands patted their waists and chests, checking for weapons. Three sofas were crammed in a horseshoe beneath a small window. A single fluorescent strip, lying on the arm of one sofa, provided the only light in the room. Omar Yussef narrowed his eyes and peered into the darkness. A lean, bearded man in his mid-thirties was performing the evening prayers in the corner farthest from the window. On either side of him, a noisy fan rushed air around the room, but it was stiflingly hot and almost as dusty as it had been outside. A rhythmic susuration of wind murmured through the gaps in the window frame.

They sat on the sofa opposite the fluorescent strip. The man who had greeted them at the door placed the light on a mahogany coffee table between the sofas. When he moved it, the icy glow illuminated his hands and face. They were the same broad farmer's features Omar Yussef had noted in Bassam Odwan. The man's high brow was alert, stiff with concentration. His eyes were black and watchful.

'You're related to Bassam Odwan?' Omar Yussef asked.

'My brother,' he said, in a hoarse, dark voice.

'May Allah be merciful upon him. I met him briefly in the jail. I think he was calm in the face of death.'

'I don't think *calm* is the right word.'

'What's your name?'

'Attiah Odwan.'

'What *would* be the right word, Attiah?'

'Prepared. That would be the right word.'

The man in the corner completed the five prostrations of the *Maghrib* prayers, but didn't stop. Omar Yussef counted two more repetitions of the motions – the standing and the kneeling, the moment of restful consideration and the bowing to the floor – that constituted a single prostration. The extra prayers signaled preparation for an imminent mission and, perhaps, death.

When the prayers were done, a woman, compelled to remain out of the visitors' sight, passed a tray of coffee through the door and Attiah set it on the table. The man in the corner greeted them. His hand, when Omar Yussef shook it, was deformed, the bones broken and barely knitted together, the skin unnaturally smooth and hairless where it had been burned. Omar Yussef flinched.

'The work of an Israeli tank shell,' the man said. His voice was low and rasping. His deep, dark eyes were dry and bloodshot. Below them were thick rings the color and texture of cinnamon bark. His beard was smooth and shone black. He pulled a tissue from a box on the table and expectorated into it. He took a packet of throat lozenges from his pocket, slipped one into his mouth, and picked up his coffee cup.

'As you were with your parents and in your home,' he said.

'You're Abu Jamal?' Omar Yussef asked.

The man nodded and retreated into the darkness.

Omar Yussef attempted to lighten the tension in the room. 'Did we come to the right place?' he said with a laugh. 'I didn't expect to find you praying here. Perhaps we arrived at the head-quarters of the Islamists by mistake.'

Abu Jamal smiled thinly. 'Among the resistance, those who never used to pray are connected to Allah now, because death seems so close. We're all ready to be martyrs before Allah at any moment. We put our souls in the hands of Allah.'

'I'm Omar Yussef Sirhan, from Dehaisha Camp. I work for UNRWA. One of my colleagues, a Swede, has been kidnapped by the Saladin Brigades and another has been killed, also by the Saladin Brigades.'

'That was the Gaza City people who did that,' Abu Jamal said, coughing and reaching for another tissue.

'The killing? Yes, well, sort of.'

'What do you mean?' Abu Jamal's head dipped, menacingly.

'The Gaza City people acted on paid orders from someone in Rafah.'

'I'd know about that, if it was true.' Abu Jamal crunched the throat lozenge between his back teeth.

Omar Yussef smelled the menthol across the room. 'Perhaps it was someone from Rafah, but not someone from the Saladin Brigades.'

Abu Jamal was silent. He drank his coffee and wiped his mustache with the back of his deformed hand.

'My colleague, the Swede, came to inspect the schools and found that one of our teachers had been arrested,' Omar Yussef said. 'It should have been a simple matter, but in some way that we don't fully understand it touched on other issues far beyond the case of the imprisoned teacher. Dangerous issues.'

'What do you want from me?'

'I'd like you to free the Swede.'

'How can I do that?'

'There's no need for you to hold him anymore, now that the brother Bassam Odwan is dead.'

'That's not what I mean. I don't have him.'

Omar Yussef tilted his head and gave his words a taunting, sarcastic bite. 'Do you mean that the Gaza City wing of the Saladin Brigades killed the UN man and carried out the kidnapping, too?'

Abu Jamal found another piece of the throat lozenge to crunch. 'Perhaps.'

'That's not what they told us.'

'What *did* they tell you?'

'That the Swede was taken by someone from Rafah.'

'By the Saladin Brigades in Rafah?'

Omar Yussef thought hard. 'They just said that it was someone from Rafah.'

'There are one hundred and sixty thousand people in Rafah. I'm only one of these.' Abu Jamal shared a scornful smile with Attiah, whose bulk was shrouded by the darkness at the other end of his sofa.

'The Saladin Brigades distributed a leaflet, announcing that the Swede would be released in return for the freedom of Bassam Odwan,' Omar Yussef said. 'Besides, I witnessed the kidnapping. The gunmen were wearing Saladin Brigades headbands.'

'Anyone can get headbands made and anyone with a computer and a fax machine can call himself the Saladin Brigades. The leaflet didn't come from us.'

'If you don't have him, where should I look?'

'It's not so easy to know who to trust and who to suspect in Rafah,' Abu Jamal said. 'Of course, we expect to come under attack from the Jews – our holy Koran says that we will be in a continuous battle with them until the Day of Judgment. But now it's other Palestinians who kill my men.'

'Like Bassam Odwan.'

'Like him.'

'These other Palestinians, do they steal your new missiles, too?'

Abu Jamal's face was immobile. *I have his attention*, Omar Yussef thought.

'If you find the Swede,' Omar Yussef said, 'you may find your missile, too.'

Abu Jamal's dark eyes flickered.

Omar Yussef puzzled out what he had to say as he went along, speaking slowly and determinedly. 'The Swede was kidnapped because he questioned the purchase of academic degrees by officers of the Preventive Security. Bassam Odwan was killed for shooting Lieutenant Fathi Salah. Fathi's brother, Yasser, is in the Preventive Security. Odwan told me he was alone with Fathi when the shots were fired by a single shooter.'

'You met Bassam?'

'In his jail cell. Another UN man, James Cree, was blown up by the Saladin Brigades from Gaza City, but it was on the orders of someone in Rafah, who may, in fact, have been trying to kill me.'

Abu Jamal winced at the mention of James Cree.

Someone powerful has blamed you for an embarrassing attack on the UN, Omar Yussef thought.

'The orders to kill the UN man came from Rafah,' Omar Yussef said. 'From Yasser Salah.'

Now Abu Jamal spoke slowly and carefully. 'Why did Salah want to kill you?'

'I had been to his family home in Rafah to investigate the kidnapping of the Swede. Yasser Salah is the one who connects all these strands. That's where we'll find the missile.'

Abu Jamal coughed and spat into a tissue. 'Lieutenant Fathi Salah came to us to sell the missile. He was a Military Intelligence officer. Perhaps they have the missile.'

Omar Yussef shook his head and stroked his mustache. 'Fathi was scared and alone when he met Odwan. That's because he was operating without the permission of his boss General Husseini.'

'Why didn't he sell the missile to General Husseini?'

'He would have, but Yasser couldn't allow that. If *his* boss, Colonel al-Fara, discovered that he'd sold such a strategic weapon to his greatest rival, it would've been the end for Yasser.'

'Selling the missile to the Saladin Brigades was the neutral option?'

Omar Yussef nodded. 'But something went wrong in the sale. It didn't matter to Yasser, because he could still sell the missile to Colonel al-Fara. But he had to get rid of his brother, first.' Omar Yussef rubbed his palms as though washing them. 'He knew

306

General Husseini would blame Odwan for Fathi's killing.'

'So Yasser Salah sold out his own brother. But why would he kidnap the Swede?'

'I don't know yet. Perhaps it had to do with his degree from al-Azhar. He bought the degree so he could be promoted. Maybe he feared being demoted or punished for corruption, if the bogus degrees were exposed.'

Abu Jamal shook his head. 'It'd be too risky for Yasser. Anyway, al-Fara's officers get promotions for corruption. You may be right about the missile though.' He leaned toward Attiah and whispered. The burly man went to the back of the apartment and spoke into a phone in a low voice. 'We'll go to look for the missile at Salah's house,' Abu Jamal said.

'When?'

'We had another mission planned for late tonight, so everyone's on standby. We'll be ready soon.'

'We'll come with you.'

Abu Jamal clicked his tongue and raised his chin. *No.*

'You're forgetting the Swede.' Omar Yussef stared at Abu Jamal.

The head of the Saladin Brigades squeezed his chin thoughtfully in his good hand. 'All right. Stay out of the way, though. I don't want another UN guy's death blamed on the Saladin Brigades.'

If I die, Omar Yussef thought, *you won't have any trouble. No one will so much as pick up the phone to call you.*

CHAPTER 27

It was eleven that night before Abu Jamal decided he had gathered sufficient weaponry to be certain of taking out the Salah home. Omar Yussef paced the darkness above the stationery store. He was sure Yasser had the missile, but he couldn't be positive that this second Salah brother was also behind Wallender's kidnapping. If he was wrong, he wanted to know quickly, so he could pursue different leads to free the Swede.

Omar Yussef gave a low growl of frustration. These were hopeless thoughts – if Wallender wasn't at Salah's house, he wasn't going to find him at all. His colleague would remain at the mercy of whichever of the different gangs might be holding him. The Saladin Brigades would reclaim their missile, have it copied, shoot it over the border fence into Israel, and draw down a new war on the people of Gaza. *At least someone will be happy*, he thought. He clenched his fists behind his back.

Heavy footsteps approached fast from the rear of the apartment. In the darkness around the far sofa, the orange tip of Sami's cigarette dipped toward the coffee table and was crushed out. He was standing next to Omar Yussef when Attiah Odwan came to the door. Across his strong, rounded chest, he braced a Carl Gustav submachine gun. He had eight grenades clipped to his belt and his vest was bulky with spare magazines for the gun. He gestured with his head for them to follow.

At the foot of the stairs, three jeeps idled with their headlights off. The men inside had wrapped their *keffiyehs* around their faces against the dust. Omar Yussef never wore this checkered scarf, but he wished he had one now, even though it was a mark of rustic simplicity. He couldn't tell if he was cold because he wore only a shirt or because the tension in his muscles cut off his blood. He coughed and sat beside Sami in the first jeep. Abu Jamal came quickly down the stairs. He put on a green forage cap and took his place in the front seat. Attiah Odwan jogged to the corner of the main street and glanced quickly along it before gesturing to the convoy to move. He slid into the back seat beside Omar Yussef.

As he edged across the seat to make room, Omar Yussef struck his head on something metal. The blow reignited the bruises from Wallender's kidnapping and he grunted with the pain. He turned to glare at one of the gunmen in the luggage space at the back of the jeep, who was withdrawing the thick tube of a shoulder-launched missile like the one Omar Yussef had seen used against General Husseini's home that morning. The gunman put the missile next to another which he held upright between his legs. The gunman tapped his knuckle against the missile launcher where it had hit Omar Yussef's head and shrugged, his apologetic eyes showing between the folds of his *keffiyeh*.

'Be careful,' Omar Yussef said. 'One bullet will be enough to blow my head off. Don't waste your missile.'

Abu Jamal glanced to the rear of the jeep and spoke to the man with the LAW anti-tank missiles. 'When we get there, stay close to me.'

The jeeps went fast down the main street. If it had been quiet in the early evening, now it was ghostly and empty. The nights in Rafah belonged to the gunmen, the smugglers and, sometimes, the Israeli undercover squads.

Sami lit a cigarette and handed the pack to the grateful gunmen in the back. Attiah Odwan declined the smokes.

'What do you intend to do at Salah's house?' Omar Yussef asked Abu Jamal.

Abu Jamal's head and shoulders rocked with the jolting of the jeep over the rough road. He was loose and relaxed. 'We will achieve revenge for Attiah's brother,' he said.

Omar Yussef knew there would be more deaths tonight. In the quiet jeep, he wondered if his reasoning about Yasser Salah was correct. What if he was bringing down this merciless, heavily armed force on an innocent family? A low hint of panic pulsed through him. He thought perhaps he should slow the gunmen down, while he ran through his logic again. 'You might need Yasser Salah alive,' he said. 'To guide you to where the missile is hidden.'

'Someone in the family will remain alive to show us,' Abu Jamal said. 'I don't expect it will be Yasser. He isn't the type.'

'Yasser knows the truth,' Attiah said, quietly.

Omar Yussef turned to the burly man squeezed onto the back seat next to him. 'The truth, Attiah?'

'The Salah family demanded the death of my brother Bassam, because they said he killed their son,' Attiah said, staring into the dusty darkness beyond the window. 'Their demand was correct under our traditions of blood vengeance. But it wasn't true that Bassam was the killer. Now, under those same traditions, I will take revenge. *My revenge is true.*'

Omar Yussef thought about that for a while. 'Do you expect the Salahs to put up much of a fight, Abu Jamal?'

Abu Jamal lifted his hands before him in a shrug. 'Those who die for the resistance go to Heaven,' he said. 'Those whom we kill go to Hell.'

I don't believe in Heaven, Omar Yussef thought. He looked into the murky night. They were in the half-demolished section of Rafah, where the walls were pocked with bullet holes, framed by jagged, blasted edges ripped by tank shells. *And Hell is right here.*

The first jeep slowed and rounded the corner of the alley that led to the Salah family home. It crept toward the sandy lot where James Cree had parked the UN Suburban a day and a half earlier. Omar Yussef frowned. It seemed so long ago, almost as if Cree had been dead as many years as his namesake in the British War Cemetery. *How old would that make me?* he thought. *I've lived lifetimes today.*

The second jeep came alongside it and the last one rolled around to the west of the house. The gunmen climbed quietly from their jeeps. Omar Yussef stepped stiffly onto the sand, rolling his shoulders after being squeezed between Sami and Attiah.

The house was dark. Through the swirling dust, Omar Yussef could see the black canvas of the mourning tent flapping in the wind and hear its low, steady resonance. The olive trees rustled above the perimeter wall. He took a few steps down the lane and looked toward the garage at the back of the house, which he and Cree had passed as they left the day before. His eyes strained into the darkness. A faint rim of light glowed around the door between the garage and the garden. The wind gusted and Omar Yussef blinked against the dust. When he opened his eyes, the light in the garage was out. Someone knew they were there.

The gunmen scuttled across the sand toward the perimeter wall. Omar Yussef went after them.

He picked out Abu Jamal by the peak of his forage cap and whispered his name. He wanted to tell him about the light in the garage. Abu Jamal turned.

A sudden burst of thick, popping gunfire spat from the house. Its baritone harmonized with the bass of the slow, flapping canvas tent. Abu Jamal dropped to his knees. He lifted his Kalashnikov and returned fire toward an upstairs window of the Salah house. His men took cover behind the wall ringing the olive grove. Abu Jamal followed them quickly, still shooting.

Omar Yussef crouched in the middle of the sandy lot, just where he had been when the firing began. He saw the orange muzzle-flashes of the gun upstairs in the Salah home, but when he looked around him in the dark, everything was black. Someone grabbed his waist and trotted him toward the cover of the wall. He fell forward, but he kept going, scrambling on all fours across the sand. He dropped to the ground at the wall and pushed his glasses back into place. He turned, panting. Sami smiled and patted his arm.

The gunmen gathered on either side of the gate, preparing to charge the house. A flash ripped out of the darkness and part of the wall disintegrated. The explosion lifted two of the gunmen and dropped them in the sand a few yards from the gate. Omar Yussef felt the explosion as a wave of deeper heat in the humid night. *Yasser booby-trapped the entrance*, he thought. One of the men on the sand cried out in pain. Another volley chattered from the machine gun in the upstairs window and both of the fallen gunmen were still. Attiah stood and fired toward the window.

Abu Jamal signaled to the man with the two LAW missiles strapped to his back. The man nodded, readied one of the missiles and edged toward the gate. His shoulders lifted as he took a deep breath. He stepped into the open and fired toward the top of the house. The shell streaked bright blue and red through the window where the gunshots had originated. It struck the cement inside with a sound like the falling of a tall tree and filled the room with light.

The gunmen lifted their heads and watched the glare turn to a smoky billow of darkness. The man with the missile turned to Abu Jamal, nodding excitedly. A rattle of shots came from another upstairs window and he fell. He dropped the spent missile-launcher and clutched his stomach. Abu Jamal dragged him out of the line of fire. He rolled the moaning gunman onto his side, pulled the remaining anti-tank launcher from his back and set it against the wall. He tore the man's T-shirt to examine the wound.

Attiah leaned against the broken end of the wall, returning fire. The smoke from the room where the missile had struck was thicker now, obscuring the top floor almost completely. The fire had spread to the other rooms. Amid the gunfire, Omar Yussef heard a woman scream. Attiah rounded the wall and, keeping low, charged toward the front door of the house.

Omar Yussef grabbed Sami's shoulder. 'There's a garage at the back. I saw a light in there before the shooting started.'

Sami nodded. They crept behind the wall, passing the side of the house.

'Lift me over into the garden,' Omar Yussef said. 'You're fit enough to follow me on your own.'

The wall was seven feet high. Omar Yussef put his foot in Sami's linked fingers and the younger man shoved him until he could get his knee over the wall. Broken glass lined the top and Omar Yussef felt it slice his hands and leg. Bellowing through clenched teeth, he pushed himself quickly over and fell to the ground hard on his back. He rolled onto his front, keeping his bloody hands out of the sand. He came to his knees and gripped the front of his shirt tightly to stanch the bleeding from his palms. 'Sami, there's glass on the wall. Be careful.'

'Okay.'

At least two guns seemed to be firing inside the house. As Omar Yussef grimaced with the pain in his hands, a man in a white T-shirt rushed out of the back door and down the steps. He fired a few rounds into the house and fled across the garden. Only when the man was close to Omar Yussef did he see that it was Yasser Salah.

An olive tree splintered with the impact of a volley fired from inside the house, and Yasser Salah dropped to one knee. Attiah Odwan rushed out of the back door, spraying gunfire around the garden. Omar Yussef went down flat. Yasser took quick aim and fired. He pulled the trigger for the briefest moment, but it was long enough to hit Attiah with six shots. The burly man went down, dead. Omar Yussef gasped.

Yasser halted. He looked in Omar Yussef's direction, peering into the darkness between the olive trees. Omar Yussef held still on the sand.

Above him, he heard a grunt and Sami came up onto the wall. Yasser lifted his rifle and fired. Sami dropped silently back from the wall. Yasser hurried to the garage, pulled open the door and shut it behind him.

'Sami?' Omar Yussef said.

'I'm okay, Abu Ramiz. I'll be with you in a minute.'

'Are you hit?'

'Not really.'

'What does that mean?'

'Just a graze on the shoulder. Give me a second, okay?'

Omar Yussef stared at the door to the ramshackle garage. He heard shots inside the house and more than one woman screaming now. He went low across the sandy garden to the garage. As quietly as he could, Omar Yussef opened the door and entered.

A small storm lantern stood on a workbench in the corner. It swung as Yasser Salah picked it up, casting a warm penumbra around him, but its light didn't reveal Omar Yussef's entry. With his other hand, Salah reached out and pulled a man toward him. The man's hands were bound in front of him and his mouth was covered with black duct tape. His wavy, grayish blonde hair was dry and unkempt.

Omar Yussef resisted the temptation to call out to Magnus Wallender. He edged through the shadows toward the illuminated corner of the room.

Salah pulled a paraffin heater away from the wall. Below was a trapdoor. *His smuggling tunnel,* Omar Yussef thought. Salah lifted the trapdoor. The entrance was only three feet square and lined with wood. He cut the twine around Wallender's hands and ripped away the tape on his face. Wallender bawled in pain, with his hand to his mouth. He bled through his stubbly beard and over his shirt. Salah stepped onto a ladder inside the shaft to the tunnel, holding the storm lantern. He pulled a pistol from the back of his pants and held it on Wallender. 'Follow me down here,' he said. Wallender nodded, exaggeratedly compliant. His feet were on the top rungs.

Omar Yussef opened his mouth to call to Wallender. Instead his words were swallowed by the roaring blast of another shoulder-launched missile. It struck the side of the garage, knocking him to the ground and bringing down part of the wall behind him.

He forced himself onto his knees and scrambled toward the entrance of the tunnel. The flimsy garage creaked with the missile's impact and he knew it was about to collapse. As he lowered himself into the tunnel, the wooden roof of the garage dropped. He looked down. At the foot of the shaft, twelve feet below, the glow of the lantern lit Magnus's upper body. The Swede's legs angled into the narrow tunnel that must have led under the border. Omar Yussef saw no sign of Salah. His hands bloodied the rungs of the ladder as he descended.

Above him, he heard another wall come down. The wooden supports of the shaft groaned and dirt puffed out through the gaps between the planks.

Omar Yussef reached the bottom of the ladder. Wallender was on his belly, edging backwards through the tunnel. Unlike the shaft, it had no wooden supports and it was even narrower – about two feet square. Omar Yussef went onto his hands and knees. 'Magnus,' he whispered.

The Swede looked into the half-light that filtered beyond him from the lantern. His bloody face registered recognition. Sweat channeled dirt into Omar Yussef's eyes as he strained to see past Wallender, but the Swede's body blocked his view along the tunnel. The earth around them murmured and dust dropped from the roof.

He had to get them to turn back. 'Yasser,' he called into the tunnel.

'Fuck your mother,' Yasser shouted. 'I'll shoot the foreigner.'

'Let's all get out of here, Yasser. It's going to collapse.'

The puff of dirt became a trickle, like rain all along the tunnel. Then the earth growled like a man taking a punch and the roof of the tunnel fell. Omar Yussef dived to grab Wallender's arm. He pulled hard and the Swede shoved himself forward. The shaft around Omar Yussef filled with thick dust. In the darkness, he tried to call Magnus's name, but he could only cough. He held the man's arm and sensed the Swede's desperate scrambling to free his legs and waist, then he felt the resistance lessen. He slipped backward against the planks of the shaft as Magnus came out of the tunnel and up onto his knees. He put his arms around the Swede and they gripped each other. He pushed Magnus up the ladder and scrambled behind him through the thick air. He heard stones clashing against each other above him.

'I can't get out, Abu Ramiz,' Wallender said, from the top of the ladder. 'It's blocked.'

When the garage roof came down, it had covered the head of the tunnel. Coughing, Omar Yussef and Wallender shouted that they were underground. They listened intently to the deep silence, then yelled again.

As they waited, Omar Yussef sensed a calm in himself. He had found Magnus. Even if they were both to be stuck in this tunnel forever with no one above them aware of their fate, he had shown the Swede the kind of man he was. *I might remain here,* he thought, *buried in Gaza with James Cree's great-grandfather.* He frowned. Something flashed through his mind for a moment, linking the old skeleton in Doctor Najjar's morgue and the British Military Cemetery. He tried to bring the two images together once more, but he was distracted by Magnus yelling through the timber and stones for rescue.

Magnus breathed heavily. He put his hand on Omar Yussef's shoulder. 'Abu Ramiz, while I was held captive, I felt very alone,' he murmured. 'Though I'm still trapped, at least I have a good friend with me.' Then he raised his voice: 'Tell me, did Sweden invade Norway?' He slapped Omar Yussef's shoulder and rolled his head back, laughing. Omar Yussef saw that his companion was so relieved to be rid of Yasser Salah that even the prospect of being buried alive didn't spoil his humor. He coughed out the dust and smiled.

The rubble above them scratched and rumbled as it was lifted away. The head of the shaft cleared and Wallender was pulled from the ladder. Omar Yussef followed him. Sami gripped him under the arms, grimacing from the light wound to his shoulder, and hoisted him onto the broken stone of the garage wall. Omar Yussef lay limp and sweating next to Magnus. The dust storm still smothered Rafah in filth and humidity, but to

Omar Yussef it felt crisp and stimulating, like the air of the mountains, after the dirt in the tunnel.

Sami leaned over into the shaft that led to the tunnel and stared into the darkness. 'No one else down there?' he said.

Omar Yussef lifted his head to speak the name of Yasser Salah, but he choked on it and coughed until his diaphragm bit into the bottom of his lungs.

Abu Jamal crossed the debris of the fallen garage, holding a flashlight before him. His men were tossing wooden beams and sections of tin roof and cinderblock into the garden, searching through the destruction. The chief of the gunmen stared at the exhausted Swede. Crouching and breathing deeply, Wallender was coated in earth from head to foot. He shielded his eyes from the beam of Abu Jamal's torch.

Omar Yussef sat upright and addressed Abu Jamal. 'This is Magnus Wallender of the UN, who was kidnapped by Yasser Salah. Yasser is dead, down in the tunnel.'

Abu Jamal looked at Wallender as though Omar Yussef had introduced him to the filthiest mongrel stray in Gaza. He turned the light on Omar Yussef, pulled his pistol from its holster and leveled it at him. 'You bastard, where the fuck is my missile?'

CHAPTER 28

Magnus Wallender rose to his feet, wheezing. The skin around his mouth, where Yasser Salah had ripped away the tape, was bleeding and caked with damp mud. His thick hair stuck up in frightful wisps and his light-blue irises stood out sharply in a face dark with dirt. He rolled his shoulders back, blinked away the grit and stepped in front of Abu Jamal. 'Whoever you are,' he said, 'put away that gun.'

Abu Jamal looked Wallender up and down. He glanced behind him, where his men were clearing wreckage, hoping to find the missile. 'I know who you are, even if you don't know me,' he said. 'It's your good fortune that I don't want trouble with the UN, because otherwise I'd kill you now.'

Wallender reached out for Abu Jamal's pistol. Abu Jamal pulled away but slid the gun into its leather holster.

The gunman scratched the back of his head and gave a surly kick at a broken cinderblock. He stepped to the side of Wallender, so he could direct his complaints at Omar Yussef. 'So where's the *Saladin I*?' he said.

'Yasser must have hidden it,' Omar Yussef said. He stood up slowly and stared at his bleeding palms. 'I need something to bandage my hands.'

'Fuck your hands. If you bleed to death, the United Nations can't blame *me* for it.' Abu Jamal headed for the house.

One of the gunmen came out of the back door, shoving the father of Yasser and Fathi Salah down the steps in front of him. Abu Jamal doubled his pace and drew his pistol as he crossed the sandy garden. When he reached Zaki Salah, he put his hand on the old man's shoulder, shoved him to his knees, forced his head back and thrust the barrel of the gun inside his mouth. 'Where's the missile?' he yelled.

Zaki shook his head. Abu Jamal yelled again, and then a third time he screamed his question. He pulled the pistol out of the old man's mouth, slapped the barrel into Salah's cheek and back-handed it onto his nose. Blood ran down the front of Salah's long, white *jalabiya*.

Abu Jamal grabbed Salah's beard and pulled him across the sand to where the body of Attiah Odwan lay. He pushed the old man to the ground beside the thick, muscular corpse. Salah looked at the dead gunman's face and muttered a blessing.

'Shut up,' Abu Jamal shouted. 'Your bastard son killed him. Your bastard son Yasser, who's dead and buried under the ground beneath your garage.'

Salah muttered again, closing his eyes and praying for the soul of his son. Abu Jamal kicked the old man in the stomach. He gestured to the gunman who had brought Salah from the house. 'Lift him up.'

Omar Yussef stepped into the sandy garden. He moved toward Abu Jamal. Sami held his wrist and shook his head. Omar Yussef ignored him. 'That old fellow doesn't know where the missile is,' he called.

Abu Jamal turned and glared at him.

'Do you think a man like Yasser would trust anyone? Even his own father?' Omar Yussef said.

Abu Jamal looked at Salah, then back to Omar Yussef. 'If he doesn't know, then how will we find it?'

'You never will.'

'Wrong answer.'

'It wasn't an answer, it was a wish.' Omar Yussef pushed his chin toward Abu Jamal. He clenched his bloody hands and felt them shaking.

'If this old man doesn't know where to find the missile—' Abu Jamal kept his eyes on Omar Yussef, as he lifted his gun to Salah's head '—I don't need him alive.' He pulled the trigger and Zaki Salah tumbled backwards over the corpse of Attiah Odwan.

Omar Yussef gasped. The old man's legs twisted unnaturally at the knees. The wound on his forehead was a small black hole, but the blood poured from the back of his skull onto the sand. Omar Yussef reached out and grabbed Abu Jamal's deformed hand. The smooth skin was cold in his palm. He pointed at Attiah Odwan's body underneath the dead old man. 'At least Attiah died bravely,' he said. 'You will never have that honor.'

Abu Jamal narrowed his eyes and looked over Omar Yussef's shoulder at Magnus Wallender. Omar Yussef wondered if the gunman was considering a new kidnapping, which might allow him to screw some kind of reward out of the government as recompense for the night's fruitless operation. But killing Zaki Salah appeared to have calmed him. He spoke quietly. 'Like Attiah, I'm ready to be martyred,' he said.

Omar Yussef smelled the menthol throat lozenges on Abu Jamal's breath. 'If Allah wills it.'

Abu Jamal put away his gun. His bloodshot eyes were distant. 'Is that also a wish?'

'Get down,' one of the gunmen yelled from inside the ruins of the garage. Abu Jamal and Omar Yussef dropped to the sand. They heard a hollow ringing as something bounced toward them. A rock, a foot in diameter, came to rest against an olive tree a yard away from them. It didn't sound like a rock and it bounced much too lightly. Omar Yussef tensed his whole body and waited.

One of the gunmen ambled across the sand from the garage. 'Sorry, chief. I was tossing the rubble out of the garage and I threw that stone without realizing what it was. I think it's a disguised fiberglass cover for a roadside bomb. As I threw it, I realized it was too light to be a rock and I thought perhaps there was already a bomb rigged up inside it. That's why I shouted.' He knelt close by the rock. 'It doesn't seem to be armed.'

'What else is in there?' Abu Jamal gestured toward the rubble.

'A few dozen Kalashikovs and a lot of grenades under the wreckage. Salah's weapons store. Quite a haul.'

'Bring the jeeps around and load it up,' Abu Jamal said.

'Now you're happy?' Omar Yussef rose to his knees.

'Now I can continue our resistance. Until my martyrdom.' Abu Jamal kicked the fiberglass rock. Omar Yussef dropped to the ground again. The rock rolled away from them. Abu Jamal laughed, soft and jeering.

Sami sheared a slice of material from his T-shirt and bound his shoulder, where Yasser Salah's bullet had winged him. He knelt by Omar Yussef with a pan of water and cleaned the dirt from his lacerated hands. 'You were nearly buried alive back there, Abu Ramiz,' he said.

'Yes, I thought it might become my eternal tomb.' Omar Yussef remembered the way the images of the skeleton in the pathologist's surgery and of the British War Cemetery had come to him in the tunnel. It was as though it had all been down there in the same hole in the ground with him and Yasser Salah. He rubbed his forehead.

'I wouldn't have left you down there. I'd have

dug you up and shipped your body back to Bethlehem. Gaza's a terrible place to stay, even if it's only your bones.' Sami ripped another piece from his T-shirt and tied it around Omar Yussef's palm.

Even if it's only your bones. Omar Yussef thought of Yasser Salah, crushed in the collapsed tunnel. Though Salah was gone, others would die when his stash of weapons was aimed at them. Beyond the grave, the men of Gaza could still wield death. He thought of the skeleton on the pathologist's dissecting table. *Who did you rise from the dead to kill?*

CHAPTER 29

Dawn lent a roseate highlight to the dust cloud, as Sami accelerated out of Rafah, north on the Saladin Road toward Gaza City. Wallender had washed the abraded skin around his mouth under a faucet, but his face remained grimy and bloodied. The pine air freshener dangling from the rearview mirror of the Jeep Cherokee battled with the scent of sweat and soil from the car's passengers. Omar Yussef wondered if his body would ever be cleansed of the dirt constricting his breath and clogging his throat.

In the back of the car, Wallender had been gabbing with the excitement of new freedom ever since they'd left the Saladin Brigades men at the stationery store, their jeeps laden with Yasser Salah's weapons and the dead bodies of four of their comrades. *I'll let him wash and rest before I tell him about James,* Omar Yussef thought. *Or about Eyad Masharawi. Perhaps I won't tell him the rest, ever. Maybe that way I'll able to forget it, too.*

He gazed across the cabbage fields. The wind had picked up and bent the isolated stands of sycamore. The dust storm was building for its final squall. Perhaps it would at last blow itself out and he would see the sunshine again before he left Gaza, after all.

As they passed Deir al-Balah, the tall palms bowed under the wind. The cabbage fields fluttered like the emerald surface of the sea, stretching to the neat green hedge around the British War Cemetery. The gusts came from the east with the dawn, as though the growing light were blowing into Gaza.

Omar Yussef stared at the hedge as they approached the cemetery. *In the tunnel, it was as though this place of tombs was down there with me and Yasser Salah. The old skeleton was there, too.* He frowned. 'Sami, pull over at the junction,' he said, pointing toward the caretaker's little farmhouse.

The mysterious skeleton in the morgue was discovered in the corner of a field near here, he thought. He recalled the desecrated graves he'd seen when he visited the cemetery with Cree. The words Khamis Zeydan had spoken to him when he first arrived in Gaza sounded in his head: *There is no single, isolated crime in Gaza. Each one is linked to many others.*

Omar Yussef stepped out of the car and trotted to the gate of the caretaker's yard, his head bowed against the wind. The caretaker stared in fright when he saw Omar Yussef, his clothes filthy and bloody and his head covered in dust.

'You remember me, Suleiman? I was here with Mister James Cree from the United Nations.'

Suleiman Jouda nodded, but his expression remained one of shock.

Omar Yussef coughed. 'This is Mister Cree's friend, Mister Wallender. Also from the United Nations.'

Jouda gaped at Wallender's gory face and his filthy clothes.

Omar Yussef edged past the caretaker. 'He's from Sweden,' he said, with a wink, as though that explained their strange appearance on Jouda's doorstep at daybreak. Jouda nodded, hesitantly. 'We need to inspect the graveyard on a very important issue of United Nations security business, Suleiman.'

Omar Yussef crossed the dirt yard, passing a wheelbarrow and some trenching tools that stood against the wall. Jouda opened the gate to the graveyard and entered. Omar Yussef picked up a long-handled spade and gave it to Sami. He ignored Sami's quizzical expression and followed Jouda onto the lush lawn of the cemetery.

Wallender stared at the neatness of the graveyard. 'This really doesn't look like Gaza. What're we doing here, Abu Ramiz?'

'We're paying our respects,' Omar Yussef said. He turned to Jouda. 'Suleiman, show us the graves that were recently desecrated. Was it these, near the end of the path?'

Jouda led them to the corner of the first block of gravestones facing the lawn's central obelisk monument. 'It was these few here, *ustaz*,' he said.

'But can you tell me, please, what's the matter? I'm sorry to ask, uncle, but the British consulate is sending someone today to inspect the repairs I've made to the damaged gravestones. Is your visit connected to that?'

'In a way. Everything will be okay. Don't worry.'

'Is that *my* shovel?' Jouda said, nervous and slightly indignant now.

'Trust me, Suleiman.' Omar Yussef stepped off the gravel path onto the grass.

Jouda had bonded the pieces of the broken gravestones and re-laid the disturbed turf around them. The one that had been marked with graffiti stood out. Jouda's cleanser had erased the vandals' slogans, but it also had scoured away ninety years of dust from the rock, leaving a chalky diagonal stripe across the crest of the stone.

Omar Yussef approached that grave. He read the inscription. *Private Eynon Price. Royal Army Medical Corps, 53rd (Welsh) Casualty Clearing Station. 28 years. 4/5/1917.* He read the inscription again. *Eynon Price, Eynon Price. How do you pronounce that name? 'Eye' or 'Ay' or 'Ee'? Eynon Price.* He was sure he knew that name. Perhaps a foreigner working for the UN had a similar name, but he couldn't recall who it might be. Then he remembered: he had heard those words, uttered by a tongue unaccustomed to English. In Odwan's cell. When the doomed man had recounted the nonsensical babbling of Lieutenant Fathi Salah before he was shot. *High Noon Price*, Odwan thought Salah had said.

Odwan had believed Fathi Salah was negotiating the price of the missile, but the frightened officer was actually telling him where to find the weapon. It was here, its burial disguised as a desecration of the graves.

Omar Yussef felt a surge of strength and excitement. He had discovered the truth and now he was about to uncover the *Saladin I*. 'Sami, start digging right here.'

Jouda protested. Omar Yussef put his hands on the man's shoulders and spoke soothingly. 'Suleiman, there has been a terrible criminal act. You heard about the bones that were found near here and taken to the morgue at Shifa Hospital?'

Jouda nodded. 'It was in the newspaper, *ustaz*,' he said. He kept his eyes on the grave, where Sami was peeling away the turf the caretaker had only lately re-laid.

'Those are the bones that should be in this grave.'

'Then what's in the grave now?'

'All the evil of Gaza.'

'Leave it there then.' Jouda didn't question that evil would reside beneath the earth.

'We can't do that. Where will the soldier's bones rest?'

Sami was working up a sweat, down to his chest in the sandy earth, the bandage on his shoulder bloody. Omar Yussef felt the air growing warm as the sun came up.

He thought of Lieutenant Fathi Salah, a good

student and later a decent officer, but a poor man with a bad brother who pressured him to make the missile deal with the Saladin Brigades. Fathi couldn't carry out Yasser's dirty trade and lost his nerve. When Fathi blurted the location of the missile to Odwan, his brother shot him dead. Omar Yussef remembered Professor Adnan Maki's dinner lecture about the alien invaders who had come to Gaza over the centuries, including these British men in the graves under his feet. But it wasn't the outsiders who exacted the highest cost in blood from Gaza; it was the men like Yasser Salah who killed their brothers.

'Abu Ramiz.' Sami tossed the shovel out of the grave. He lifted a plywood box onto its end. It was the length of a coffin, but it was bound with wire and the wood was bright and new.

Wallender helped Sami lift the box onto the grass. Sami sent Jouda back to his yard for wire clippers. He smiled at Omar Yussef, admiring and puzzled. When Jouda returned, Sami cut the wire and beat open the nailed lid of the box with the handle of the spade.

The missile was gray and surprisingly narrow – no wider than a toddler's torso. A yellow stripe circled it near its pointed tip and another by the fins at its base. Three foam inserts held it in place and it was packed tight with plastic ballast bags.

'Suleiman, call the hospital and talk to Doctor Najjar, the pathologist. Tell him you've found where the missing bones belong,' Omar Yussef said.

'Tell him I'll call the morgue to explain, as soon as I can.'

The caretaker hurried toward his house.

Omar Yussef bent to close the lid of the missile crate.

'What's this all about?' Wallender asked.

'This is the *Saladin I*,' Omar Yussef said. He knocked the lid into place with the heel of his hand.

Sami came close to Omar Yussef. 'How are you intending to destroy this missile, Abu Ramiz?'

'Destroy it?' Omar Yussef laughed. 'We're going to sell it.'

CHAPTER 30

As the wind dropped, the dust cloud settled in a final gritty film over Emile Zola Street. Omar Yussef blinked at the sky. A deep blue came through the dirt for the first time in four days. The tricolor at the French Cultural Center, next door to Maki's house, dangled from its pole as though it were wilting in the early morning heat. Sami idled the Jeep at the curb. He rapped his fist on the plywood missile crate, which rested over the folded rear-seats, and gave a thumbs-up. Omar Yussef nodded to him and pressed the buzzer at the professor's gate.

The blue metal door swung open and Omar Yussef entered the garden of luxuriant bushes and tall palms. He calmed himself with a deep breath and noted that it was the first time in days he had inhaled without also swallowing a handful of sand. By the fountain, the plastic doe stretched her neck from behind a bush, and Omar Yussef let her snout nuzzle into the crust of blood and sweat on his bandaged palm.

The Sri Lankan maid awaited him at the wide mahogany door. She paid no attention to the dirt

335

that covered his face and hair, or the blood smeared across the belly of his shirt where he had stanched the flow from his slashed palms. He wondered what strange people came through this entrance that the tiny woman could take in, with a polite smile, such a horrific apparition as he must surely have presented.

'Professor Adnan is not yet up,' she said. 'But, if you're in a hurry, I will tell him you're here.'

'Please do. Thank you.'

The maid went to fetch Adnan Maki. Omar Yussef pulled one of the bentwood chairs from under the dining table, so as not to dirty the sofa and make work for her. His back ached and his head pounded. Magnus would be washing and shaving back at the Sands Hotel now, and he wondered how soon he would be able to do the same thing. He rubbed the stubble on his chin and it showered a dusting of dirt onto the shiny tabletop. He wiped the earth away with the edge of his hand. His bandage left a damp smear on the polished surface. He drew in his breath and shook his head.

The Sri Lankan returned. She smiled and suggested a coffee. Omar Yussef asked her to make it without sugar and she went to the kitchen. He was listening to the muted sounds of her preparations, when he noticed Maki watching him from beside the Chinese cloisonné screen that masked the hallway. Maki wore a red silk dressing gown and cream silk pajamas. His gray hair was tousled. Omar Yussef looked at his wristwatch. It was eight-thirty.

'Morning of light, Abu Nabil,' he said.

'Morning of joy,' Maki said. His voice was quiet. He stared at Omar Yussef, yawned and rubbed his hands across his face to wake himself up.

'I'm sorry to disturb you.'

Maki seemed to shake off his sleepiness in an instant. He was as loud and vivacious as ever. 'Not at all, Abu Ramiz. I welcome you to breakfast with me. If good company is rare in Gaza at dinner-time, then at breakfast it's something never to be experienced.' He leered.

Omar Yussef wondered what kind of company Maki kept at breakfast in his Paris apartment, away from the conservative watchers of Gaza. It probably wasn't much more classy than Omar Yussef must have looked at the moment. 'I apologize for my appearance.'

'Would you like to clean up in the bathroom? What on earth has happened to you?'

The Sri Lankan brought the coffee. Maki told her to bring out a plate of croissants and toast.

'I'm really not hungry, Abu Nabil,' Omar Yussef said.

'No, no, I insist we enjoy an unhurried breakfast, the two of us.' Maki sat at the table. 'I very much welcome your excellent company. The Revolutionary Council meetings are over. My cultured friends among the delegates are returning to the West Bank. All is once again deathly quiet in Gaza. Deathly, deathly, deathly.'

Omar Yussef detected a deeper layer of meaning

in the repetition of Maki's last word. Perhaps Maki had seen Omar Yussef's notes on the back of the Saladin Brigades leaflet after all. But it didn't matter now. Omar Yussef held the trump card.

'I didn't come for cultured talk. I want to do business,' he said.

Maki tilted his head and opened his hand.

'I have something to offer, as a trade,' Omar Yussef said.

The Sri Lankan came with a plate of pastries. Maki pushed it across the table to Omar Yussef, smiling. 'Is this another deal for the freedom of your friend Professor Masharawi?' he said.

'You know as well as I do that Masharawi's dead,' Omar Yussef said.

The smile was gone from Maki's face. He pulled the plate back across the table and bit into a chocolate croissant. As he chewed, the wet, black, tadpole eyes narrowed until they were hard and cunning. He wiped a few flakes of pastry from his wide upper lip. 'I don't know that *quite* as well as you do, but it's true that I do know it.'

'I have the *Saladin I.*'

'The what?'

'The prototype missile that you and Yasser Salah stole from the Saladin Brigades.'

'I don't know what you mean. Who is Yasser Salah?' Maki lowered his chin like a dog preparing to pounce.

Omar Yussef fought against his tiredness for concentration. 'Yasser Salah was a Preventive

338

Security officer in Rafah. You sold him his university degrees, so he could obtain promotion.'

'He *was* a Preventive Security officer, you said?'

'He's dead now. Buried alive in his smuggling tunnel beneath the Egyptian border. I went to his house last night and found my kidnapped Swedish colleague there, thankfully still in good shape.'

'The Swede is safe? So everything is completed to your satisfaction.' Maki threw his arms wide, exposing the gray hairs on his chest at the neck of the pajamas.

'Not quite. I want to sell you the Saladin missile.'

Maki shook his head, as though deeply puzzled. 'Why should I want it?'

'Because if you don't buy it, I'll sell it to Colonel al-Fara.'

'So?'

'He'll want to know how this missile, which was smuggled into Gaza by the Saladin Brigades, ended up in the hands of a UN schoolteacher.'

'And what will you tell him?'

'That his ally on the Revolutionary Council, Professor Maki, wanted a piece of the arms trade. He arranged for degrees from al-Azhar University to be conferred on a nobody down in Rafah named Yasser Salah, so that the man could be promoted to a powerful position in the local Preventive Security branch.'

Maki laughed and clapped his hands. 'Abu Ramiz, the dust storm has affected your brain, perhaps. This is all most fantastic.'

Omar Yussef ignored him. 'With his status in the security forces to protect him from rival smugglers, Salah could smuggle weapons and sell them readily. When he heard that the Saladin Brigades were bringing in a new missile, Salah figured it was an opportunity to snatch the prototype and sell it back to the gunmen.'

Maki stopped laughing. His jaw was tight.

'Salah used his brother, a Military Intelligence officer, to carry out the trade,' Omar Yussef said, 'so the Saladin Brigades would blame Military Intelligence for the theft. His brother lost his nerve and blew the sale, so Salah killed him. He was preparing to sell the missile to Colonel al-Fara, I believe, when things started to go wrong.'

'I don't know anything about this missile.'

'Yes, you do. Yasser Salah had two bogus university degrees, but he was no historian. The missile was hidden in a grave in the British War Cemetery. That was your touch, professor. You're the history man.' Omar Yussef watched Maki closely. 'Do I need to remind you of your lecture over dinner about the British in the First World War?'

The professor pulled a croissant into pieces. He laid the strips on his plate, side by side.

'The degrees you sold to Preventive Security men like Salah gave you a strong network all over Gaza. These men owed their promotions and power to you. You used them to sell the weapons Salah smuggled under the border.' Omar Yussef raised his finger and looked hard at Maki. 'But if

Colonel al-Fara found out you were using the sale of degrees for more than just a little extra cash, he'd squash you. He wouldn't want his people to owe even partial allegiance to anyone else.'

'I sold a degree to al-Fara, too.' Maki smiled. 'So stop behaving as though you have the upper hand here.'

'I have the missile, remember,' Omar Yussef said.

Maki waved his hand dismissively. 'All missiles look the same to me. Salah handled that end of things.'

'You've gone too far, Abu Nabil,' Omar Yussef said. 'When Professor Masharawi made his accusations about corruption at the university, you had your network in Preventive Security frame him as a spy. In the end, you kidnapped the Swede, blew up James Cree and had Masharawi killed, because you saw that we were getting too close to the truth.'

'I didn't order the UN fellow to be blown up,' Maki said. 'That was Salah's stupidity. In any case, he thought you'd be in the car, rather than the foreigner.'

'But you *did* want me killed?'

Maki lifted his chin arrogantly, then he dropped it and it was as though the fight had gone out of him. 'I found a Saladin Brigades leaflet in my office after you left, with notes about the Salah brothers on the back. I knew then why you were in my office with my secretary. There was a phone number on the leaflet, too, so I had Salah call it.

When you answered, he put the Swede on the line, to scare you off. It didn't work, so I issued the order to have you killed.' He shrugged. 'But your friend the Scotsman was already dead. At the time he died, I assure you I didn't wish you killed. That roadside bomb was too much.'

Omar Yussef felt his shoulder twinge where the stone had hit him by Cree's burning vehicle. It was one bruise among many, but he sensed it deep in his muscle now. 'It was too much for *me*,' he said. 'For you, it was only part of Gaza's long, fatal history.'

'I'm not a monster, Abu Ramiz. I'm a politician.' Maki placed both hands over his heart and frowned. 'How do you think politics is conducted in Gaza? With reasoned debate between men who call each other "the honorable gentleman"? I hoped you'd see that you were involved in something more than a trivial argument between a part-time professor and the head of the university. Masharawi's torture should've shown you it was much bigger than that.' Maki shook his head slowly. 'If you had been smarter, your friend the UN man would still be alive. It wasn't his fault that he didn't understand the way Gaza works. But you're a Palestinian – I told you to guide the foreigners away from the Masharawi case. Still you went ahead with your stupid investigation. If anyone killed the Scotsman, it was you.'

Omar Yussef's jaw quivered and his hands shook with rage. 'You admitted that you were prepared to go even further,' he said, as calmly as he could. 'You put out an order for me to be killed.'

'That was a lesser thing than the murder of the Scotsman. Do you think anyone at the United Nations would worry about your death?' Maki said. He smiled, seeming to gain energy from Omar Yussef's evident anger. 'Even so, the Scotsman's killing will come to nothing. If the UN found out that I was involved in his death – which they couldn't prove, believe me – their diplomats would hush it up.'

'One of their colleagues is dead.'

'Oh, yes, you might expect them to want justice for their departed comrade. But they'd be far more concerned about the peace negotiations. They aren't about to blame a senior member of the Revolutionary Council for the murder.' Maki gestured around the room, as though its luxury were proof that he was above justice and law. 'The UN will close its eyes to this, agree that it was the result of some internal battle between criminal gunmen, and pay a pension to the poor man's family, if he has one.'

Omar Yussef recalled bitterly how swift the UN negotiating team had been to turn back to Jerusalem, after the bomb killed James Cree. 'Perhaps you're right. They'll allow the incident to be buried,' he said. 'Why should it only be Palestinians who're corrupted by Gaza?'

'Did you come here to listen to me confess? You think three thousand years of death in Gaza will be ended if you take me in to the police? I gave you a lesson in Gaza's history when we had dinner the other night. But you didn't pay attention.' Maki leaned over the table and wagged his finger at Omar Yussef. There was a smear of melted chocolate on the knuckle. Maki sucked it away. He smiled and smacked his lips. 'Yasser Salah and Eyad Masharawi and your UN man, these are all small issues. These three men all benefited from the violence and corruption here – Salah ran guns, Masharawi was the principled defender of justice, and your UN man got a tax-free salary and the warm feeling that he was helping the poor, dark natives.'

'It cost them their lives.'

'That was the risk they took. While they lived, they thrived on the same system that killed them.'

Omar Yussef waved his bandaged hand. 'Let's forget that we're both history teachers. I don't care about ending Gaza's violent story. When you invited me to your house for dinner, you said you could offer me incentives to bury the Masharawi case. I know what you meant by that, and I'm prepared to let you buy my silence now.'

Maki was still. He smiled tentatively, then he raised his eyebrows and laughed. He slapped the tabletop with both hands and laughed harder. 'Abu Ramiz, I liked you from the moment I met you.' He pointed a finger at Omar Yussef. 'You're a very, very bad man, my friend. My dear, darling friend. A very bad man.'

Maki called to the Sri Lankan for a whisky. She brought it before he'd finished laughing and he paused in his laughter only long enough to slug it down. He held out his glass. 'One for you, Abu Ramiz?'

Omar Yussef shook his head. 'I want twenty thousand dollars,' he said.

'That much?'

'That's the price at which you offered the missile to the Saladin Brigades.'

'Well, I'm sure I can manage that.'

'In cash. Now.'

Maki stopped laughing and sighed. He smiled. 'How do I know that you have the missile?'

'Open the door of your garage. My assistant will bring our car inside and leave the missile there for you.'

Maki took Omar Yussef through the kitchen to the side entrance of the garage. He rolled up the street door and pulled his Mercedes out into the sunlight to make room. Omar Yussef beckoned to Sami, who reversed into the garage. With Sami, he maneuvered the plywood missile crate out of the rear of the Jeep and onto the oil-stained floor. Maki came back in and pulled down the door. Sami pried open the lid of the crate.

Maki looked inside and smiled. He ran his hand along the missile, breathlessly, as though it were a naked woman. 'The *Saladin I*. Close it up, Abu Ramiz. I'll get you the money.'

In Maki's living room, Omar Yussef paced the

shiny marble floor. The professor returned with a black leather briefcase. He laid it on the dining table and opened it. Inside were twenty bundles of U.S. dollars. Omar Yussef riffled the end of one wad of bills. 'No need to count it, Abu Ramiz,' Maki laughed. 'I consider this a fine price and an excellent deal.'

'What'll you do with the missile?'

'I'm sure that Colonel al-Fara will consider this an excellent deal, also.'

'You'll give it to him?'

'Give it? Abu Ramiz, you and I are both engaged in the arms trade now, so let's not be coy. Colonel al-Fara knew about the Saladin Brigades' attempt to smuggle in a new prototype. He was concerned, because it would have given them an important weapon with which to threaten the Israelis.'

'And, therefore, a tool with which to blackmail money from the party and the government,' Omar Yussef said.

'If they weren't paid off, they would've bombarded Israel with *Saladin* I missiles, and then the Israelis would've invaded Gaza.' Maki laughed.

'That would've embarrassed Colonel al-Fara.'

'If al-Fara lost control of security in Gaza, soon it would be all over for him.' Maki punched a fist into his hand. 'I had intended for Yasser Salah to do the deal, keeping me out of it. But it will work just as well if I use my personal relationship with al-Fara to make the trade. As soon as you leave, I will call the colonel and tell him that an intermediary has offered to sell him the *Saladin I*.'

'At a small profit to you.'

Maki bowed, with a smile. 'He won't mind a little premium, a consulting fee, if you like. The colonel shall be quite pleased with his week's work. First, a Military Intelligence man is killed and the Saladin Brigades are blamed for it. As a result, a Brigades man, this Bassam Odwan, is murdered by Military Intelligence and in revenge the Brigades execute General Husseini, Colonel al-Fara's biggest rival. Now the colonel is able to purchase the missile over which everyone else was fighting. A very satisfactory outcome for him, wouldn't you agree?'

Omar Yussef picked up the briefcase and went to the door. He was in the garden with his hand on the doe's snout when Maki called to him from the doorstep.

'How does it feel to hold that money, Abu Ramiz?'

Omar Yussef shrugged.

'You don't feel a bit dirty, even a little excited? You're accustomed to holding a large amount of cash from an illegal transaction?'

'No. But I'm used to carrying school books.' Omar Yussef lifted the briefcase and tapped its side. 'This is the textbook of Gazan history.'

CHAPTER 31

O mar Yussef struggled up the lane, sand sifting over the tops of his loafers, and leaned his hand against the graffiti of the Dome of the Rock encased in swathes of black barbed wire. He smiled. Even if the wire were real, it couldn't have cut his palm any worse than the glass along the wall at Salah's house already had done. Perhaps death had tracked him through Gaza, as he had imagined, but only as a reminder of his mortality, spurring him to better actions. In any case, it hadn't caught him. He tightened his bandages, pushed open the gate and went slowly through the lemon and olive trees to the Masharawi house, Maki's briefcase tapping against his knee with every step.

The sandy yard outside the front door was shaded by a black canvas awning, under which the family would receive mourners. Beneath it, Naji sat on a plastic garden chair with a flask of bitter coffee and some tiny polystyrene cups, ready to greet visitors. The boy didn't notice Omar Yussef. He was alone, miserably twiddling the ear that, by its odd angle, marked him as his father's son, the son of a man rubbed out as a collaborator. The boy stared at the tangle of shadow beneath the olive trees. The soft trilling of his doves floated on the hot air. Omar Yussef went quietly into the house.

In the sitting room at the end of the hall, he found Salwa Masharawi and Umm Rateb. The two women sat hand in hand, Umm Rateb staring at her friend's fingers with the desperation of a parent tending a sick child. Salwa gazed at the photo of her husband on the bookshelf. With her free hand, she touched a small, lace handkerchief to her eyes. Omar Yussef would have left them in peace, but he needed to speak to Salwa. He stepped through the door.

'Abu Ramiz, morning of joy,' Salwa said. Her voice was dreamy and slow. She seemed not to notice Omar Yussef's dirty clothes and bandaged hands.

'Morning of light, my daughter,' Omar Yussef said. 'May Allah be merciful upon your departed husband.'

'Thank you, Abu Ramiz. Welcome, welcome,' she said.

Umm Rateb stood. She lifted her palms as though she held Omar Yussef's bandaged hands in them and looked at him with concern. He shook his head. 'You must have some coffee, Abu Ramiz,' she said. 'Didn't you see Naji in the mourning tent?'

'He's grieving for his father, Umm Rateb. He's not a waiter. Leave him be.'

'I'll make you coffee, *ustaz*. Sit down with Salwa.' Umm Rateb went to the kitchen.

Omar Yussef lowered himself onto the sofa. His thighs ached and he groaned as he came to rest. 'I'm sorry that I wasn't able to attend the funeral this morning,' he said. 'I found my kidnapped Swedish friend and was able to free him. We brought him back from Rafah just now.'

'May Allah be thanked.'

'I want to tell you that, with all my heart, I worked to prevent what happened to your husband.'

'I know, Abu Ramiz.' Salwa dabbed at a tear beneath her eye with the handkerchief. 'In Gaza, a man like Eyad can speak his mind and pay a terrible price, or he can ignore the wrongs in the world and his life feels no better than death. Eyad chose his way. That's why I loved him.'

'You're right, my daughter.' Omar Yussef lifted the briefcase and laid it on Salwa's lap. She glanced at him and he nodded for her to open the case.

Salwa unclipped the clasps and gasped. 'Abu Ramiz, what have you done?'

'I hope this will help you in difficult times.'

'Where is this money from?'

'This is the nearest thing to a life insurance payment the university is likely to make. Of course, our Swedish friend will be in contact with you about a United Nations pension.'

Salwa caught another tear at the corner of her eye. She opened her mouth to ask another question, but Omar Yussef clicked his tongue. She returned her gaze to the photograph of her husband. 'Thank you, Abu Ramiz.' She closed the briefcase and slipped it behind the sofa. Umm Rateb brought in a small cup of coffee.

'Allah bless your hands,' Omar Yussef said.

'Blessings,' Umm Rateb said.

Omar Yussef caught the rosewater scent of the woman's soap and felt the guilt of his attraction to her once more. *And in a house of mourning, too,* he thought, shaking his head. But he forgave himself right away. He had no reason to doubt that he was a good man, whatever his less commendable urges.

Umm Rateb lowered herself onto the armchair opposite him, blowing out her cheeks. She cleared her throat. 'Abu Ramiz, I hope it isn't too late, but you remember the leaflet you left in Professor Maki's office?'

'I know what happened to that.'

'You do? I found it on the floor behind his desk. There was a dirty shoeprint on it. Perhaps he stepped on it without seeing it.'

'He certainly found it, Umm Rateb.'

'I'm sorry. I tried to reach you at your hotel to tell you I had it, but you were out.' Umm Rateb's look of concern lifted and she smiled knowingly. 'The lady who answered the phone at the reception desk laughed and said you were "out on a case."'

Meisoun. Agent O. Omar Yussef felt his neck grow

hot and cleared his throat. 'I wonder what she meant.' His coffee cup rattled in its saucer.

He said goodbye to the women and went out into the humid shade of the awning. He sat on the plastic chair next to Eyad Masharawi's lonely, awkward son.

The boy barely looked up. He reached out for one of Omar Yussef's bandaged hands and laid his skinny fingers across it. Naji's shoulders shook. The sobs came with the same rhythm as the call of the doves in their cage upstairs. He rested his forehead on Omar Yussef's chest. The schoolteacher stroked the boy's dark hair with the fingertips of his other hand. He sat still and firm for an hour, until the boy's weeping was done.

CHAPTER 32

Sami stopped the Jeep outside the Sands Hotel to pick up Magnus Wallender and Khamis Zeydan. The Swede was quiet and grave – Omar Yussef had asked Khamis Zeydan to tell him the details of Cree's death, while he visited Salwa Masharawi. The Bethlehem police chief, however, was positively frothing with excitement, as he handed a clean shirt to Omar Yussef.

'Professor Adnan Maki's dead,' he said.

Omar Yussef twisted in his seat and dropped his jaw.

Khamis Zeydan slapped his good hand into his gloved prosthesis. 'There's a special meeting of the Revolutionary Council this evening to discuss the situation. After all, this is the second Council member assassinated in two days.'

'How did it happen?' Omar Yussef slipped awkwardly out of his bloody shirt and put on the fresh one.

'The official explanation won't be available until after the Revolutionary Council meets, of course.'

'Of course.' Omar Yussef lifted his chin in a quick gesture of cynicism.

'Maki told Colonel al-Fara he could arrange for him to buy the new prototype missile, the one they're calling the *Saladin I*. Al-Fara handed over the cash to Maki, who brought him the missile. But it wasn't a new missile. It was one of the old *Qassam* missiles. There're hundreds of them in Gaza and al-Fara recognized it immediately as an old one. He already has a stockpile of his own.'

'Couldn't Maki talk his way out of that?'

'Maybe he could have, but al-Fara had received a call from Abu Jamal down in Rafah. He told the colonel about Yasser Salah and the theft of the new missile.' Khamis Zeydan slapped his thigh with excitement. 'Abu Jamal accused the colonel of stealing the missile, because Yasser Salah was his officer, after all. It seems Abu Jamal blamed Yasser Salah – and, therefore, al-Fara – for the deaths of several of his men in the gunfight where you rescued Magnus.'

When he had left Wallender at the hotel with Khamis Zeydan, Omar Yussef had recounted the night's events to his friend only as far as the Swede's rescue. He had told Wallender to keep quiet about their discovery in the graveyard, and the sale of the missile to Maki was between him and Sami only. 'So it was either to be all-out war between Abu Jamal and al-Fara,' Omar Yussef said, 'or blame someone else.'

'That's right. The colonel remembered that Salah was recently promoted after obtaining his law degree. He'd known all along about Maki's sales of academic degrees – apparently he'd even bought his own law degree. The sales enabled him to connect Salah and Maki. He knew he'd been double-crossed, and he also had his scapegoat.'

'He killed Maki?' Omar Yussef said.

Khamis Zeydan nodded. 'Maki was found less than half an hour ago in his garden, lying in the fountain. He was shot Mozambique-style.'

'What does that mean?'

'A bullet in each breast and another in the forehead. It's a highly professional assassination technique. The CIA trainers taught it to al-Fara's agents. No one else does it that way in Gaza. It'll be clear to Abu Jamal that al-Fara ordered the hit to make amends for the theft of the missile.'

'Is that what the Revolutionary Council will decide?'

'Look, al-Fara killed Maki. Maybe he also had something to do with the death of General Husseini. If you were on the Revolutionary Council, would you finger him?' Khamis Zeydan snorted. 'We'll blame it on one of the Islamist groups, and we'll all be very, very polite to Colonel al-Fara.'

They drove south on the Saladin Road toward Deir al-Balah. Sami pulled up in the shade of the tall date palm outside the caretaker's house at the British War Cemetery. An ambulance was parked by the hedge and Doctor Najjar was standing at the gate to the caretaker's yard, shouting instructions to the medics. The pathologist greeted

Omar Yussef with five kisses and led him into the cemetery.

Omar Yussef looked up at the sky. The dust storm had abated fully as the morning went on. The sun seemed to bore right through the few strands of hair across his scalp and into his brain. It was noon, high noon, like the mysterious price Bassam Odwan had puzzled over in jail.

The grave of Private Eynon Price was dug in a neat rectangle, ready for the soldier's remains to be interred once more. In front of the furthest cluster of graves, Suleiman Jouda threw his spade onto the grass as he climbed out of a second hole. Sweating from the work, he approached Omar Yussef. 'When I took this job, the graveyard was eighty years old. I didn't expect to be digging any more graves,' he said, wiping his forehead on the sleeve of his T-shirt.

'You seem to have made a good job of it,' Omar Yussef said. 'You would think you had been digging graves all your life.'

'I'm from Gaza, *ustaz*. It's in my blood.' Jouda said. 'Anyway, I hope I dug this one in the right place.'

Omar Yussef stepped over to the new grave. It lay in line with one of the first headstones: *Private James Cree. 4 Battalion Queen's Edinburgh Rifles. 21 years. 5/11/17.* 'Yes, Suleiman, you dug this in precisely the right place. Good job.'

'The gentleman from the British consulate will be here soon for the reburial of Private Eynon

Price,' Jouda said. 'He said there's no need to delay the funeral until he arrives, as Mister Cree wasn't a current member of a British organization. He said he'd let Mister Wallender handle it, as the representative of the United Nations.'

The medics brought two caskets from the courtyard of the caretaker's house. The first was a simple coffin of rough pine. Doctor Najjar instructed them to lay it next to the grave of Eynon Price, until the British consular official arrived. The second was a long plywood crate, which they brought to James Cree's grave.

'That's a strange material for a coffin,' Khamis Zeydan said, quietly.

Suleiman Jouda jumped down into Cree's grave and took the weight of the casket from the ambulancemen. He climbed back out and waited for Magnus to speak.

The Swede didn't look at the coffin. He stared up into the sky, poked a finger behind his spectacles to wipe a tear from his eye, and read a brief service from a small prayer-book. He closed the book. 'The events that James and I were part of this week have taught me that people from the West, like me, have a very simplistic view of what's right and wrong here in the Middle East. We believe good must triumph over evil, but then we back bad men, when it's politically convenient. James never accepted that, because he cared deeply about the land and its people. So I will always remember him, here in his grave in Gaza.'

Jouda shoveled the dry earth down onto the plywood box.

Doctor Najjar shook Wallender's hand. 'May Allah be merciful upon him, the departed one,' he said.

'Thank you, doctor,' Wallender said. 'Thank you for looking after his body.'

The doctor cleared his throat. 'Yes, yes, it's nothing. Now, I do need you to sign some papers. There're some official requirements, and you're the representative of the United Nations.'

'Of course.' Wallender took the papers. He frowned. 'These are for transfer of the body.'

'That's correct.'

'But we're burying him here.' Wallender flipped over to the second page. 'These are for submission to the Israeli authorities. For transfer of the coffin through the checkpoint out of Gaza.'

Omar Yussef took Wallender's arm. 'Doctor Najjar, you had better prepare the second coffin for burial, while Magnus looks over these documents.'

The doctor crossed the lawn with a smile.

'Abu Ramiz, what's going on?' Wallender said.

'James's body will be transferred to Israel and from there it will be flown back to Scotland. This has all been arranged by the United Nations people in Jerusalem. They only need you to sign the clearances on this end.'

'I don't understand.'

'James's body is still at the morgue.'

'Then who's in that grave?'

358

'Not *who*, but *what*.'

'I don't get it, Abu Ramiz?'

'We just buried something that people have been prepared to kill for. Buried it where it will lie for a century, or perhaps forever. At least long enough to make it obsolete.'

Wallender stared at the grave, until it came to him. 'The new missile?'

Omar Yussef nodded. 'I switched it for an old *Qassam* missile, which Maki then tried to sell to the colonel.'

'Where did you get the old one, so that you could make the switch?' Wallender asked.

Omar Yussef tapped the side of his nose and thought of the two Saladin Brigades men from Gaza City, Walid and Khaled, who had surrendered a single missile from their stockpile and now counted themselves in the clear with the United Nations for their attack on Cree. The *Saladin I* had never left the graveyard. 'Let's go and lay this poor soldier to rest,' he said.

Suleiman Jouda packed the small mound of earth over the new grave with the back of his shovel and pushed in a temporary cross marked with the name of James Cree.

A tall, chubby, florid man in a khaki summer suit entered the cemetery. He waved cheerily and made for the grave of Private Eynon Price. It was the man from the British consulate in Jerusalem. He wiped the sweat from his neck and face with a handkerchief. 'Bloody hot down here today,' he said.

'Still, I gather I just missed the dust storm. Thank Christ for small mercies, eh?' He pulled some printed sheets from his jacket pocket and read the burial service, as the others gathered around the grave with their heads bowed.

The sky was deep blue. Omar Yussef recalled Nadia's tale of Atum's tears. If the ancient Egyptian deity had wept and his teardrops had become human beings, he was not, after all, a god in which Omar Yussef could believe. *His* god had cried dust, a tempest of dust that had denied him his sight and choked him until he was forced to end the weeping himself. As the caretaker shoveled earth into the soldier's grave, Omar Yussef looked at the blue sky and smiled. The god's eyes were finally dry from too much crying.